"I won't do it!" she cried.

"My lady—" Denny Mallon interrupted urgently, "let me tell you about two villages. One is a backward place dominated by a medieval type of tyrant and his clique of sycophants. This tyrant's father debauched every bride in the village on her wedding night on the pretext of exercising his *droit du seigneur*. And the tyrant's son hopes to pursue the same lustful course despite the protests of good folk like yourself.

"The other village is the only place I know of where babies are suckled, infants play in the street, and children go to school as they used to do the world over. Moreover, it's a place where married couples can hope to have a child of their own to love and cherish. In fact, it's a village where the inhabitants can look forward to the future."

The doctor bit his lip and lowered his head.

"Both these communities exist because of a fortuitous arrangement of one man's gene's, and the determination of people to practice self-deception on a heroic scale—because they are both aspects of the same place, and it depends only on your prejudices which one you choose to inhabit. Becau̶—̶ ̶ ̶ ̶ ̶ ̶
the same pla̶—̶ ̶ ̶ ̶ ̶ ̶ ̶-
ther, depend.̶ ̶ ̶
old fool that I ̶
in the village ̶

D1051568

...e, my dear, they are both
...ace, and you may live in the
...ing on your beliefs. I still
...am, happen to think we live
with a future."

EDWARD P. HUGHES

MASTERS OF THE FIST

BAEN
BOOKS

MASTERS OF THE FIST

Copyright © 1989 by Edward P. Hughes

A Baen Books Original

Baen Publishing Enterprises
260 Fifth Avenue
New York, N.Y. 10001

First Baen printing, February 1989

ISBN: 0-671-69806-0

Cover art by Ken Kelly

Printed in the United States of America

Distributed by
SIMON & SCHUSTER
1230 Avenue of the Americas
New York, N.Y. 10020

CONTENTS

Acknowledgements

"In the Name of the Father" originally copyright © 1980 for *The Magazine of Fantasy and Science Fiction*

"A Cure for Croup" originally copyright © 1985 for *Far Frontiers, Vol. II*

"A Test for Tyrants" originally copyright © 1987 for *New Destinies, Vol. II*

"The Wedding March" originally copyright © 1986 for *There Will Be War, Vol. V*

"Crown of Thorns" originally copyright © 1987 for *There Will Be War, Vol. VI*

Introduction

No society could endure if, as is sometimes implicitly assumed, its members became hostile to it by reason of and in proportion to their lowly status within it. Should you so plan a society as to establish and maintain equality in every respect you can think of, there would naturally be a restoration of scarce, desirable positions, by nature attainable only by a minority. You can allot equal time to each member of an Assembly: but you cannot ensure that all will command equal attention. You can chase unequal (more or less log-normal) distributions out of one field after another: they will reappear in new fields. Nor are men so base as to be disaffected from any order in which they are low-placed: they are indeed lavish in the precedence they afford to those who excel in performances they value. What exasperates them is a system of qualifying values which seems to them scandalous, a social scaling which jars with their scoring cards.

1

—Bertrand de Jouvenal, *The Pure Theory of Politics*

Edward Hughes is a telecommunications engineer specialist for a national newspaper. He lives in Manchester, England. Some years ago I visited Manchester, where I was taken to a perfectly delightful Real Ale pub owned and operated by one Ray Bradbury. (Among Manchester science fiction fans, he is known as "the other Ray Bradbury.") The Manchester science fiction club meets in an upstairs room of his tavern. This is appropriate, since the tavern harbors a ghost, fortunately more mischievous than malevolent.

We had a delightful time in Manchester; but there was one prophetic experience.

Mrs. Pournelle and I went to Manchester from Glasgow, traveling by the excellent British Railway system. This is a good way to travel. The trains are comfortable, on time, and connect nearly everyplace in Britain to everywhere else. We found ourselves wishing there was something comparable in the United States, although it's hard to see how a nation several thousands of miles in dimensions can be served by rails as Britain is. Still, regions of the US certainly could be.

When we reached Manchester we were met by the owners of the local book store. It was late afternoon, and I would be speaking shortly, so they had made dinner reservations at a nearby restaurant.

Before we could enter the restaurant we were searched. The doorman wore North African Campaign service ribbons, and was very polite. He was obviously embarrassed about having to search ladies; but he did it.

We were told that all establishments near the railroad station had similar rules. Manchester is in the west of England, near Ireland.

A few days after our stay in Manchester, Lord Louis Mountbatten was killed by a bomb.

Civilization is a fragile thing; once gone, it is not easy to rebuild. Those who found a civilization traditonally have unique privileges. Patrick O'Meara, Master of the Fist and onetime sergeant of Her Majesty's Forces, certainly does. . . .

Edward Hughes has created a new twist to the post-disaster story. The disaster isn't completely spelled out. Certainly there has been a war; there appear to have been environmental disasters as well. If so, they must have been enormous, and acted in a energy of destruction with effects of the war. The Earth is, after all, pretty big, and it's not all that easy to affect it permanently and globally. Any given hurricane expends megatons of energy, while a large volcanic explosion, such as Krakatoa, releases more energy than all mankind has been able to expend in war or peace.

This is not to say we cannot, with ingenuity, muck things up. Harrison Brown long ago showed that if our civilization falls far enough, it will be exceedingly difficult to rebuild. Social structures are delicate. The late H. Beam Piper postulated two different ways for planets to "decivilize." If we work at it, we can make the Earth hard to live on. Hughes postulates that we did, and now must live with the results.

In Hughes' world everyone knows the magnitude of the disaster: but the inhabitants of Barley Cross are determined that life shall be normal for all that, no matter what the cost. That cost has been high. For as long as most remember, the town has been dominated by the fortress known as The Fist, outside which stands the tank brought in by Patrick O'Meara, onetime sergeant of Her Majesty's Forces. As Lord he took it on himself to lead the town militia in raids to recover aspirin, antibiotics, and other supplies, so that soon the town was indeed independent. O'Meara was the founder and savior of the town: and as such, exercised the rights of lordship, including *droits du seigneur*—the rights of the elder. He slept with every newlywed bride of the village.

Except for that peculiar arrangement, Barley Cross was as nearly normal as a village in a world of universal disaster could be; and all the men of the village were pleased to have it so, now and forever.

But nothing lasts forever.

—Jerry Pournelle

Cross Purposes

Barley Cross nestles at the foot of Kirkogue Mountain in the far west of Ireland: a hamlet of less than five hundred souls, boasting one main street, a handful of shops, a public bar, a market hall, and a school. The little community has no police station, no post office, no hospital, and no hotel. But it has something which makes it unique among the villages in Ireland. Despite its small population, its lack of size, its patent insignificance, Barley Cross has its own Lord and Master.

It all began when children stopped being born. . . .

Evidence of the catastrophe was slow to reach the isolated hamlet. Barley Cross's birthrate had always been low: the younger citizens usually emigrating to seek work rather than staying at home to marry. So for years no one remarked on the absence of births. Instead they saw an increase in road merchants, rascals and scallywags visiting their village—and all displaying scant regard for law and order. The guardai patrol from Galway, attention fixed on villainy nearer

5

home, ceased to make a daily appearance on their main street. Starved of police protection, the long-suffering inhabitants of Barley Cross confronted the activities of lawless predators with little success . . . until Patrick O'Meara arrived with his tank.

Sergeant O'Meara, ex–2nd Battalion, Grenadier Guards, had grown weary of patrolling Belfast's docklands, weary of terrorist bombing and shooting, weary of seeing human life sold cheap. One fire-bright night, he stole the Chieftain tank attached to his unit and headed for home in Connemara. He found a welcome and a title in Barley Cross. . . .

In an upstairs room at Mooney's bar, Patrick O'Meara discussed administrative problems with the trio which had tried to govern the village before he arrived.

"The snag is, me lord," pointed out General Desmond, "Bernard Flatley flatly refuses to pay his taxes."

Patrick O'Meara ignored the general's wit. "Have you explained that we need money to pay for a guard on the village?" he asked. "Flatley can't expect a man to do eight hours sentry a day for nothing."

"Bernard don't exactly live in the village," explained the general. "His smallholding is two or three miles out along by Corrib."

"But he expects to be protected from villains, doesn't he?"

The general lowered his eyes. "He says he can handle his own troubles, me lord—and ye can stick yer taxes."

The sergeant frowned. Farmer Flatley wouldn't be the only citizen to reject the new lord's taxes if he was let get away with a refusal to pay. The new lord addressed a small wizened character seated on his right. "What do we know about this fellow, Denny?"

Doctor Denny Mallon's face twisted in concentration. "Ach—he's normally a dacent body. We don't see much of either him or his wife. He's far too busy on his farm. He helps keep us in milk and eggs and bacon, you see. A few turkeys around Christmas time— "

"Does he supply meat to Tom Burke?"

Tom Burke was Barley Cross's butcher. That was one of the names Patrick O'Meara had already learned.

"Ah, no." The doctor sucked at his pipe. "Bernard has no more than half a dozen cows. He'd maybe sell you a bit of veal if you were to ask. But he keeps the beasts mainly for their milk."

Patrick O'Meara chewed a lip. When government demands for income tax ceased to drop through letter boxes, his subjects had quickly grown accustomed to living tax free. They would be equally ready to forget their contributions to the village budget if this man Flatley got away with it. The rebellion had to be nipped in the bud. He looked up. "Any suggestions?"

"Lock him up 'til he changes his mind," urged Larry Desmond.

Patrick O'Meara refrained from comment. That kind of action wouldn't do much for a new lord's image.

Kevin Murphy, the third of his counsellors was visibly hesitating. The sergeant eyed him. He knew from experience that the vet's solutions tended towards the unorthodox.

"Let's have it, Kevin," he urged.

"We could fabricate a raid on Flatley's place," murmured the vet.

"Ye mean we should scare him with a bit of noise?" queried the general. "Put a few bullets through his chimney pot? A fertilizer bomb in his privy?"

"No," said Kevin Murphy. "I mean we should steal his cows."

"And where could we hide them?" The general's voice was scornful. "Sure everyone knows Bernard's beasts."

"Hold it!" commanded their new master. "We don't

dismiss anything out of hand. Let's kick it around a bit."

"No need for talk," grunted the vet. "Ye could lose Flatley's cows in Brendan McCarthy's herd."

"Who's Brendan McCarthy?" queried their lord.

"He's the wealthiest man around here," volunteered the doctor. "He has forty or fifty cows."

"Would he cooperate?"

"As long as we put him in the picture. But he'd not be party to stealing another man's beasts."

"Half a dozen volunteers," reflected the sergeant. "We could swing it."

"And what if someone got hurt?" queried the doctor. "Bernard Flatley's quick with that up-and-over he keeps loaded."

"I've a couple of flack jackets in the tank. Surely we could make up another four?"

"And what would we do about heads or limbs?"

Sergeant O'Meara sighed. "Okay, Denny. Let's forget Kevin's idea. I'll take Larry's advice and put Flatley in the cooler."

"Hold on, now," urged the general. "I'll come rustling with ye. We need only another four volunteers. And I reckon we could manage with fewer than that."

The new lord stared from the vet to the doctor.

"Count me out," mumbled Denny Mallon. "Not that I'm scared. But there are too many people depending on me."

Kevin Murphy squirmed. "Sure 'tis me own idea, I know. But the beasts would miss me—if Flatley didn't."

Larry Desmond wasn't listening. He counted on his fingers. "There's Andy McGrath and Kev Kennedy. Young Jemmy Boyle and Pete O'Malley—they'd all be game for a lark."

Their lord frowned. "It won't exactly be a lark,

Larry. If Bernard Flatley is as sharp with a shotgun as you say he is, someone might get hurt."

"Ach!" snorted the general. "No one ever got kill't by a shotgun. A few pellets in the arse is all the harm ye could come to."

Patrick O'Meara was unconvinced. "I've seen some nasty wounds from nail bombs—"

"Beggin' yer pardon, me lord," interrupted the general. "But ye're not dealing with thim IRA boyos now. Bernard Flatley is the sort of felly who wouldn't hurt a fly. And, anyway, we'll take good care to stay out of range."

Patrick O'Meara meditated. Larry Desmond was right. A farmer with a shotgun could not be equated with an armalite-carrying gunman. He would have to remember that Barley Cross was not like Belfast. "If we wait until dark—" he began.

"That's the stuff!" approved the general. "Flatley's cows will be spirited away afore the stubborn fool knows it. And he'll have to cough up to see 'em again."

His lord sat back. "Right, Larry. You know the lads better than I do. Pick your volunteers. Kit them out with hoods and flak jackets. And let me know when you're ready."

Larry Desmond beamed. "I will, me lord. Just lave all them fiddly bits to me. 'Tis to be a night operation, then?"

Patrick O'Meara nodded. "There's less chance of being recognized at night. Especially if we wear hoods."

The general rose to his feet. "Very good, me lord. If that concludes the business in hand, I suggest we adjourn to the regions below."

Patrick O'Meara smiled. In the room below, Fechin Mooney would be drawing pints of Guinness or glasses of poteen for thirsty customers. And Larry Desmond's thirst was notorious. "Get along then," he said. "I'll be down in a minute."

The general departed, the vet hot on his heels. The doctor hung back. "A quick word with you, Patrick," he said.

The sergeant paused, one arm in the sleeve of a camouflaged smock. "What is it?"

"I don't think you should go gallilvanting out to Flatley's place. What if you were to get a charge of buckshot in the wrong part of your anatomy?"

Patrick O'Meara shrugged. "Sorry, Denny. I take your point. But it's a risk that can't be avoided. Maybe later on, when the lads are better trained—"

The doctor sighed. "I wish you'd remember why we made you our lord. If Barley Cross is not to be peopled with childless couples, you have an important role to play. And that's not as a target for idiots like Flatley."

Patrick O'Meara shook his head. "None of your lasses have offered me an opportunity, yet."

The doctor grunted. "Give them time. We can hardly advertise your abilities. They know what to expect on their wedding nights. I'll put another whisper out about your virility if you like."

The sergeant buckled on a webbing belt. "That's enough of that, Denny. I've high hopes of Maureen Neary. She looks after Killoo Farm on her own, I'm told. And she's quite keen on this Flinty Hagan chap. If Flinty would only shape—"

The doctor got up. "In that case, Patrick, let me buy you a drink. I've half an hour to spare before evening surgery."

Curracloe Farm on Corrib's shore slumbered under the moon. The nights were still warm enough for cattle to sleep in the open. Hooded figures crossed a field towards the recumbent animals.

"Mind you don't rouse that dog," cautioned Andy

McGrath. He had but recently come to live in Barley Cross, and had not yet established amicable relations with all the farmyard sentinels.

"Ach—old Tuathal won't bother me," boasted Kevin Kennedy. "Didn't I rear him as a pup?"

Everyone knew that the Kennedy brothers bred Irish wolfhounds. And everyone knew that, despite their being the size of a full grown donkey, Irish wolfhounds were quite gentle creatures.

Pete O'Malley wasn't reassured. "I've a Valium capsule here would help to settle his suspicions," he murmured.

"Sure—ye'll give no drugs to friends of mine!" declared Kevin Kennedy.

"Give the dog the Valium," commanded their lord. "We're supposed to be villains, remember!"

"Let me have the bloody pill, then," muttered Kennedy. "Tuathal will take yer arm off if ye go near him."

A shape as big as a pony came bounding towards them.

"Here Tuathal!" whispered Kevin. "Sweeties for ye."

The dog gobbled the capsule noisily.

Kennedy put his weight on the animal's back, trying to persuade it to lie down.

Slowly Tuathal grew torpid. His tail dropped, his legs quivered, his eyes grew heavy. Finally, grunting, he subsided.

"He's away," approved the general. "Now let's stir up the ladies."

They stole towards the animals. "Hup!" the general urged in an urgent whisper. "Get up, ye silly creatures!"

The cows stirred reluctantly.

On a distant fence, disturbed by the activity, a roosting hen clucked in its sleep.

Jemmy Boyle thrust among the cows, tugging and pushing at them.

Larry Desmond's scowl disappeared. "Ye see how it's done?" he indicated to Sergeant O'Meara. "Jemmy gave Flatley a hand with the milking this summer. Them beasts remember him."

Hat flapping, arms waving, murmuring encouragement, Jemmy got his charges moving across the field towards the gate. In the road, Tom Burke sat at the wheel of a borrowed cattle truck.

As the cows appeared, he skipped down from the cab, lowered the tail ramp, then swung wide the gate.

In ten minutes, Flatley's herd was packed in tight. Larry Desmond squeezed into the cab beside Andy McGrath and their new lord. Kevin Kennedy and Pete O'Malley clung to a door at each side. Jemmy Boyle could be heard soothing the beasts within. Tom Burke eased into gear. They lumbered towards the McCarthy acres.

"Not a drop of gore spilt!" exulted the general.

Patrick O'Meara pulled off the hood which had hidden his face. "I hope you're not disappointed," he murmured. Come morning, Bernard Flatley would find the dog drugged and his cows gone, and would hopefully jump to the wrong conclusion.

Patrick O'Meara's bedroom had belonged to a Mooney scion long emigrated. The door had no lock. Patrick O'Meara woke to see a pair of lenses, one of them fractured, looming over him. Mooney handed him a mug of tea. "There's a wumman below wants a word with ye, me lord."

Patrick O'Meara leaned on one elbow while he sipped. "Do I know her?" he asked.

" 'Tis the Flatley woman from Curracloe," Mooney told him. "Shall I tell her ye're not up yet?"

The lord of Barley Cross blew on his tea. "Give me five minutes," he said. "What does she want?"

Fechin Mooney flapped his hands. "She didn't say, me lord. But she's terrible worried. She's pedalled all the way from Curracloe, and it's not yet seven o'clock."

Patrick O'Meara kept a straight face. He could guess what was bothering Missus Flatley. He swung a leg out of bed. "Tell her I'll be down shortly."

Imelda Flatley was a big, heavily-muscled woman. Sweat still moistened her upper lip. She was waiting in the public bar.

He said, "I'm Patrick O'Merea. What can I do for you?"

She stood up, hands fluttering. "Me lord—Bernard's gone off without a bite of breakfast. And he's taken his gun with him!"

Patrick O'Meara fingered an unshaven jaw. "Has he now? Why would he do that?"

Imelda Flatley's bosom heaved. "We've been rustled, that's why. Some villains went off with all the cows during the night. Bernard thinks it's them tinkers that are camped along the road. Oh, me lord, ye must do something—he'll murther 'em for sure."

Patrick O'Meara pondered. Larry Desmond had assured him that Bernard Flatley wouldn't hurt a fly. But then, Larry Desmond's judgment was often less than accurate. He said, "Did Bernard tell you where he was going?"

"He said he'd make sure those tinkers niver rustled no cows again."

Tinkers were a nuisance. They were dirty, unsanitary, and light fingered; stealing anything that wasn't nailed down. Sergeant O'Meara was tempted to let Flatley work his will on them. But a farmer seeking vengeance for stolen cows was too much of a menace to loose even on vagrants. Someone might get killed—

and it might not be a tinker. He daren't allow that to happen.

"Could I borrow your bike?" he asked.

She gestured at the window. "It's outside."

He said, "Don't worry about your Bernard, Missus. I'll see no harm comes to him or anyone. Just wait here until I get back. Mister Mooney will no doubt make you a cup of tea."

He slipped up to his room. Hurriedly he buckled on the Webley revolver he preferred to a regulation Browning automatic. He clapped on his uniform beret, then clattered back downstairs. Fechin Mooney carrying a cup of tea into the bar watched him wide-eyed.

"Ye've had no breakfast, me lord!"

Patrick O'Meara slammed through the street door. "Keep it warm for me, Fechin."

Through the bar window Mooney and his guest watched their new lord wobble down the main street on a lady's bicycle far too small for him.

"There's a broth of a man for ye," murmured the publican admiringly. "It don't take him a week to make up his mind."

"He didn't give me time to think," confided Imelda Flatley.

By the time he gained the Mambridge road, Patrick O'Meara's legs were going like pistons: the bike wheels shimmering discs. Vaguely he recalled seeing a tinker's caravan the previous night. His heart thumped. Sweat streamed into his eyes. Iron bands encased his chest. His boots were soled with lead. He began to respect Imelda Flatley's determination in making the ride before breakfast. What man was worth such punishment! He should have taken the tank, instead of this fatuous conveyance.

Smoke drifting across the road warned him that he was close to a campfire. He ceased pedalling, tried his brakes, then put a boot on the road, and came to a jerky halt. He laid the bike quietly on the verge, and crept towards the source of the smoke.

Farmer Flatley had found his tinkers. A grimy character stood with his back to a caravan wall, arms raised above his head. Flatley was pointing a shotgun at him. Before Patrick O'Meara could intervene, a woman stepped from behind the vehicle. She, too, carried a shotgun. The woman raised her voice. "If ye don't put down that gun, Bernard Flatley, I'll blow your head off."

The shotgun wavered in Flatley's grasp. He turned to see who threatened him. "Watch what you're up to with that thing, Minnie Thomond," he called.

Her eyes narrowed. "Last warning, Flatley. Drop it, or I'll do something I may regret."

Flatley's shotgun clattered to the ground.

The tinker lowered his arms. "Ta, Minnie. Now I'll show this bugger what I think of nosy farmers."

Flatley moved to retrieve his gun, caught a warning twitch of the woman's weapon, and changed his mind.

The tinker rolled up his sleeves. "This ain't going to be murder like you was planning, Flatley. But it'll be bloody close to it."

The farmer was slightly built: the tinker at least three stone heavier. Sergeant O'Meara unholstered his Webley. He stepped from concealment. "Hold everything!" he called.

The tinker froze. Bernard Flatley gaped. The woman fingered her shotgun.

"Don't!" cautioned Patrick O'Meara. "I kill professionally."

Minnie Thomond recognized a real threat. She lowered the gun until its stock rested on the ground.

The tinker studied Patrick O'Meara's uniform. "You're in the British army!"

The sergeant lowered the revolver. "Not quite," he corrected. "But I'm authority 'round here. And I don't permit murder." He addressed Flatley. "Pick up your gun and go home. I'll find your cows for you."

Flatley broke his gun before tucking it under his arm. "You must be the new lord they've picked themselves in the village," he challenged.

Patrick O'Meara nodded.

"How did you know about my cows?"

"Your wife requested my help this morning."

"To find me cows?"

"To stop you committing murder. I hang murderers."

Flatley paled. "Ye'll get nothin' out of me for yer taxes."

Patrick O'Meara eyed him stonily. "Then find your own cows."

"I'll do that."

"And bear in mind what I told you about murderers."

He watched until Flatley was out of sight, then turned back to the tinkers.

"That's my wife you threatened," grumbled the man.

Patrick O'Meara holstered his revolver. "Be grateful to her. She probably saved your life." He addressed the tinker's wife. "You're a rash woman, Missus Thomond. You may have prevented a murder. But, in future, don't do it with a shotgun."

Then Patrick O'Meara mounted Imelda Flatley's bike, and rode back to Barley Cross and breakfast.

The news spread quickly. The new lord had personally stopped Bernard Flatley from killing tinker Thomond. Flatley's cows had been stolen, and the farmer had suspected the tinker. The admiring glances which followed Patrick O'Meara around the village were embarrassing. For his conscience troubled him. Bernard Flatley might be hasty tempered, but it was Patrick O'Meara who had organized the disappearance of his cows, and it was Patrick O'Meara who should bear the blame for the contretemps on the Mambridge road. Patrick O'Meara wasn't accustomed to feeling ashamed of himself. He went looking for the general.

Larry Desmond was dead-heading roses in his garden.

At the sight of his new master, the general straightened. He slipped a pair of kitchen shears into his pocket, and came to the gate. "Can I do anything for ye, me lord?"

"You can, Larry." Patrick O'Meara hesitated. He scratched his head. He massaged the back of his neck. He stared around, as if to ensure he could not be overheard. "It's about those cows—"

The general grinned. "Sure, thim cows is safe as houses where they are."

Patrick O'Meara groaned. "That's the trouble, Larry. Flatley would never dream of searching McCarthy's pastures. He'll never find them."

The general shrugged. "So let him pay his taxes."

Patrick O'Meara gulped. "He's a stubborn man, Larry."

The general seemed unimpressed. "We can all be stubborn, me lord. It's knowing when not to be stubborn is the main thing."

His lord sighed. This was going to upset the general, but it couldn't be helped. Patrick O'Meara had to live with his conscience. He said, "If we return those cows without insisting on payment, Flatley might be grateful enough to pay his taxes."

Larry Desmond looked as if he'd swallowed something unpleasant. "Ye don't know our Bernard very well, me lord."

Sergeant O'Meara studied his hands. "I'm aware of that, Larry. But the other day I stopped Flatley from killing someone, or from getting killed himself—I'm not quite sure which. But I didn't take on the running of this village to organize that sort of situation. We'll have to find another way of solving the problem."

Larry Desmond knew when to capitulate. "Would ye like me to go up to the McCarthy place, and fix up for the cattle to go back?"

His lord nodded. "I would, Larry. You can tell Flatley you found them wandering in the hills. He won't ask too many questions."

Larry Desmond lowered his eyes. He scrubbed his hands with a soiled handkerchief. "I'm just about finished here, me lord. I'll get young Jemmy, and we'll set off right away."

Patrick O'Meara knew he had sold the pass, and that he had no excuse. He mumbled his thanks, and made a rapid escape.

Doctor Denny Mallon met him as he slunk back to Mooney's. Briefly he told the doctor of his decision to return Flatley's cows. Denny Mallon nodded approval. "Sure t'was a mistake, Pat. Kevin gets these wild ideas. I'm sure it's those Bolshie books he reads. We should never have gone along with him. The sooner things are put right, the better."

His words failed to console Patrick O'Meara. "I didn't think the thing through, Denny. The Flatley's are having to buy milk, now—assuming they've the cash put by. And the people they used to supply milk to are seeking new retailers. I've probably ruined them."

The doctor wagged his head. " 'Tis just like medicine, Pat. Everything has side effects that you don't expect."

His lord looked glum. "Maybe I should never have taken on the job."

The doctor patted his arm. "Because of one mistake? When we ran the Cross t'was like a comedy of errors. You couldn't do worse if you tried. And, you are still the only man who can repopulate the village."

Patrick O'Meara had almost forgotten that aspect of his job. "It takes two to make that sort of bargain,

Denny," he complained. "And the ladies seem to be shy of me."

Denny Mallon smothered a cough. "Give 'em time. You've only been our lord and master a couple of weeks."

"Perhaps it's because I've no place to take them to?" reflected his lord. "I could hardly bring them back to Mooney's for a session of *droit du seigneur*."

The doctor pondered. "You have a point there, Pat. We promised to do up that old Higgins place for you, didn't we? Perhaps we'd better make a start on it."

The Higgins place was a stone fortress erected by some thirteenth century O'Flahertie chieftain. It stood atop Barra Hill, at the far end of the village. Some years previously, an English couple had put in wooden floors and modern plumbing to make a home for themselves. When the troubles began, the Higgins had departed for more civilized latitudes, leaving their dreams to decay.

"It might help to undermine some bride's resistance." Patrick O'Meara's voice held slight conviction. He didn't relish forsaking the comforts of Fechin Mooney's hostelry for the draughty barracks towering above his realm. "Is there a water supply up there?"

"I believe there's a well," said the doctor. "Sparkling, fresh water—never runs dry, I'm told." He coughed. " 'Tis pumped up—by electricity, I believe."

"Jasus!" murmured his lord. Mooney's electric had failed four times that week. And the prognosis for an uninterrupted supply was far from optimistic.

"Ach—we'll get a man to do the pumping for you," the doctor assured him. "They tell me you get a marvellous view of Corrib and Leckavrea from the bathroom window."

"That's splendid," murmured his lord. "There is a bathroom, then?"

The doctor hesitated. "I'm not sure you still have a bath in it. There's been a deal of pilfering since the Higginses left."

"There had better be a deal of restoration, then, before I move up there," added his lord darkly.

Denny Mallon smiled. "Ah, don't be worrying, Pat. We'll soon have you settled in. And the village brides will be queuing up demanding their droits."

Patrick O'Meara's eyes lacked the doctor's twinkle of optimism. "Who's your Clerk of Work?" he demanded. If the roof leaked or the garbage wasn't cleared, it would be handy to know who to complain to.

Denny Mallon lowered his eyes. "I guess that will be Larry," he confessed.

His lord groaned aloud.

Larry Desmond called on his master later that evening. Patrick O'Meara had climbed Barra Hill that afternoon to examine the ivy-clad tower his advisers hoped to foist on him. He was making a note of its defects when the general knocked.

Larry Desmond was annoyed. He dabbed his forehead with a large, checkered handkerchief. Evidently he had been hurrying. "We've been gazumped, me lord," he complained.

Surely "gazumped" meant an unsanctioned price increase? Patrick O'Meara frowned at his general. "Who's done what to us, Larry?"

"Them villains have stolen our cattle, me lord."

"You mean Flatley's cows?"

Larry Desmond towelled his neck. "Aye—had a few of Brendan McCarthy's, too. I'm just back from Gortnageelah—that's Brendan's place. He's hoppin' mad."

"When were they stolen?"

"Last night. The divils must have been watching the place. They took Flatley's cows from the pound where we left them, and helped themselves to a few of Brendan's beasts as well."

His lord folded his notes, and tucked them into a pocket. Complaints about the O'Flahertie castle could wait on a more suitable occasion. "Who goes in for rustling around here?" he asked.

Larry Desmond scratched thinning hair. "Tom Burke reckons it could be a gang that peddles beef in Galway. Thim town butchers aren't too particular where their meat comes from."

Patrick O'Meara drummed on the table, his brow furrowed. "How many animals did they snatch?"

"Brendan reckons about a dozen."

"Would they sell them alive? Or would they slaughter them first?"

"I reckon they'd be slaughtered and butchered before they're sold. That way the thieves would get a steak or two for themselves. There's no way of identifying meat after it's cut up."

"Then they'd hold the animals somewhere until they were ready to dispose of them. Beef keeps better on the hoof."

Larry Desmond looked sideways at his lord. "Sounds like ye've maybe done a bit of cow catching yerself, me lord."

Patrick O'Meara smiled. "Only in your company, Larry." He thought a moment. "So they'd need a slaughterman. And possibly a butcher?"

"I wouldn't argue with yer logic, me lord."

"And a truck to shift the animals."

"That too, me lord."

"So we're looking for a butcher and maybe a slaughterman. A fellow who can lay his hands on a truck. And a man who has the facilities to conceal stolen cattle until he's ready to sell them."

The general brightened. "Bejasus—that's half the gang identified already!"

Patrick O'Meara got up. He reached for his jacket. "Let's go and talk to Tom Burke."

Tom Burke was not home. His wife recommended they try Mooney's bar. They retraced their steps, and discovered the butcher in the snug, playing cribbage with Eddie Pearce. The sergeant waited until the butcher triumphantly pegged out, then put his question.

Tom Burke shuffled the cards while he considered. "There's only one fellow I know might fit the bill," he mused. "Name of Joe Lynch. He has a shop in Galway. He can always let me have half a carcase if I'm stuck for meat—at his price, of course. He lives out along Clifden road."

"On his farm?" asked Patrick O'Meara.

"Ah, no." Tom Burke scratched a tight-stretched shirt front. "It's a house and a few acres, set well back from the road. He built the place for his wife, before she died."

"Could he keep cows there?"

Burke laughed. "What do you think he does? There's always a few head of cattle in the field at the back. Who they belong to is anyone's guess."

Sergeant O'Meara eyed his general. "We might pay the man a visit, Larry."

Tom Burke began to deal. "Lynch will be home tomorrow—it's early closing in Galway. Don't mention my name. Meat's getting tight. I may need to pay him a visit soon."

That evening Sean O'Rourke called at the new lord's lodging. Patrick O'Meara was eating his evening meal.

"I've just finished me stint at the post," O'Rourke reported. He tendered a slip of paper. "That tinker fellow left this for you."

Patrick O'Meara had organized checkpoints on the roads into the village. The post which Sean referred

to stood between Barley Cross and the main road.
Anyone leaving or entering the village had to pass
the guard hut. The tinkers had evidently left Barley
Cross.

Patrick O'Meara put down his knife and fork. He
studied the message. It contained only one word.

He looked up. "What's *Fintona* mean?"

Sean O'Rourke shrugged. "It has me beat, me
lord."

"Maybe Doctor Denny will know. He gets around."
Patrick O'Meara pocketed the paper. "Was this the
tinker fellow that Flatley wanted to shoot?"

O'Rourke nodded. "Minnie Thomond's man. He's
been pottering around the district for donkey's years."

"Did he say anything to you?"

O'Rourke wrinkled his brow. "Well, now—I says
to him, 'What's this mean, man?' Thomond says,
'None of yer business, Sean. Just give it to his lordship. 'Twill help him find Flatley's animals.'"

"Nothing else?"

"Not a word, me lord."

Tinker Thomond must have appreciated his deliv-
ery from Flatley's ire, and had left the note as a
token of his gratitude. He must believe that *Fintona*
would convey something to his benefactor. Patrick
O'Meara decided to see the doctor.

He picked up his knife and fork. "Leave it with
me, Sean. I'll find out what it means."

Denny Mallon, in shirt sleeves and carpet slippers, studied the message. "It rings a bell, Pat." He
rubbed his jaw. "'Tis probably a place name. That
Thomond fellow gets around. Ah, yes—I have it! A
couple of years ago I treated a woman for jaundice.
I'm sure the place was called *Fintona*. Hold on—I
sent a bill." The doctor opened a desk crammed with
papers. "There'll be a record of it in here—Jasus,
what a system!" He leafed through a ledger, scatter-

ing loose papers. "Ah!" He read aloud. "Here we are. May Lynch. Six visits to *Fintona*." He sighed heavily. "I see she died of hepatitis. My last visit was to sign her death certificate."

Patrick O'Meara said, "And where is *Fintona*?"

Denny Mallon pondered. "I'd estimate it's a couple of miles along the Clifden road. A fine, modern house, I recall, with a few acres of land."

Patrick O'Meara nodded. "The tinker must have seen this Lynch fellow stealing Flatley's animals."

Denny Mallon dropped the ledger on the desk. "I wouldn't be surprised. Lynch has a butcher's shop in Galway. He used to buy up beasts to fatten before slaughtering." The doctor sniffed. "Are you intending to get the animals back?"

Patrick O'Meara nodded. "That would be the general idea."

The doctor got out a pipe and tobacco pouch. "Better take some good lads with you. If I recall rightly, Mister Lynch has a couple of brawny sons. You might meet opposition."

His lord showed no surprise. "No doubt," he said. "Villains don't like their plans being frustrated."

"Least of all a town councillor," added the doctor, digging into his pouch.

"Lynch is a town councillor?"

"He was the last I heard. You might find he has police protection, these days."

Patrick O'Meara stood, considering possibilities. "Maybe we'd better get a move on."

"I shouldn't dally," agreed the doctor.

The raid on *Fintona* took place at first light the following day. The Lynch boys and their father were taken by surprise. Threatened by half a dozen FN rifles, they offered no resistance as the Barley Cross volunteers rounded up the stolen cattle.

Jemmy Boyle examined the ears of several beasts. "They've burned over the brands, and put their own on instead," he complained. He slapped a meaty flank. "Hup, milady. I'd know you even if they cut yer ears off altogether. Into the truck with ye. Yer holiday's well and truly over."

Mark Brophy, the McCarthy cowman snarled. "Who are they trying to kid? As if I'd not know me own beasts, with or without brands!"

Patrick O'Meara faced Joe Lynch. "I'm taking these cows back to their owners. We don't like cattle thieves in Barley Cross. If you come snooping around again, don't be surprised if you get shot at."

Lynch blustered. "Ye've no right to those animals. They're my property. I bought them from a farmer out by Screeb."

Patrick O'Meara swung up the barrel of his Webley. "Okay—show us your receipt."

Lynch's face darkened. "God damn you, soldier! Who do you think you are? What gives you the right to come onto private property, and steal my cattle?"

Patrick O'Meara saw that the cows had been loaded into McCarthy's truck. His men were ready to leave. He said, "I'm running things in Barley Cross." He holstered his gun. "And my policy is to hang cattle thieves. Just watch your step in future."

Lynch shook his fist. "Ye've not heard the last of this! I'll show ye who's boss around here!"

Bernard Flatley met them at the farm gate. Eyes wide, he watched the ramp come down, and his cows being chivied out.

"So ye found them after all!" He counted bovine bodies. "And ye've brought back more than I lost."

"The rest belongs to Brendan McCarthy," snapped Jemmy Boyle. "He don't make a fuss of things like you do."

Brendan Flatley ignored the dig. He addressed Patrick O'Meara. "What do I owe you?" His voice was gruff. "I don't expect ye to retrieve me cows for nothin'."

Patrick O'Meara gave him a stony glance. "There's no charge," he said. "Some of us put the welfare of the village above personal convenience." He raised his voice. "Let's get on to Gortnageelah!"

They left Flatley in a cloud of dust, his cattle milling around him.

"I don't see that ould divil ever coming 'round to a sensible way of lookin' at things," ruminated Larry Desmond.

"Let him be," murmured the Lord of Barley Cross. "I've had enough of Flatley and his cattle to last me a lifetime."

Sergeant O'Meara was taking the top off a boiled egg in Mooney's kitchen the following morning when he heard a police siren. He recalled Denny Mallon's warning. Why would the gardai protect a bent butcher? Were they more concerned with keeping a food shop stocked, than the means by which it was accomplished?

He was spreading jam on a crumbling slice of soda bread when heavy boots clumped into the bar next door. He heard loud voices and Mooney's ineffectual bleating. Then the door swung open.

A large police sergeant stood in the doorway. He fixed the army sergeant with a hard, official eye. "Are ye the man in charge around here?"

Patrick O'Meara put down the bread and the knife. "You might say that I am," he admitted.

"Are ye the fellow they call the Lord of Barley Cross?" persisted the sergeant.

Patrick O'Meara sighed. "That's one of my titles."

The policeman gave him a sour smile. "Well, me lord, will ye kindly step along to that barricade ye've had fixed across the road, and instruct yer fool of a man to raise it to that I can drive me motorcar through."

Patrick O'Meara stood up. "What's the trouble, officer? Has someone broken the law?"

The policeman hooked thumbs in his belt. "Well, now, that's a point that has yet to be established. The nub of the matter is that a gang of hooligans visited Mister Lynch at *Fintona* yesterday, and took off with a dozen cows he had bought." The policeman's eyes narrowed. "Those beasts were destined for his shop in Galway, and their theft is tantamount to taking meat from starving people—in addition to being a criminal act."

"There are no cows in my village," stated the O'Meara.

The sergeant's smile broadened. "Ah, but ye're surrounded by farms. And I've no doubt that we'll find our missing cattle on one of them. Mister Lynch is positive he will recognize them."

"I'm sure he will," murmured Patrick O'Meara. "I'll bet he knows just where to look for them, too. You have the fellow with you?"

"And another armed officer." The sergeant patted his holster. "And let me warn you, Mister Lord of Barley Cross, any shenanigans will be firmly dealt with."

"I'll get my jacket," said Patrick O'Meara.

The policeman stared at the chevrons and the medal ribbons. "Ye're a goddamn British soldier!" he accused. "A sergeant at that!"

Patrick O'Meara nodded equably. "*Was*," he corrected. "I resigned recently."

The police sergeant eyed the holster. "Have ye a license to carry that weapon?"

Sergeant O'Meara straightened. Suddenly he was as tall and broad as the policeman. "As much license as I need," he said coldly.

The police sergeant decided not to pursue the matter. "Let's get moving," he commanded.

They walked along the main street towards the checkpoint. People opened doors a crack, or peered from behind curtains, to watch their new lord with the policeman. And various gentlemen hurried to their emergency stations.

A patrol car waited at the barrier. Close behind it stood a cattle truck. In the cab of the truck, Joseph Lynch hunched over the wheel. One of his sons sat beside him.

The two sergeants halted before the wooden hut by the barrier. At the sight of Patrick O'Meara, Volunteer Toomey came to attention.

"At ease, Eamon," ordered his lord. "These gentlemen wish to drive through our village. I've given them permission. Please raise the barrier."

The policeman swung 'round. "Hold on, now," he commanded. "What's this about permission? I'll remind ye that ye're talking to the law, and we need no permission to drive through here."

Patrick O'Meara regarded him evenly. "That depends. Have you a warrant to search for those cows?"

"God dammit!" snarled the sergeant. "Who needs a warrant to snatch back stolen beasts?"

"I think you do." Patrick O'Meara loosened his holster flap. "If you can't show me a warrant, I suggest you return to Galway city, and get a magistrate to issue you one."

The police sergeant also loosened his holster flap. "I warned you, soldier," he whispered. "Trouble will be firmly dealt with."

Patrick O'Meara was stalling for time. He had detected a familiar clanking sound. He turned to see a long, large barrel poke from behind the schoolyard railings. A sloping glacis followed, and an armored turret. The head of Volunteer Andy McGrath projected from a hatch in the glacis. General Larry

Desmond and Pete O'Malley manned the turret above, Pete's finger curved round the trigger of the turret machine gun. Inside the tank, Sean O'Rourke slotted a round of APFSDS into the breech of the main armament, whilst Kevin Kennedy lowered the muzzle until the police car rose into his sights.

Patrick O'Meara tapped the law's shoulder, pointing.

The man swiveled to face a British Army Main Battle Tank. His mouth opened, unbidden. "Jasus!" he murmured.

Larry Desmond halted the Chieftain. "I'll give ye five minutes to turn your motor 'round and beat it," he called. "This is the Free and Independent Village of Barley Cross. And we don't admit unauthorized visitors."

Patrick O'Meara saw the smirk on Pete O'Malley's face. The general's declaration was inflammatory to say the least. Barley Cross independent? Of what? The guardai? The rest of Ireland? The powers that be would have something to say about that.

The police sergeant found breath enough to blaspheme.

Larry Desmond consulted an old fob watch. "Ye've four minutes."

Cab doors opened in the truck. Two figures in civilian clothes emerged, and legged it up the road.

The policeman turned back to Patrick O'Meara. "Tell that madman he can't threaten the law."

Patrick O'Meara reflected. If he didn't support the general now, they were truly sunk. Maybe it was time to burn a few bridges. He said, "I'm sorry, sergeant, but he can, and he does. That's General Desmond of the Independent Barley Cross Volunteers. No foreign official tells him what he can or cannot do." He raised his voice. "Take cover Eamon! The general has his dander up."

Volunteer Toomey saluted before heading for cover.

"Foreign official?" choked the sergeant.

"Three minutes!" called the general.

Patrick O'Meara decided to rub it in. "Excuse me, officer," he murmured. "I must take cover myself."

He left the policeman to face the tank alone.

The man reached for his gun. "In the name of the law—" he began.

The turret machine gun chattered. A row of holes marched across the tarmac.

The law forgot his weapon. "Dick!" he shouted. "Get that bloody car turned 'round!"

Sergeant O'Meara grinned. Pete O'Malley was reckless with the turret gun. But it seemed to have persuaded the law.

The driver of the patrol car jerked into action. The engine roared into life. The car reversed into the fender of the truck behind. It came forward again, and bumped the barrier. Barley Cross's striped frontier boom was not an obstacle to be brushed casually aside. It had been adapted by their blacksmith from the metal leg of an old goal post.

The patrol car driver lowered a window, face pale. His voice quavered. "I've no room to turn."

"One minute left," advised Larry Desmond.

"Get out of the car!" roared the sergeant.

The door opened. Both representatives of the law dived for cover.

"Fire!" commanded General Desmond.

The Chieftain's main armanent spouted flame. An armor piercing shot sped beneath Seamus Murray's homemade barrier, pierced the grille of the patrol car, and struck the engine block. Designed to penetrate several inches of armor, the shot vaporized a passage through the block, encountered the case-hardened contents of a gear box, and ricochetted upwards, emerging, velocity scarcely diminished, through the car roof. The vehicle lurched backwards. Its rear end crumpled on the cattle truck fender to the accompaniment of breaking glass. Moments later, the errant projectile threw up a plume of peat far beyond the Clifden road.

Patrick O'Meara's jaw dropped. General Desmond hadn't been joking after all!

The Chieftain's turret swung to cover the ditch in which the law cowered. "Ye have five more minutes to clear off, before I take further action," warned the general.

Sergeant and driver scrambled from the ditch. The sergeant raised a fist. "I'll have the law on ye for this!"

"Ye are supposed to be the law, for what ye're worth," Larry Desmond reminded him. "But ye've no authority in a sovereign village. And ye have four minutes to get out," he added.

Sergeant and driver surveyed the wreck of their vehicle. Then the sergeant eyed the large muzzle of the Chieftain's 120mm gun. "Get in the truck!" he ordered his companion.

"And take yer rubbish with ye!" called Larry Desmond.

The truck motor rumbled, reverse gears whined, and, metal screeching on the road, the law retreated backwards from Barley Cross, dragging the wrecked patrol car with it.

General Larry Desmond climbed out of his cupola, and scrambled to the ground. "Thank heaven that's over," he sighed. "That bloody contraption of yours gives me claustrophoby."

Patrick O'Meara stared after the vanquished police with regret. "You've put your foot in it this time," he told the general. "They'll be back, with every available cop in Galway."

"I doubt it," disagreed the general complacently. "I know that sergeant. I was a cop meself, ye know. He had no search warrant. But he had a cattle truck. And he knew where to look for his beasts."

"His bosses won't be bothered about cattle,"

brooded Patrick O'Meara. "They'll be looking for a fellow with a tank who shoots at police vehicles, and has funny ideas about who runs the country."

Larry Desmond shook his head. "Those cops are not concerned with Barley Cross. Sure we could declare independence twice a week and not be noticed. Who gives a damn about Barley Cross? When did we last see the guardai? Didn't that Healey gang burn down your folk's home without a murmur from the police? I tell ye, that sergeant has been taking handouts from Lynch, and looking the other way when it comes to stolen animals. All he's worried about is how to explain that wrecked patrol car. I bet he dumps it in an alley and sets fire to it, so he can tell his boss it was wrecked in a riot."

Patrick O'Meara sighed. Larry Desmond might just be right. Surely he couldn't foul *everything* up!

Fechin Mooney interrupted breakfast the following morning. "There's a delegation to see ye, me lord," he announced.

Patrick O'Meara's heart beat faster. This was it. The general had trespassed far too far the previous day. The police sergeant had kept his promise. Shenanigans were about to be firmly dealt with. And the Independent Village of Barley Cross was going to get its collective collar felt. He put down his fork. "Is it the gardai?" he queried.

Mooney's mournful face creased in surprise. "Ah, no, me lord. 'Tis General Desmond and the Flatleys. They're waiting in the taproom."

Relieved, but puzzled, Patrick O'Meara pulled on his smock, and followed Mooney through the doorway.

A smiling general awaited him. Flatley looked embarrassed.

"Bernard has decided to pay his taxes," explained the general.

The farmer pulled a wad of bills from his pocket.

"I've included a punt or two extra," he muttered, face lowered, "on account of the trouble ye went to getting me cows back."

Feeling awkward, Patrick O'Meara accepted the money. He wasn't a tax collector. "I think Miss Larkin is acting as Chancellor of the Exchequer," he told Flatley. "I'll see she sends you a receipt."

Flatley shuffled his feet. "Ach, there's no need for that."

He stood silent. His wife watched him. She nudged him with a leg of mutton arm. "Get on, ye booby," she commanded. "Say yer piece!"

Bernard Flatley glanced at his audience.

Imelda Flatley flourished a fist under her husband's nose. "Do I have to show ye how?"

Bernard Flatley lowered himself on one knee. His voice faltered. "I've come to swear fealty to my liege lord and master," he whispered. He met Patrick O'Meara's eye. "I heard about Lynch and his cattle truck, and what you did. I realize I've been an ungrateful bugger. Ye'll hear no more grumbles from me."

Patrick O'Meara pulled the man to his feet. "Get up, Bernard," he told the farmer. "This isn't the middle ages."

Bernard Flatley flushed red. " 'Tis Imelda insisted on me doing it," he confessed. "She's hot on history."

Imelda Flatley threw back her muscular shoulders. "Sure, the O'Meara's our lord and master, isn't he? So ye've given him yer oath of fealty in a fit and proper manner." She glared at Patrick O'Meara, challenging him to contradict.

Patrick O'Meara knew better. Corrupt coppers and cattle thieves—yes. Angry farmers or Gadarene governments—maybe. But females inspired by historical novels—never.

He reflected. Bernard and Imelda Flatley were straws in the wind. Their submission was spontaneous. Perhaps it was possible to maintain a place where law was respected, where folk could live in peace, and where children might grow up in a sane society. If only a jealous world allowed . . .

Patrick O'Meara smiled bleakly. "You're quite right, Imelda."

Imelda Flatley bowed like a born lady. "Thank 'ee, me lord."

Behind them, Larry Desmond put a hand on her husband's shoulder. "Well spoke, Bernard. The master is going to need all the support we can muster to protect our independence."

"God save Barley Cross," breathed Fechin Mooney.

The general flashed a surprised glance at the publican, then studied the floor. "Amen to that," he whispered.

The Flatleys eyed each other uneasily.

The lord of Barley Cross forced a smile.

They all knew the gardai were never coming back.

The Incompleat Angler

Denny Mallon, clumping across the fields behind Barley Cross, bumped into Kevin Murphy. The doctor carried a shotgun and an empty bag. The vet had no guns, but a brace of rabbits hung over his shoulder.

The doctor eyed the trophies. " 'Morning, Kev! I see ye've had better luck than I have this morning."

The vet halted. "I've been doing me snares," he confided. "They beat all yer guns for filling the pot."

Denny Mallon pushed back his hat to scratch his head. "You could be right," he admitted. "I haven't set a snare for years."

The vet unknotted a cord, and held out a rabbit. "Tess can make ye a tasty stew with it."

The doctor accepted the gift. Fresh meat was not to be sneezed at in the Cross. He said, "I've been waiting to talk to you."

The vet scraped mud from his gumboots onto a tussock. "Now's yer chance, man."

Denny Mallon hesitated. Kevin Murphy was not exactly a confidant, but the doctor respected the

35

vet's common sense. "It's the lasses of the village," he confessed. "They have me puzzled."

Kevin Murphy slung the remaining rabbit back over his shoulder. "Ye're not the only one. I've been trying to understand them for years. Just what has you bothered?"

The doctor gnawed his lip for a moment. "It's this droyt of Patrick's. He had no trouble with Missus Hagan—Flinty not being sexually competent, if you take my meaning—but . . ." He eyed the vet. ". . . he's not been required to demand his rights since. And, if we're going to repopulate this village, he ought to be kept busy."

The vet stuck his hands in his pocket, and turned his back to the wind. "Ye're complaining that we haven't enjoyed any more nuptials since Flinty Hagan and Maureen Neary got wed?"

Denny Mallon nodded. "That's about the size of it. And I can't figure out why. We've at least three or four eligible couples, and they're all dragging their feet."

The vet made a mental calculation. "It's not more than three months since the wedding. Even if the Master fertilized Maureen, she wouldn't be showing yet."

"I've examined her. She's pregnant," stated the doctor.

The vet hawked and expectorated. "Well, maybe she's keeping it to herself. Maureen was always a reticent lass."

The doctor frowned. Few knew about Flinty Hagan's handicap, and they wouldn't split for fear of hurting the man's pride. "But if Maureen keeps quiet about who got her pregnant, it could be months—" he began.

"Years, more like," corrected the vet. "There's not much call for matrimony now that we've lost the knack of getting lasses in the family way."

"So how do we let the woman know who managed it with Maureen Neary?"

The vet ruminated. "Bit difficult. Ye could whisper it into your Tess's ear, and trust her to spread the word—but truth to tell, I think the ladies were upset at the way the Master whisked Maureen off to his bed on her wedding night."

"But if they knew the reason—?"

The vet shrugged. "I'm not sure they'd believe it. Any case, we don't want his sexy skills advertising too widely. Our plan was for the husband to get the credit for any children that came along. Some of the villagers wouldn't approve of our plan, anyway. Father Con would be down on us like a ton of bricks."

"So what do we do?"

"Try tipping off your wife. Tell her it's confidential. That usually does the trick."

The doctor appraised the cynic with a judicial eye. "No wonder you never married, Kev."

The vet gave him a lopsided grin. "Mares, cows, ewes and sows and the odd bitch are trouble enough for me."

In the dark evenings, the Mallon's often dined by candle light. Candles, in Tessie Mallon's opinion, were a deal more civilized than oil lamps, and burned with a less objectionable smell.

Over his evening meal that night, the doctor was grateful for the gentler illumination. Manipulating his wife was a task that didn't require flood lights. He dabbed a napkin to his lips, coughed for attention, and said, "I wonder we've had no more marriages since the Hagans got wed!"

Tessie Mallon, disappearing into the kitchen with the used plates, said over her shoulder, "And no wonder with that brute up at the Fist waiting like a spider for the next innocent lass to fall into his clutches."

"You sound a bit peeved with the O'Meara," said the doctor mildly.

"I need to be," retorted his wife. "He may have saved the village from rape and pillage, but he's substituted his own version instead."

"Ah, now," persisted the doctor, "that's maybe just because we don't understand his motives."

"And what are his motives?"

"Mmm . . ." The doctor got out his pipe. "I examined Maureen Hagan last week. She's three months pregnant."

His wife's startled face appeared at the kitchen door. "She's what?"

The doctor repeated his statement.

Tessie Mallon clasped her hands together. "Well, good for Flinty! It'll be grand to see a child about the place again."

The doctor poked his pipe into a mixture of tobacco and dried herbs, and prodded the bowl full. He coughed.

" 'Twasn't Flinty did it."

Tessie Mallon's hands unclasped. "Then who was it?"

Denny Mallon put away the punch. "Can't you guess?"

She placed her fists on the table. "Are you trying to tell me that the Master is responsible for Maureen Hagan's condition?"

He nodded.

"I don't believe it. You're just trying to justify his dirty antics."

Denny Mallon lowered his head. "It couldn't be Flinty because he . . ."

Her voice rose. "Because he what?"

Denny Mallon's mouth shut like a trap. "I'm not at liberty to reveal. Any case, it's confidential."

She glared at him. "What's confidential? That the Master got Maureen pregnant?"

"Yes," he lied.

She placed her hands on her hips. "You expect me to swallow that?"

He sighed. "No, I don't."

She jerked the table cloth from beneath his nose, bundling it under her arm. "Then you'll not be disappointed."

Denny Mallon groaned theatrically.

Tessie Mallon met Claire Dooley outside Curzon's Knitteds on Main Street the following day. Tessie succumbed to an irresistible temptation. "Have you heard?" she whispered. "Maureen Hagan is going to have a baby."

Claire Dooley's eyes opened wide. "You don't say!"

Tessie Mallon looked smug. She felt relieved now it was out. "It's true," she insisted. "Denny told me—but you mustn't tell a soul—they're keeping it quiet."

Claire Dooley nodded. Tessie could trust her. "How did Flinty manage that, I wonder?" she mused.

"Denny tried to persuade me the Master was responsible," continued Tessie, "—and that's pure eyewash. I don't believe him."

Claire Dooley was no longer listening. "Fancy," she murmured, "a baby in the village!" She clutched her bag tighter. "I'll be seeing ye, Tessie, I have to go."

Tessie Mallon waved a reluctant farewell. It was a contest now who could spread the news the fastest.

Claire Dooley buttonholed Cissie Flanagan at the door of Burke's butchers. Tessie snared young Mary O'Toole on the step of Pearce's bakery. The secret spread like floodwater.

Flinty Hagan, who delivered fresh eggs from his wife's farm, was puzzled by the smiles and knowing winks he received from his customers the following day. "There's something queer going on," he told his wife later on. "All the wives are smiling at me fit to bust this morning. I even got a grin from Missus Sourpuss Doyle—which is tantamount to a twenty-one gun salute."

Maureen Hagan smiled. " 'Tis your personal charm, Flinty. Sure, I'm not the only one who appreciates you."

Flinty hung his cap on the door besides his Fist Volunteer's uniform. "Well, you're the only one that counts with me," he assured her.

His wife eyed him shrewdly. Earned or not, deliverymen always gained a reputation for loose morals. "Just make sure those smiling wimmin' know that, too," she told him.

Later that week, over a pint of main barrel in Mooney's, Flinty Hagan confessed to his friend Andy McGrath. "I don't know if I can stick it much longer. Sure, I swear, one of these mornings, I'll be dragged in and raped."

Andy McGrath showed scant sympathy. Wasn't Flinty's predicament a setup most men would dream of? He said, "Any time you need an assistant, Flinty, I'm not be too busy to spare you a hour or so."

"You're not a married man," complained Flinty. "I've a wife at home keeping an eye on me morals."

"But you got her in the family way," pointed out Andy McGrath. "That's what is making you so popular. There's no one else in the village has pulled off that little trick recently."

Flinty peered into his drink. Pride was a funny thing. He knew who was really responsible for Maureen's condition—but damned if he'd admit it to anyone. "How do they know they can't do it, if they won't try?" he demanded.

Andy McGrath smiled crookedly. "Who says they are not trying? You don't have to marry a lass to get her to bed. We're not all as naive as you are."

Flinty spluttered over his beer. "Who are you calling naive?"

Andy McGrath waved a deprecating hand. "Don't take on, lad. I meant it to be a compliment. There's nothing smart, to my mind, in exploiting a state of sterilty."

Flinty drained his glass. "It's me state of virility being exploited that has me worried."

Around the same time, a part-time schoolteacher climbed Barra Hill to visit the Master of the Fist. Patrick O'Meara conducted Celia Larkin to his upstairs parlor. He sent Michael to make tay, then he drew the schoolteacher to him and kissed her.

After a moment, she pushed him off. "I've something to tell you, Patrick O'Meara."

"Tell on, Larkin," he commanded.

"You have a revolt brewing in the village. The Barley Cross Ladies Sewing Circle wants to supplant you."

Patrick O'Meara's eyebrows shot up. "Me? Why?"

She shook her head impatiently. "Oh, not as our Master. You're secure enough in that position. But they don't like you exercising your *droit du seigneur*."

He frowned. "What's it to do with them? I've only done it with Maureen Hagan, and she was perfectly satisfied."

Celia Larkin sighed. "They think it's Flinty that put her in the family way. They want him to exercise his droit on them, not you."

"But Flinty can't—"

"I know. But they don't. So Flinty's their man, and you're out."

He chewed his lip. "What do we do? I promised Flinty and Maureen that I'd keep Flinty's handicap a secret. And Denny won't split."

She shrugged. "Can't help it—the word has got around among the ladies that Maureen is pregnant, and Flinty is getting the credit. No one has done anything desperate yet, but, sure as fate, they'll be dragging him into their beds if you don't do something about it."

The Lord of Barley Cross stared at her. "What can I do? If those silly women want to deceive themselves, they'll have only themselves to blame when nothing happens after sleeping with Flinty."

"They are not silly women," snapped Celia Larkin. "They are nice, ordinary women who want a child of their own to love and cherish, and they think Flinty can provide them with one."

The lord of Barley Cross scratched his head. "Beats me. If I tell them it was me got Maureen pregnant, I destroy Flinty—"

"They wouldn't believe you anyway. Denny tried to convince Tessie that it was you, and she wouldn't listen."

The O'Meara's face hardened. "I knew those three would be involved in it somewhere! Have the general and the vet been extolling my virtues, too?"

The Master was referring to the triumvirate who had run Barley Cross before he and Celia arrived. She put up a hand. "The general has had nothing to do with it. Neither he nor Kevin—"

A discreet cough from without warned of Michael's approach. The schoolteacher hurriedly perched on the settee. In silence, they watched Michael lay a silver salver laden with teapot, cups, milk jug and sugar basin on the table.

"Will that be all, me lord?" asked the servant.

"That'll do nicely," said the Lord of Barley Cross. "I'll ring if we want anything else."

"A wee drop of the craythur?" suggested Michael.

"Not just now, Michael."

"Would ye like me to pour for you?"

"Get out, Michael."

"Yes, sor. At once, sor."

When he had gone, Celia said, "What was I saying—?"

The O'Meara shook his head. "It doesn't matter. I was being psychopathic about Larry and Kevin as usual. What do you suggest I do about this Flinty business?"

Celia Larkin had been waiting for this moment. She put milk into the cups, then poured the tea. Patrick O'Meara watched her without speaking. She put two spoonsful of sugar into his cup, stirred it, then put the cup on the table close to a chair.

He sat down. "Well?"

She eyed him acidly. She knew how to handle this soldier. "I would write them a letter," she told him.

"About what?"

"I would write that in view of their reluctance to grant you your legal rights, you will no longer demand your *droit du seigneur*, and, if you've hurt anyone's feelings in the past, you humbly extend your apologies, and promise to behave better in the future."

"Damned if I do," he muttered.

Her mouth tightened. "This village is damned if you don't."

He looked startled. "How do you make that out?"

"You won't get the chance to make any more babies as we planned."

"If I write the sort of rubbish you're dictating, I certainly won't."

She sipped her tea. "Trust my judgement, Patrick."

He spooned a floating tealeaf from his cup. "What do you know that I don't?"

She shrugged. "Let them sack you. Someone has then to ask Flinty to do the honors in your stead. They may chicken out at the last minute. Or Flinty may not accept. Because he will be deceiving them if he does, and Flinty likes to be an honorable man. If he isn't an honorable man, they are going to be disappointed. And after two or three disappointments, they will think again."

He swallowed. "That might take a long time."

She pursed her lips. "Not necessarily. Some of those lasses have been postponing marriage only because of what you have threatened to do on their wedding night. If you had shown a bit more finesse with Maureen Hagan—"

He spluttered. "Finesse? I talked it over with her. She agreed. Why should anyone get upset?"

She sighed. "Don't ask me to explain women to you, Patrick. Just accept that they think you acted like a boor."

He grinned. "Or a boar?"

Her cup tinkled in the saucer as she placed it on the table. "You're getting warm, my lad," she told him.

The letter provoked comment among the ladies of the village. "Well, at least it's an apology and a promise," said Tessie Mallon at the Sewing Circle's weekly meeting. "And we won't have to submit to the indignity of—"

"There's no danger of ye submitting to any indignities," interrupted Brigit Cullen, who was engaged to Tom O'Connor. "Ye're already wed."

Tessie Mallon subsided, hurt.

"So—who's going to approach our candidate?" asked Martha Brennan, who competed with Eleanor Dolan for Pete O'Malley's affections.

"It should be one of you younger women," ruled Cissie Flanagan. "I certainly couldn't talk to Aloysius Hagan about anything like that."

"How about Tessie getting the doctor to have a word with him?" suggested Mary O'Toole, who had her eye on Barley Cross's blacksmith. " 'Twould be easier for a man to do it. They are always on about sex anyway. And Doctor Mallon would be the ideal choice."

Tessie Mallon briefly considered letting Biddy Cullen stew in her own impudent juice, then, reflecting that Mary's plan would keep Teresa Mallon in the limelight, decided to go along with the idea.

"I'll ask him," she promised.

Denny Mallon was packing for an evening's fishing with the lads when his wife came home. "What is it, woman?" he asked testily. "Can ye not see I'm busy?"

Tessie Mallon ignored the rebuff. She was quite aware of the importance of wifely gossip compared to fishing trips. "It'll only take a minute," she assured him. "Will you ask Flinty Hagan to take the Master's place when Brigit Cullen gets married?"

"Will I what?" demanded the doctor.

His wife repeated her request.

Denny Mallon straightened up from his packing. "What in the name of heaven are you talking about?"

Flinching, she stuck to her guns. "You know the Master has decided not to claim his droyts anymore? He wrote a letter to our Sewing Circle telling us so. Well, we women want Flinty Hagan to take his place."

"But Flinty can't—" he began, then stopped. Denny Mallon peered narrowly at his wife. "Have ye gone completely mad?"

She gulped. "I'm speaking for the women of Barley Cross. We—they . . . want Flinty Hagan to have the Master's droyts."

"In God's name, woman!" stormed the doctor. "Flinty isn't our Lord and Master! He has no legal right to such license."

She hesitated. "You mean the Master can legally demand—?"

The doctor clenched his fists. "Why do you think we agreed to this *droit du seigneur* in the first place?"

Tessie Mallon recovered fast. It was only man's law they were talking about. "Well, we don't care," she snapped, burning her boats. "We want Flinty Hagan to do it."

He peered at her from beneath bushy eyebrows, gnomish features suspicious. "Who's put ye up to this?"

"No one in particular," she lied stoutly. "We ladies are united."

"Then ye can find someone else to do your dirty work," he growled.

"Denny!" she pleaded.

"Not on your life," he refused, adamant.

"But Flinty has given his wife a child—" she protested.

"He has not," growled the doctor. "I told you—'tis the O'Meara that's fertile."

Tessie Mallon's face screwed up. She sniveled. Her eyes grew moist.

"Ah, give over, woman," snapped the doctor. "There's nothing for you to cry about."

"But I promised I'd ask you—and I thought you would do it for me. Now they'll all know I can't keep my promises."

Denny Mallon was silent, thinking. Flinty Hagan was one of a party going out on Corrib that evening. Two rods to a boat was the norm, and there were plenty of boats. It would be easy enough to ensure he shared Flinty's craft. He eyed his wife's contorted features. "Lave off whimpering," he commanded. "I'll do what I can. But I make no promises, mind you."

Tessie Mallon's face straightened magically. She threw her arms around him. "Denny, you darling—I knew you wouldn't disappoint me!"

He struggled to free himself. "Lave off, woman. Sure—I'm not sure I don't prefer ye when ye're whingein'!"

Corrib lay black and calm under a fitful moon. The air was mild. Flinty Hagan pulled half a dozen vigorous strokes, then stowed the oars. The boat drifted on under its own momentum. Denny Mallon balanced the lantern on a thwart. Squinting against the light, he began to assemble his rod.

"Easy there, doctor," cautioned Flinty, "or ye'll have us over!"

Denny Mallon stood motionless until the boat ceased rocking. Over the water from a distant glimmer rasped the voice of Kevin Murphy urging Tom Burke to show a bit of sense. Further away Danny Pearce could be heard berating Malachy Kennedy for his habit of catching crabs.

Flinty Hagan snorted. "Them noisy buggers will frighten the fish away."

The theory was that the fish would be attracted by the lights. Denny Mallon got his line in the water, and settled down to wait. In the distance half a dozen dim beacons bobbed silently on Corrib's black bosom as the Barley Cross Angling Society settled to business.

The doctor gave his man time to relax. "Have ye heard what the women are saying?" he said at length.

Flinty Hagan was reluctant to chat. Did the doctor think the blessed fish were deaf? He grunted. "No. What are they up to now?"

Denny Mallon wedged his rod under a thwart. He leaned towards his companion, and hissed. "They want you to take over from the O'Meara!"

The boat swayed.

"What, me? Run the village?"

Denny Mallon grabbed the gunwhale. "Ah, no, Flinty. Not that. They want you to take 'em to bed on their wedding night, like the Master did with your Maureen."

"But—!" Flinty stared past the lamp into Denny Mallon's puckish features. As his doctor, Denny was privy to Flinty's unusual marital arrangements. "—I can't! Ye know that."

Denny Mallon cleared his throat. "Aye, Flinty—I know. But the villagers don't."

Flinty sniffed. "They ye'd better tell them!"

The doctor shook his head. "Not I, Flinty. I've sworn me Hippocratic oath. Your secret is as inviolate as the confessional so far as I'm concerned."

"Then let the O'Meara tell them!"

"The ladies have upset our Master. He don't want anything more to do with them."

The boat dipped. The lamp flamed high, and began to smoke. "Ye can't expect me to tell them," objected Flinty. "I did a deal with the Master so me and Maureen could have a family. But the result of me wound was supposed to be kept a secret. . . ."

Denny Mallon hesitated. Here came the ticklish bit. "What if you agreed to do what they want, Flinty? And don't tell them about your handicap?"

Flinty meditated a moment. "But, then—nothing would happen . . . afterwards."

The doctor nodded wisely. "And that would serve the silly besoms right." He chewed on a fingernail for a moment, before continuing. "But what if you let on you were shy—and won't cooperate unless the deed is done in the dark—without any talk?"

Finty scowled. "What difference would that make?"

A smirk twitched the doctor's mouth. "Why then—you needn't be there at all."

"But someone has to—"

"Exactly." Satisfaction rang in the doctor's voice. "Someone who wouldn't disappoint them."

Flinty shook his head. "It won't work."

"Why not?"

"They'd know it wasn't me."

"How? All cats are black in the dark."

"Maureen would give me away."

"She would not. Has she told anyone about your wound?"

"Well—the Master wouldn't agree."

"Leave the Master to me."

Flinty peered at the doctor. "Ye're a devious devil, Doctor Mallon."

Denny Mallon gripped his rod, and prepared to concentrate on the fish. "I'll take that as a compliment, Flinty."

Late the following morning, the doctor's hunched figure toiled up the hill to O'Meara's Fist. The Lord of Barley Cross led him upstairs. "Let's sit where there's a bit of light, Denny." He rang for Michael. "Tay for two, Michael," he ordered, "with a drop of the craythur in it." He turned to the doctor. "Now," he said grimly, "what have you been up to?"

The doctor got out pipe and pouch. The O'Meara was evidently feeling touchy. Denny Mallon waved a pipe stem at the Master. "I've been discussing our predicament with Flinty Hagan. The man is willing to take over your seigneural duties, so long as he doesn't have to actually exercise your droits."

The Master of the Fist frowned. "I don't get you, Denny."

Denny Mallon explained.

"So I do clandestinely, what we had planned I do openly?"

"That's the shape of it," agreed the doctor.

"And how does that affect my position as lord of the village?"

The doctor grimaced. "I told Tessie that you are legally entitled to demand your *droit du seigneur*. She wasn't impressed."

Patrick O'Meara pondered. This wasn't the British Army. Out here in civilian country, one had to rule by consent. And the women hadn't had time yet to get used to his tyrannical ways. Not that he was bothered about going to bed with any of them. But there was a plan to attempt the repopulation of Barley Cross. Blast these amateurs! If he handled it wrong . . .

"I doubt it'll work," he mused. "But I'll give it a go."

Denny Mallon swallowed with relief. "I knew you'd cooperate, Patrick. And when you've got one or two of them in the family way we could—"

Patrick O'Meara wasn't listening. The doctor was an incurable optimist. "Have you considered when, how and where the deed will be done?" he demanded. "Is Flinty supposed to visit the bride in her home? Or do we take the cow to the bull as is customary?"

Denny Mallon winced. "We're not animals, Patrick—"

The O'Meara's eyes were hard. These folk weren't living in the real world. They thought wishing could make it so. "My point exactly," he snarled. "And I want to know how I substitute my carcase for Flinty's at the crucial moment."

"Jasus!" breathed the doctor. "I knew I'd missed something."

"Suppose," said the O'Meara patiently, "the bride comes up to the Fist. We use that bedroom along the corridor for the fertility rite. I stay out of sight. Flinty presumably is lurking somewhere in the background waiting to do what is required of him."

Denny Mallon sucked on his pipe. "I see no snags in that," he murmured.

"I do," snarled the O'Meara. "For a start you're forgetting Maureen Hagan. I expect she'll have pretty positive views on the starring role you are planning for her husband. Then there's the groom. If I was doing the deed, he'd be my problem, and I'd sort out some way of dealing with him. But the problem is Flinty's. So he'll have to be seen doing something, even though it'll only be a pose. Those women will expect it. They'll all want to be in the act."

"Jasus!" gasped the doctor again.

"Who is the groom?" demanded Patrick O'Meara.

"Lord man—I don't know," confessed the doctor.

The Lord of Barley Cross wagged his head wearily. "You tell those women that our man will be delighted to oblige. Find out who's marrying who, and I'll fix up Flinty's moves for the day. Also I'll have a confidential word with Maureen. With luck, we might pull the wool over a few eyes. But," he added, "I'm damned if I send any presents."

Word of Flinty Hagan's consent to act as stud bull spread fast round the members of the Sewing Circle.

"Now," said Cissie Flanagan, chairing an emergency meeting of the group. "Who's going to put young Hagan to the test?"

The Sewing Circle fell silent.

"Wasn't you thinking of getting wed?" Cissie demanded of Brigit Cullen.

"I'll be taking the plunge when I'm good and ready," Biddy retorted. "Tom O'Connor and me don't need no pushing."

"Well, how about you?" Cissie turned to Martha Brennan.

Martha colored. She stared round the room. "I'd prefer someone else to go first," she said firmly.

Cissie clicked her tongue. "Maybe we didn't need Tessie to talk to the doctor? 'Tis a pity no one has the gumption to—"

"I'll do it," volunteered Sally Keegan, who was courting Malachy Kennedy. "My man's been working on the Croom house for months. If I wait 'til he says it's ready, we'll never get wed. I'll give him the hurry up."

"Tell him ye're pregnant," leered Brigit Cullen

"Won't Malachy mind about Flinty?" asked Tessie Mallon.

Sally tossed her curls. "He won't know, will he? As far as he's concerned it'll be the O'Meara having his wild way with me."

"You'll go up to the Fist?"

"How else would we work it? I'm certainly not going out to Killoo Farm for no ceremony. Missus Hagan would have the skin off me. And Flinty ain't coming to our place. My Malachy would murder him."

"I—I'd better talk to the O'Meara," muttered Tessie Mallon.

She found the Lord of Barley Cross leaning on a gate watching Brendan McCarthy's cabbages.

"Are you busy, my lord?" she asked.

He smiled at her. "Do I look it, Missus Mallon?"

She felt flustered. She should have got Denny to do this for her. "You don't, my lord. Could I talk confidentially to you?"

He waved a hand. "Only the cabbages are listening."

"It's about Sally Keegan—she's getting wed to Malachy Kennedy."

The O'Meara nodded. "And—?"

"She wants to come up to the Fist for . . . for—"

Tessie Mallon's voice faltered. She stood wordless.

The O'Meara let her sweat for a long minute. Then he said, "You mean for the *droit du seigneur* you ladies have refused to allow me to enjoy?"

Tessie Mallon nodded mutely. This was going worse than she had anticipated.

"It seems a little one-sided," he continued. "Expecting me to cooperate in my own deprivation."

"But Flinty—" she ventured.

He nodded. "Ah, of course! Flinty is our wonder stud."

She bridled. "There is no need to be vulgar."

His eyes opened wide. "But that's why you want me to let him use my facilities. Perhaps I should charge a stud fee?"

She realized he was tormenting her. "Will you let her come up, my lord?"

He admired her courage. Tessie Mallon was getting nothing out of this. "There are conditions," he said. "Flinty Hagan is a shy man. He insists that the deed must be done in the dark, in silence. There must be no conversation. Not even an exchange of greetings. There must be no discussion of the matter with his wife. And if Mal Kennedy doesn't like wearing horns, he must lump it. I'll punish any attempt to take it out of Flinty. Will they accept those conditions?"

Tessie Mallon inwardly cursed the Barley Cross Ladies Sewing Circle. "My lord," she said, "I begin to think it would be best if we let everyone believe that you are insisting on your *droit de seigneur*. Flinty Hagan's role can be kept quiet."

The Lord of Barley Cross kept a straight face. "In that case, Missus Mallon, you could have a deal. You are suggesting that we carry on as if I am still the star performer. Only the ladies of the sewing circle will know it's not the truth."

"I think that would be best, my lord."

He held out a hand. "Let's shake on it, Tessie."

Tessie Mallon began to understand what her husband saw in the man. She took his hand. "And mum's the word, my lord," she whispered.

The Lord of Barley Cross sent for Flinty Hagan as soon as his visitor had left.

"Flinty," he told the man, "you're off the hook."

"Me lord?" queried Flinty, who had forgotten his conversation with the doctor.

"You told Doctor Denny that you were nominally prepared to stand in for me regarding a certain commitment at the next village wedding—"

Flinty frowned, then his face brightened. "Oh that! Doctor Denny mithered me so much we'd have got no fishing done if I hadn't agreed. Anyway—" Flinty sounded aggrieved. "He told me I wouldn't have to do anything!"

"Doctor Denny was being optimistic. You would have had to do enough acting to win yourself an

Oscar." Patrick O'Meara eyed Denny Mallon's victim with grim humor. "But I've been wheelin' and dealin' with the village ladies, and all you need to do to satisfy them is keep your mouth shut and your face out of sight on wedding nights."

"Yes, me lord," acknowledged Flinty, who had no intention of doing anything else.

"Well, then, that's settled," said the O'Meara. "Can I offer ye a drink before ye go?"

"It's very kind of ye, my lord," murmured Flinty. He clutched his cap tighter to his chest. "Will this wheelin' and dealin' business ye've been up to put a stop to them women ogling me on me egg round?"

Patrick O'Meara shook his head. "I'm afraid you're going to be more popular than ever, Flinty."

The day chosen for the wedding dawned wet, but by two o'clock, the drizzle had ceased, and a watery sun warmed the congregation which assembled to watch Sally Keegan wed Malachy Kennedy. After the service, a bemused Malachy was given notice by a smartly turned out Sergeant McGrath that his new-made wife was required to present herself forthwith at the Fist for their lord's *droit du seigneur*.

Malachy Kennedy was a biddable man. He had been warned about the lecherous antics of their new Master, and had decided not to dispute the inevitable. He kissed his new wife, then helped her into the car loaned by Doctor Mallon. He watched her drive off with her military escort, then returned to the reception to get thoroughly drunk. Around six, when most of the guests had departed, he found himself in the company of Flinty Hagan

"What are ye going to do tonight?" asked Flinty, knowing how Malachy must be feeling.

"Ach—I'll sod off on me own somewhere," confessed Malachy. "Sure I can't face all these people knowing what's happening to my Sally."

"I have to disappear, too," mumbled Flinty, hazily recalling the O'Meara's instructions. "Got to stay out of sight all bliddy night."

Malachy felt a twinge of sympathy for his friend. Maureen Hagan must be a hard woman to treat Flinty so. He squinted through the uncurtained window. " 'Tis a fine night," he observed. "We could put a boat out on Corrib?"

"Now there's an idea," approved Flinty, relieved at finding his problem solved so conveniently. "We might take a bottle or two along with us, eh?"

Malachy stared round the almost empty Market Hall, noting the uneaten food that was left. "We could certainly find a home for some of this stuff."

Unsteadily, they toured the tables, laying in provisions.

"Damn!" murmured Flinty. "I'll have to traipse up to Killoo Farm for me rod."

"I'll lend ye a spare," volunteered Malachy. "Let's be off. The fish'll be biting like midges tonight."

In a small room at O'Meara's fist, Sally Kennedy got into bed. Her feet found the warm brick wrapped in a towel that Michael had placed beneath the blankets. Recalling Tessie Mallon's instructions, she blew out the candle, and snuggled down. Later she heard the door creak as someone entered the room. Sally nerved herself for the ordeal.

The figure halted by the bedside, then threw back a corner of the coverlet.

"Is it you, Flinty?" she whispered.

"Hush!" said a masterful voice.

It wasn't as bad as she expected.

A little over a month later, in the still unfinished Croom cottage, Sally Kennedy decided that her husband should be let into a secret.

"I was at the doctor's this morning," she told him.

He shot her an apprehensive glance. "Is there something wrong, Sal?"

She smiled. "Ah, no—'tis good news. I'm pregnant."

Malachy Kennedy's frown disappeared. He grabbed her, and swung her off the floor. "That's great! Aren't things bucking up in the village at last? First Flinty Hagan's missus. Now you . . ."

She couldn't keep it a secret. She stared down at him, hands on his chest. "And 'tis Flinty ye can thank for what's happened."

He stared back up at her. "Come again, lass!"

She bit her lip. "When I went up the hill for the Master's droyts, it wasn't the Master I went to bed with, it was Flinty. Tessie Mallon arranged it all with the O'Meara. But we haven't to let on to anybody, because Flinty is a shy man."

Malachy Kennedy's brown furrowed. Carefully he lowered his wife to the floor. "And how often have ye been to bed with our Mister Hagan?"

Her mouth opened. "Why, just the once—and only so he could—"

"And when was that?"

"I've just told you—on our wedding night."

"The night him and me fished all night on Corrib?" Malachy peered incredulously at his wife.

It was her turn to frown. "You mean he wasn't up at the Fist with me?"

"Not unless he can be in two places at once."

Her hand flew to her mouth. "Then who was it that—?"

Malachy didn't know whether to feel relieved or not. At least the O'Meara had a legal right to do what he did to a fellow's wife. But not Flinty Hagan. That was going too far! " 'Twas the O'Meara for sure that got you pregnant," he told her. "Flinty had nothing to do with it."

The word soon got around. A month later, Tessie Mallon climbed Barra Hill again. "Brigit Cullen and

Tom O'Connor are having the banns called," she told the O'Meara. "Ye'll be invited to the wedding."

"Will I now?" said the Lord of Barley Cross politely.

Tessie mallon wavered. "The Ladies Sewing Circle have released you from the promise you made, and we hope you will condescend to practice your droyt after the wedding," she gabbled desperately.

The Lord of Barley Cross smothered a smile. "Does Biddy Cullen subscribe to that view?" he queried.

Tessie Mallon flushed. Had the Master heard about the flaming row which had well nigh wrecked the Sewing Circle? "I think she would insist on it, my lord," she murmured.

"And what about Flinty Hagan?" asked the Master.

Tessie Mallon stared at him blandly. "I don't know if he'll be invited, my lord."

Patrick O'Meara smiled. He knew.

A Flight of Fancy

Tinker Tarbert Thomond toiled up Barra Hill to the revamped O'Flahertie stronghold known as O'Meara's Fist. The tinker envisaged a deal with the fortress's tenant.

Overhead, in his ivy-clad eyrie, Patrick O'Meara, Lord of Barley Cross and Master of the Fist, persevered with an interview more painful than the one the tinker planned for him.

"But, Andy," he demanded, "Where will you go? What will you do?"

Sergeant Andy McGrath shifted uncomfortably on a hard chair. "I dunno, me lord," he confessed. "I've got to get away. Maybe I need a change."

The Lord of Barley Cross compressed his lips. "God dammit, Andy—what sort of change to you want? You're the only professional soldier I have in my cockeyed army. What'll I do without you? And where else in Ireland will you find another community like ours? Where law and order are upheld?

58

Where the poor and the weak aren't exploited? Where people can look forward to a nearly normal future?"

Andy McGrath twisted a uniform cap in his anguish. "Nowhere, me lord," he admitted. "It's just that . . ."

"It's Flinty Hagan's wife, isn't it?" the O'Meara accused. "You've had your eye on her for ages."

Andy McGrath lowered his head. "God forgive me, me lord—but ye're right. I fancied her long before she married Flinty . . ." The sergeant's voice trailed off into a significant silence.

The Lord of Barley Cross sighed. "Dammit, Andy—I never thought you were a ladies' man. If I'd known you were keen on the lass, I'd wouldn't have pushed Flinty at her."

Andy McGrath sniffed. "Trouble is, Flinty is me pal, too. I get on well with both of them. Didn't I stand godfather to their little Liam?"

The Master of the Fist stood up, his face hard. "Well, I'm accepting no week's notice from you—as if you were chucking up an ordinary job. You'll have to give me time to train someone to take your place."

Andy McGrath got to his feet. "I'll help ye train whoever ye want, me lord. But I must tell ye—if I stay much longer in Barley Cross I'll go out of me mind."

The Lord of Barley Cross scowled at his sergeant. "As far as I'm concerned, you've gone already." He paused, struck by a thought. "Don't let on about this to General Desmond. I'll tell him when I'm ready."

The sergeant got up. "Ye can rely on me to keep quiet, sir."

To the guard on the gate, tinker Thomond explained, "I've important information from Oughterard for the O'Meara. He'll murther you if ye don't let me in . . ."

Patrick O'Meara studied his visitor with distaste,

the sour taste of Andy McGrath's resignation still in his mouth. Tarbert Thomond was not a citizen of Barley Cross. No doubt he would expect payment for any news he brought. But buying pigs in pokes was not an O'Meara habit. And, in any case, the Lord of Barley Cross didn't trust the fellow. These days, tinkers like Thomond traded where they could. But the man wouldn't have ventured this far without something of real value.

"Tarbert," said the Lord of Barley Cross, temporizing, "Will you take a drink?"

"That's kind of ye, me lord." The tinker squatted, uninvited, on the chair recently warmed by Andy McGrath.

Patrick O'Meara restrained an impulse to throw the man out, and instead busied himself at the sideboard.

"Well now, Tarbert." He handed the man a tumbler half full of poteen. "I must tell you that I'm not greatly concerned with what goes on in Oughterard. . . ."

Ever since Patrick O'Meara had hijacked the Healey gang's fuel reserves almost two years previously, an undeclared truce had prevailed between Barley Cross and the neighboring village. Other villians had come and gone, but the villains of Oughterard had kept away from Patrick O'Meara's bailiwick. During those years, the last shreds of law had disappeared from Connemara. Central government, preoccupied with anarchy closer to home, had ceased to concern itself with the west coast peoples, leaving them to sink or swim as best they might.

Most of them, reflected Patrick O'Meara, might as well have sunk.

And in Connemara, Moran Healey, despot of Oughterard, had held back from war, deterred by the fire-power of the O'Meara's Chieftain tank . . . .

Tarbert Thomond seeing Patrick O'Meara's lack of interest, feared a deal was slipping through his fingers.

"Me lord," he murmured, " 'tis important news."

"So you say," agreed the O'Meara. "But shouldn't I be the judge of that?"

"Well, me lord—" Tarbert Thomond knew when to cut his losses. This hard bastard who had grabbed the reins in Barley Cross might have a sense of honor as yet undiscovered.

"If I tell ye what I know, will ye pay me what ye think it's worth?"

"Now there's a fair suggestion," approved the Lord of Barley Cross, urbane as any man holding four aces. "Why not try me?"

"Well, me lord, 'tis like this . . ."

Lucy Nolan, Praty Coughlin's married sister who resided in Oughterard, and to whom Thomond had recently delivered a letter from her brother now resident in Barley Cross, believed that mob-master Healey had found himself a secret weapon.

The O'Meara showed some interest. "Does she have any idea what sort of weapon?"

The tinker stared into his potion to conceal a smile of triumph. Finally he had the bastard's attention. Now, he had to build the rumor up into a tidbit worth of recompense. "She didn't like to say, me lord, for fear of getting her husband into trouble, but one of Healey's men told Nolan it would put paid to yer tank!"

The warmth of the study caused Tarbert Thomond to exude a distinctive aroma. The Lord of Barley Cross got up to pace the carpet and, ostensibly, to think. The tinker's news was certainly worth money. Sooner or later, Healey would have to be dealt with. He and his gang deserved to be put down. But Thomond's story was rumor. It wouldn't do to encourage a belief that the O'Meara was a sucker for gossip.

He halted several paces from the tinker. "Tarbert,

you'll have to go back, and get your ear closer to the ground. You've fetched only half a story, and that's not much use to me."

"Yes, me lord." Thomond's voice lacked enthusiasm.

"Och—there's little danger for you there," coaxed the O'Meara. "Healey won't touch you. Everyone knows you're a free agent, beholden to no one." *Free to run with the hare and hunt with the hounds—* added the Lord of Barley Cross to himself.

"True, me lord."

"Bring me the rest of that story—what sort of weapon Healey has got—and I'll allow you to carry on trading in the village."

Tarbert Thomond blinked. Until that moment, he hadn't been aware that he needed permission to tinker in Barley Cross.

"If ye insist, me lord," he muttered.

"Oh, I do." The Lord of Barley Cross was smiling now. "Find out what Healey has up his sleeve, and I'll make it well worth your while."

The tinker stood up, and swallowed his drink. He had been a fool to come up to the Fist thinking this hard bastard would pay for his information. But then, who else would buy it? Perhaps he could persuade Ambrose Nolan to ferret out a few more facts. He grunted, "Leave it to me, me lord."

Face grim, the Lord of Barley Cross watched him go. Two encounters like this morning's were enough to upset any man's temper.

Later that day he leaned on a gate alongside Doctor Denny Mallon, watching O'Leary's pigs at lunch.

"Handy things, pigs," observed the Lord of Barley Cross, "for converting waste into food."

"More or less the antithesis of what people do," agreed the doctor.

The O'Meara raised his eyebrows. "Maybe it would be possible to set up some kind of cycle between the species?"

The doctor fumbled a pipe bowl into his pouch. "Hardly likely, Pat. Remember, the pigs don't survive their part in the conversion process."

The O'Meara nodded. "True, Denny. I'd overlooked that small matter." He paused for a moment, eyes studying the swine. Then he said, "I had a chat with Andy McGrath and a visit from that tinker fellow Thomond this morning."

Doctor Mallon put a match to his pipe, puffing out clouds of noxious smoke. "Did you so? I hear the tinker's been trading in Oughterard. He brought back a letter for Praty from his sister. Apparently our Tarbert operates some sort of a postal service."

"Our Tarbert would sell shares in cobweb mines if he could find suckers to buy them." The O'Meara stared in the direction of Oughterard. "He tells me that friend Healey has found some sort of weapon that will be a match for my old tank."

"Like what?"

"He didn't know. I sent him away with a flea in his ear to see if he could find out more about it."

Denny Mallon valued what the O'Meara's Chieftain tank had done for Barley Cross. He said, "What could hurt it?"

The O'Meara shrugged. As an ex-Grenadier guardsman, he knew only too well what could hurt tanks. "Healey might have got hold of a rocket launcher and ammunition."

The doctor rubbed the bowl of his pipe against his chin, eyes shut in thought. "You worried?"

The O'Meara stretched over the gate to scratch the back of a friendly pig. "We're getting low on gas, Denny. I've just about enough left to run the tank to Oughterard and back."

"I hope Mister Healey isn't aware of that."

"Ach—Healey knows all about shortages. Praty Coughlin told me that some of his crowd are carrying crossbows instead of guns."

Denny Mallon snorted with contempt. "Bejasus—those buckos are never happy without a weapon to wave about! How are *our* military resources holding up?"

The O'Meara ticked the pig's ears. "Apart from a bit of bad news this morning, we're managing, Denny. General Desmond has our soldiers terrified of wasting a shot without his authority, 'though we've plenty of bullets in stock. There's that Bofors-type gun I took from Healey—for what use the thing is. I'm sure the British navy never left it in the condition Healey had it. And I've ammunition enough to deal with him—as long as I can maneuver. An immobilized tank would be a different story."

"Could you not get McGuire to distill you something?"

Patrick O'Meara laughed. "If I asked Mick McGuire for two hundred gallons of ninety octane poteen he'd revolve faster than his own mill wheel!"

The doctor sucked at his pipe. "Then you'd better call a moratorium on tank maneuvers until Thomond finds out what Healey is cooking up. What was the bad news you had?"

The O'Meara dilated on Andy McGrath's pusillanimity.

The doctor frowned. "We can't spare him, Pat. He's the only real soldier we have, after yourself. You'll have to talk him out of it."

The O'Meara kicked at the gate. "Easier said than done, Denny. The man's infatuated with Maureen Hagan."

"Damn!" The doctor's brow wrinkled in thought. "Could we not talk Maureen into an illicit relationship? After all, Flinty can't—"

Patrick O'Meara grinned in spite of his depression, wondering just how far this man beside him would go to protect his beloved village.

He said, "I'm surprised at you, Denny—suggesting such a thing. Our Maureen is a good girl."

Denny Mallon showed no signs of repentance. "Is she, Pat? I seem to recall you talked her into a little indiscretion a while back."

Patrick O'Meara tugged thoughtfully at the friendly pig's ears. "That was necessary. How else can we prevent Father Con's christening font from rusting?"

The doctor's eyes twinkled. "Father Con's christening font is carved from Connemara marble. It can't rust."

"Well—grow verdigris, or whatever happens to unemployed marble basins."

Denny Mallon stared skywards, mouth pursed. "Do we now equate morality with the state of a christening font?"

The O'Meara concentrated on the pig. "It's better than having no standards at all. I could try having a word with our Maureen."

Denny Mallon groaned. "That might help. If you can't think of anything better. And, try to do something about our fuel stocks, too."

The O'Meara drummed on the gate, flinty-eyed. The tank's maneuverability had to be husbanded. If Healey had got hold of anything like that British 17-pounder which could shoot through nine inches of armor, Barley Cross would need every drop of fuel he could lay his hands on!

The Master of the Fist sighed. "I'll put the word out. Anyone that's hoarding diesel or gas had better hand it in. I'll need every drop if we bump into Healey's tank killer."

The doctor tapped out the dottle from his pipe, scattering ashes on the pig below. "Have you told the general about this new weapon?" Denny Mallon was aware that General Larry Desmond and the Lord of Barley Cross did not always see eye to eye on military matters.

The O'Meara contemplated the haunches around O'Leary's troughs. "Och—Larry is too busy building fortifications at the Fist to be bothered about Moran Healey's plans."

The doctor gave his lord a long look, then he shrugged. "Perhaps it's as well. Larry might go charging off to find out what's brewing." He sucked on a dead pipe for a moment, then tucked it into his pocket. "Lucy Nolan says they are near starving in Oughterard."

The Lord of Barley Cross grunted without sympathy. "Let 'em starve. We've enough to do feeding our own people."

"I don't mean the Healey gang," protested the doctor. "That lot are probably living well enough. I mean people like Praty's sister. She writes him that most of the young adults have left the village, and there aren't hands enough now to work the fields. It's getting, she says, like the famine times when they lived on potatoes."

It was not often the O'Meara could catch the doctor out. "You mean when they *didn't* live on potatoes," he corrected. "It was only when the crops failed that they starved."

"We can do without your didactism," reproved the doctor. "You'll be lecturing me on the cultivation of lazy beds next. I was merely pointing out that we have a bounden duty to feed the hungry. And there are people here who have relatives in Oughterard."

The O'Meara grimaced. "I won't argue with you Denny. We've had plenty of food and seed from Oughterard in the past. I agree, we should reciprocate."

Denny Mallon's puckish face twisted in what Patrick O'Meara recognized as a smile. "I knew you'd see it my way—eventually."

Patrick O'Meara scowled. Denny Mallon tended to lecture at times. He said, "I'll have a word with

Andy McGrath, while I still have him. We should be able to figure out a way of sending food without it falling into Healey's hands."

"Good man." Denny Mallon straightened up. "By the way—Lucy Nolan also mentioned in her letter that Moran Healey has built a big shed on their hurley ground . . . and put up signs saying that 'Snoopers will be shot.' She's been puzzling her head, trying to imagine what they could hide in such a building . . ."

The Lord of Barley Cross found Sergeant McGrath checking the mechanics of the naval gun now standing beside the unfinished gun pit in the kitchen garden at the rear of the Fist. Willie Flanagan was chipping rust from the flared muzzle. Pete O'Malley tinkered with the angle of the gunner's seat.

The O'Meara indicated the weapon and then the half-built barbette. "Is *that* going in *there?*"

Sergeant McGrath saluted. "Yes, me lord. The idea is to have this at the back of the Fist and yer tank at the front—"

"Whose idea?"

"General Desmond's, me lord."

"And where is the general?"

Andy McGrath's face was expressionless. "He told me he was off to wet his whistle at Mooney's, sir. I don't know how ye missed him."

Patrick O'Meara frowned. Perhaps it was as well that he had not encountered the general. He pointed to a window half-hid in ivy on the wall above the gun emplacement. "That's my bedroom up there. Will I be enjoying the music of gun drills and practice firings when you get that thing finished?"

"Not while ye're asleep me lord." Sergeant McGrath wasn't without diplomacy. "Any case, we can't get the thing to shoot yet. The feed mechanism don't work as it should. And it won't elevate or traverse without the electric. I'll have to be having a go at it."

The Master of the Fist scowled. "Look for rust, Andy. The gun came off a warship wrecked on the rocks below Clifden, and it's seen not a drop of oil since then. It needs lubrication!"

"Yes, me lord." Andy McGrath waited patiently. Judging by the Master's tone, requests for demob weren't popular with him.

"And you should be able to elevate and traverse manually. Power lines can get shot away." The Master of the Fist jerked a thumb at his residence. "Now, come in for a drink. I want to talk to you."

In the Master's study for the second time that day, Andy McGrath stood at parade rest, and waited to be spoken to.

Patrick O'Meara handed him a half glass of poteen, and snarled, 'For God's sake, sit down, Andy. This isn't about your bloody resignation. I've done nothing about that, yet. I want someone to sneak food into Oughterard for me."

Clutching his glass, Andy McGrath perched himself on the edge of a hard chair. "How much food, me lord? And who to?"

Patrick O'Meara explained doctor Denny's good neighbor policy. "I think a cart load, for a start. A pig, a couple of lambs, some bread, milk, cabbages . . . I'll make a list for you, and write out some requisitions. Brendan McCarthy might even supply what we need without an order. You can tell him that all donations will qualify for tax reductions. It'll be delivered at night. Lucy Nolan, who is Praty Coughlin's sister, is the contact. I'll be satisfied if the food is left with her. She can distribute it round the village."

Andy McGrath wrinkled his brow. "You mean she'll have to make sure the Healey crowd don't get hold of it?"

The O'Meara nodded. "Exactly. Now, I can't order anyone to do the job. You can hardly call it defending Barley Cross. Could you find me a volunteer?"

Andy McGrath sighed. Sometimes the Lord of Barley Cross was pretty naive. He said, "I'll do it, me lord."

The O'Meara looked dubious. "It could be dangerous, Andy. And you're—sort of working your notice."

Andy McGrath was still feeling guilty about his resignation. "I don't mind, me lord."

"Do you know Oughterard well enough to find Praty's sister?"

"I'll take someone with me who does."

The O'Meara sighed. He was going to miss this dependable man who could be relied on not to make mistakes. He said, "While you're there, try to get a look inside the shed they've built on their hurley ground. I believe there's something interesting inside it."

The light of Sergeant McGrath's lantern revealed an entrance way wide enough for a cart.

"You go first, Flinty," whispered the sergeant. "They don't know me."

Corporal Flinty Hagan pulled the donkey into the alley after him. At his knock, the Nolan's door opened the width of a security chain. Lucy Nolan peered through the gap, holding her candle high in an attempt to see who waited outside.

"It's me, Missus Nolan," Flinty whispered. "Aloysius Hagan. I went to school with your Ambrose. Is he in?"

Lucy Nolan backed away. "Ambrose is out. What do you want?"

Flinty Hagan moved forward. "We've a cart load of food here. Praty told us you were getting hungry. The food's a gift from the folk of Barley Cross. We'd like you to share it out for us."

Lucy Nolan returned to the door to peer through the gap. "Who's that with you?"

Sergeant McGrath pulled off his billycock, and tried not to look like a tinker despite his disguise. "You can trust us, Missus Nolan," he told her. "Just tell us where to dump this grub."

Lucy Nolan fought a battle with her qualms. Then she put down the candle, and unchained the door. "You can leave it here in the lobby. Who did you say it was for?"

"It's for anyone that needs it," Flinty explained. "Just see that none of Healey's crowd gets any."

"*Them!*" Lucy Nolan's voice trembled. "Ambrose has gone to see if he can find what they're hiding down at the hurley field."

"That's where we're—" began Flinty, before a dig from the sergeant took his breath away.

"We'll leave the cart here if you don't mind, ma'am. We've another job to do," interrupted Andy. "We'll be back to unload it in half an hour."

Lucy Nolan missed very little. She said, "I'll get a lamp. You gentlemen do whatever you intend to do. The cart will be empty when you get back."

"The donkey could do with a drink, too," added the sergeant.

"Leave everything to me," said Lucy Nolan.

A gibbous moon made the hurley ground a mystery. Sergeant McGrath had doused the lantern. He and the corporal lurked behind a hedge bordering the field. The shed shone silvery in the moonlight.

" 'Tis big enough to hold an elephant," murmured Flinty. "But I don't see no lights in it."

"Perhaps elephants can see in the dark," murmured the sergeant.

"Har, har."

"That's enough of that, *Aloysius*," reproved the sergeant.

"And that's enough of the *Aloysius*," warned his corporal.

Andy McGrath ignored Flinty's insubordinate tone. No point in waving stripes about on his last few days as a volunteer. Did Flinty know he had given notice to quit?

"I wonder if there's a guard?" pursued Flinty, mollified by the sergeant's silence.

"Bound to be if they shoot snoopers like the notice says."

Flinty Hagan searched the shadows round the shed. "Where's Ambrose?"

"Snooping around, waiting to get shot at, most likely." Andy McGrath pulled off his coat, and threw it across the hedge. "I'm going over."

Flinty's teeth chattered momentarily. "I'm coming with ye."

"Keep quiet, then."

"I can't—I'm cold."

Andy McGrath believed him. Corporal Hagan had been attempting to rescue a general under fire when he forfeited his manhood.

They scrambled over the hedge, protected by the sergeant's jacket.

The activity allowed the corporal to forget the cold. He crouched in the grass. "There's someone on the roof, Sarge!"

Andy McGrath strained his eyes. They weren't as sharp in the dark as they used to be.

"There!" pointed the corporal. "On the roof—Christ! He's slipped."

A distant clatter betrayed the snooper's downfall. A door opened in the gable end of the structure. Indistinct figures emerged.

"Looks like your pal's had it," murmured the sergeant.

The figures spread out, searching.

Flinty Hagan half rose to his feet. "What are those things they are carrying?"

"Keep down! They're crossbows. We'll have to wait until . . ." Sergeant McGrath shut up.

"Until what? Until they've shot Ambrose Nolan? No bloody way!"

Flinty Hagan stood erect.

A light flashed on them. Flinty waved his arms.

Andy McGrath hugged the earth. "Get down, you fool!"

Flinty began to run

Andy McGrath heard the twang of bow strings, and the hum of arrows. The thudding of Flinty's feet on turf ceased.

The Sergeant rolled onto his side, peering along the grass. Figures clustered round a recumbent form, playing lights on it.

"He's a goner," said a voice.

"I don't know him," said another.

"Let him lie," said a third. "They'll find him in the morning, and understand we don't joke about snoopers."

Andy McGrath waited until they had gone before he dared look for Flinty. He carried the scarcely breathing body back to the Nolan's. The man of the house had got home first.

"Was it ye distracted 'em?" Ambrose Nolan demanded. "Jasus! Will ye look at *him!*"

"Bring him in!" commanded his wife. "Is he hurt?"

"Bad enough," grunted Andy McGrath.

Lucy Nolan peered at the limp body. "Looks like he needs a doctor."

"What bloody doctor have we?" snarled Ambrose Nolan.

Andy McGrath carried his limp burden into the house.

"Put him on the couch," ordered Lucy Nolan. "We'll have to do what we can for him."

Her husband stooped over the body. "He's got six inches of bliddy arrow stuck between his ribs, and the barbs won't let ye pull it out. He needs surgery."

Andy McGrath felt himself trembling. "I'll get a doctor," he promised. "We have a good one in Barley Cross. Look after him 'til I get back." He turned blindly towards the door. "Damn you, Nolan. Did you *have* to fall off that roof!"

Ambrose Nolan colored. "Don't blame me. I near broke me neck trying to see what they're keeping in that damn shed!"

"And what did you see?"

"Not a damn thing. They were sitting there in the dark."

Andy McGrath swallowed a blasphemy. A man's life put at risk because of Nolan's recklessness. He gritted his teeth. "Have ye a bike I can use?"

"Round the back. By the privy."

The sergeant nodded to Lucy Nolan. "Keep saying your prayers. I'll be as quick as I can."

Patrick O'Meara had gone to visit Maureen Hagan while her husband was off adventuring with Andy McGrath.

The Lord of Barley Cross was hardly a stranger to Maureen Hagan. She had been the first Barley Cross bride to suffer his *droit de seigneur*, and since she had been willing to be thus victimized, the experience had created something of a bond between them.

Patrick O'Meara said, "I need your help, Maureen. Sergeant Andy McGrath has given me his notice."

She flushed as she poured tea from a massive brown teapot. "What can I do about it?"

The O'Meara said simply, "Andy McGrath's in love with you. That's why he's leaving."

She said, "Oh, Jasus!"

He looked up. "Did you know?"

She bit her lip. "I guessed. He's been acting sheepish lately."

The O'Meara pondered a moment. "Does Flinty know?"

Maureen Hagan sat down, hands grasped together in her apron pocket. "Those two are great friends. I don't imagine Flinty gives it a thought."

The O'Meara hesitated. Flinty Hagan was unable to fulfill all a husband's duties because of the wound he got rescuing Larry Desmond . . . and Andy McGrath had been hanging around Killoo Farm for some time. The O'Meara said, "Is there anything between you and Andy?"

She colored again. Conversations with the Master were often embarrassing. She murmured, "There is nothing between us. But he may have got the idea something was possible, knowing how Flinty is fixed."

"*Would* anything be possible?"

She shook her head, lips tight together.

He said, "I don't want to lose Andy—he's the only real soldier I have."

Her eyes glinted. "Are you suggesting that I deceive Flinty?"

He stared at her coolly. "You've deceived him before—with me!"

"You told me Flinty knew about that."

"True." He paused a moment. "If I could get Flinty's okay to it—would you . . . ?" Patrick O'Meara knew she liked his sergeant. And, human nature being what it was . . .

Her cup clattered against the saucer. "Flinty would never agree to such a thing!"

He shrugged. "Who knows what anyone will agree to until they're asked? I have to do things I don't agree with. Will you—for the sake of Barley Cross?"

"Has Andy McGrath asked you to proposition me?"

The O'Meara shook his head. "Andy is an honest slob. He wouldn't dream of such underhanded conduct. If I get your agreement, I've still to talk him into it afterwards."

She glared at him. "Patrick O'Meara—you're a wicked bastard—and you have the morals of a tomcat!"

He sighed. "I know. We can't all afford the best sort of morals in Barley Cross these days. Will you do as I ask?"

She hid her face in her hand. "If Flinty and Andy agree . . . and you are sure it will help the village—I might."

He picked up his cup. "Good enough. Might could be right!" He gulped the hot tea, then lowered the cup. "Now, Maureen Hagan, have you any of those cookies left in your cupboard?"

Sergeant Andy McGrath found Doctor Denny Mallon having an early night in bed with a book.

The doctor answered his knock in pyjamas. "What's the trouble, Andy?"

The sergeant told him of Flinty Hagan's plight.

Denny Mallon closed his eyes for a moment. Then he said, "Round the back with you, and get the gig out quick. I'll put a few clothes on, and be with you as fast a I can."

Andy McGrath said, "I have the bike."

The doctor snorted. "You've pedalled twelve miles I haven't the patience to keep waiting for you to catch up. You'll come in the gig!"

Urged continually, the pony got them back to Oughterard in twenty-five minutes. By then, Flinty Hagan had been bleeding internally for over an hour.

Denny Mallon stooped over the corporal. Flinty lay face down on Lucy Nolan's couch, the shaft of the arrow projecting from his side, Lucy Nolan's cushions black with blood beneath him. The doctor felt briefly inside Flinty's shirt front, then turned him over. Flinty's head lolled, like a rag doll. The doctor peeled back the lid of a sightless eye. He shook his head. "We're too late. Wrap him in a blanket. We'll take him back with us."

"Is he dead?" whimpered Lucy Nolan.

The doctor wiped his hands on a rag from his pocket. "As a doornail. His lungs will be full of blood," he told them. "Flinty Hagan had drowned himself."

The Lord of Barley Cross walked back from the churchyard with the new widow. He said, "I'll send someone down to give you a lift with the farm work."

Stiff-lipped, Maureen Hagan mumbled, "I'll manage. I managed before. I can manage again."

"You didn't have a baby to look after then," the Master said gently. "I'll send Andy McGrath down to help you."

Maureen Hagan turned a bleak face to him. "Flinty told me Andy was leaving the village."

Patrick O'Meara's mouth twisted grimly. "Andy McGrath will leave Barley Cross when I let him. Right now his place is at Killoo Farm, helping you. He's baby Liam's godfather, and has a duty to look after the child. He's a single man, with no family to worry about. So I'll release him from his military commitments on the understanding he shoulders his other responsiblities."

Maureen Hagan shifted her infant to the other arm, as though to shield him from contamination. "You wouldn't still be trying to use me, would you, my lord?"

He looked surprised. "Why should I do that, Maureen?"

She glared ahead, stony-faced. "I'm thinking about our interview a couple of nights ago—when you pestered me to deceive my husband."

Patrick O'Meara's face betrayed a momentary embarrassment. He cleared his throat. "I deserve your bad opinion Maureen." He wagged his head sadly.

"Sometimes my determination to keep Barley Cross alive leads me into error."

"Andy McGrath didn't put you up to this—suggesting he comes to Killoo Farm?"

His laugh seemed spontaneous. "Nobody puts the O'Meara up to anything, I can assure you."

Maureen Hagan's expression softened. "Andy is a reliable man. I wouldn't mind his help. Flinty got rid of both our hired hands when we married." She sighed. "It all seems so . . . so damned *convenient*—thinking about that other suggestion you made."

Patrick O'Meara trudged beside her, head down, in silence. Then he looked up, breathing hard. "I didn't plan Flinty's death," he said curtly.

Later, he called a meeting of his advisers.

"We lost a good soldier and citizen," he told them, "trying to find out what Healey is cooking up for us. I'm not waiting any longer. I'm taking the tank to Oughterard. A couple of shells through that shed they have on the hurley ground should put a stop to whatever Healey has in mind."

"Ye don't usually consult us on military matters," commented Kevin Murphy from the corner of the settee. "Is there a special reason for this condescension?"

"My military problems are not usually as critical as this one could prove to be," responded the O'Meara. "We're down to the last of our fuel. If the Chieftain has more than twenty-odd miles in its tanks, I'll be astonished."

The vet stared gloomily into his glass. "I take it ye've scraped the barrel?"

"Thoroughly."

"Let's hope ye'll be astonished then."

"I'd like all the women and children up at the Fist as usual," resumed the Lord of Barley Cross, "and the street barricaded at both ends."

Celia Larkin looked up from her knitting. "Who will be in charge here?"

The O'Meara nodded at the silent figure at the other end of the settee. "Larry will defend the Fist. He prefers that to being squashed in a noisy, smelly tank."

The general raised his glass. "Every man to his taste, me lord!"

The O'Meara waved acknowledgement. "If we run out of gas, we'll abandon the tank, and come home on foot."

"You'll spike the guns before you do that, I hope," commented the doctor.

The O'Meara grinned. "We don't spike guns these days, Denny. We remove the breech blocks. But the question won't arise. I'm only taking enough shells for the job. If Healey wants to shoot an abandoned gun, he'll have to cadge his ammunition off me."

"And the machine guns?"

"We'll bring the turret-mounted gun home with us. The ranging gun will just lose some of its works."

Denny Mallon grunted, and put a match to the grass mixture in his pipe. "It all sounds pretty desperate to me. I hope you know what you're doing."

Patrick O'Meara studied his boots. "I'm not sure that I do, Denny. But, if I don't do something, that Healey fellow is going to spring a surprise on us, and I've a feeling we won't like at all."

Andy McGrath was hoeing potatoes at Killoo Farm when he heard the racket only one machine in the village was capable of making. He looked up to see dust clouds hanging above the far hedge.

Andy McGrath dropped his hoe, and ran.

The tank had to pass Killoo Farm Lane to reach the main road. Andy McGrath reached the junction first. He stood in the road, facing the approaching monster, and waved his arms.

The tank halted fifteen yards from him. The noise of the engine stilled.

Acting-corporal Pete O'Malley, lounging in the cupola, raised a negligent hand. "Hi, Andy!"

Andy McGrath lowered his head, lungs heaving. "Where . . ." he panted. ". . . where in blazes are ye going?"

Pete O'Malley patted the machine gun beside him. "We're off to give that Healey lot 'what-for' at last."

Andy McGrath clenched his fists. "Who's driving you?"

Patrick O'Meara's head appeared through the driver's hatch. "I am, Andy, since there's only you and me can handle this contraption."

Andy McGrath's mouth opened and closed several times. "If ye'll excuse me, me lord, driving that tank is *my* job."

Patrick O'Meara shrugged. "You're not in the army any longer, Andy. I accepted your resignation."

"Me lord . . ." Andy McGrath fought for breath. ". . . I want to come with you."

The O'Meara looked reluctant. "I'm not sure I can allow a civilian to take part in hostilities, Andy—there's the Geneva convention and all that—"

Andy McCrath spluttered. "I'll rejoin the Volunteers, me lord—as a private, if you like. So long as you let me come with you. I want a go at them bastards what murdered Flinty."

Patrick O'Meara decided that the time for joking was past. He wanted this man back in his army, and he wasn't particularly fussy how he achieved it. This time, though, he would tie a tighter knot. He frowned at the man in the road. "Do I understand that you are applying to rejoin the Fist Volunteers?"

Andy McGrath stiffened to attention. "Yessir."

"For keeps, this time? Not just while you get your own back on the Healey gang?"

Andy McGrath squared his shoulders further. Flinty

Hagan's widow might fancy another soldier husband. "For keeps, me lord," he confirmed.

Face stern, the Lord of Barley Cross donned his Grenadier Guard's beret, and pulled himself erect in the hatchway. "Raise your right hand, and swear it!"

Andy McGrath raised his right hand. "I so swear, me lord."

Andy McGrath had been a full-time soldier in the Irish army. He was reliable. And he had been a good sergeant. The O'Meara jerked a thumb over his head. "Up to the turret with you, then. You keep your old rank. Pete will be gunner."

Andy McGrath, hand on a lamp bracket, and one foot in a towing eye, paused. "Who's going to drive then, me lord?"

The O'Meara started the engine. "I am, Sergeant—because this could be the Chieftain's last outing, and it's *my* bloody tank!"

Oughterard was quiet. Its citizens, awed by the sight of a British Army Main Battle tank clanking along their main street, lay low. Rubble from a battle two years ago littered the street. Treads crunched over stone, glass and plaster. All timber had disappeared, noted the O'Meara—probably for firewood. He spoke over the intercom. "Whereabouts is this hurley field, Andy?"

"Keep going, me lord," responded Andy McGrath. "Just folly your nose for a while."

They passed the crater where, two years back, the O'Meara had blown a heavy machine gun and its crew out of existence.

"Does no one sweep up in this place?" murmured the O'Meara, surveying the rubbish.

Flashes winked from the windows of a building on the corner ahead. Metal spanged off the armor.

The O'Meara ducked, and closed the driver's hatch. "Button up, Sergeant. They've saved some ammo for us."

"Permission to shoot the cannon at them, me lord?" requested Andy McGrath, who had never fired the Chieftain's main armament.

"I've only fetched half a dozen rounds," objected his master. "And they're for the shed on the hurley field."

"Just one shot, me lord," coaxed the sergeant. "If this is our last run out."

"One armor-piercing, then," conceded the O'Meara. "Aim low, so it'll hit something really solid, or it'll go right through the place."

Sergeant McGrath tapped his loader on the shoulder. "Load AP."

Curly Phelan, ladies' coiffeur when not on Fist duty, slid a bottle-shouldered round into the breech. Curly wore knitted gardening gloves to avoid soiling his hands. "Gun loaded, Sarge," he reported.

Andy McGrath put an eye to a periscope. The range was point blank. "Aim at the bottom of the front door," he commanded.

Corporal O'Malley depressed the long barrel until it almost touched the glacis above Patrick O'Meara's head.

"On target, Sarge," he announced.

Andrew McGrath thought briefly of Flinty Hagan, and the face of Lucy Nolan as she watched him bleed on her cushions. His mouth tightened. He squeezed the trigger. Flame gouted from the gun muzzle, the explosion deafening, even through his ear muffs. The door vanished in splinters. He heard the shot bounce around inside the building. Then the roof dipped in the middle. Gable-end chimney stacks nodded briefly to each other. The structure began to tumble down.

Healey's men, hands high, spewed from the hole where the front door had been.

Andy McGrath opened his hatch, and removed an earpiece. He heard their voices.

Someone shouted, "You're too late, you bastards!"

The driver's hatch below swung open. "Too late for what?" queried Patrick O'Meara.

"You'll know when you get home."

"What will we know?" pursued the Lord of Barley Cross.

"The plane flew off twenty minutes ago. We're bombing shit out of your bloody Fist right now."

The O'Meara appeared not to hear him. He fumbled for something inside his cubby hole. "Tell me," he said, "were you at the Kilcollum massacre?"

The man ceased mouthing curses. "What do you know about Kilcollum? You weren't there."

"Thank you," said the O'Meara, face pale. His hand appeared, holding a large service revolver. Carefully, he shot the man dead.

From the steps of the Fist, General Larry Desmond watched an airplane buzzing Barley Cross.

Tom Burke, village butcher and acting lance-corporal, stood beside him. "Niver thought I'd see one of them things again," he murmured.

A small object dropped from the plane, struck the roadway, and rolled under a cart outside M'Glone's creamery. Came a flash, and the cart was flinders. Moments later the crack of the explosion followed, muted by distance.

"Well, I'm damned!" said Tom Burke.

The general fumbled in his pocket, then handed the lance-corporal a large iron key. "Nip down to the cellar, Tom," he instructed. "Fetch up a box of rifle ammunition, and start dishing it out."

Round the back of the Fist, lounging in their new gun pit, Willie Flanagan, poacher, and Eamon Toomey, simpleton, heard a sound they had never expected to hear again, and searched the sky in vain.

"I tell't ye we should've built this bloody brock at the front," complained Willie Flanagan. "Ye can't see a damned thing round this side."

"We will if it flies over us." pointed out Eamon with devastating logic.

They heard the thudding of Larry Desmond's boots on the flagstones. "Get that bloody cannon loaded!" he commanded. "Someone's bombing the village."

"All the ammo is up in the house," complained Willie. "Didn't ye order us not to leave it out in the rain."

"Then go and get some quick!" screeched the general.

Willie Flanagan departed at a run.

"Does it work properly now?" queried the general, who was aware that the gun had been reluctant to perform.

"Sure we gave it a good oiling," Eamon assured him. "And the Master told us we don't need the electric to move it. We can turn it with these little wheels." He slipped into the gunners seat, and rotated a handle. The gun muzzle swung round to point at the general.

Larry Desmond ducked instinctively. "Be ready to shoot at that airplane if it comes round this side," he ordered.

"Yes, sir," agreed Eamon. "Just the one bullet?"

"No, dammit!" howled the general. "Fire off the bloody lot if ye have to!" He left at a run, seeking volunteers to post on the roof.

In the two-seater monoplane circling above Barley Cross, the pilot spoke to his passenger behind him.

"Must you keep opening the window? I dislike drafts."

Moran Healey paused with another grenade in hand. "Just keep flying in circles, Mister Parnell— tipped over a bit, so I can see what's happening down there."

The pilot craned his neck. "What the devil are you dropping?"

Moran Healey released his missile. Their eyes followed its descent, and saw it explode in the Kennedy's chicken run.

"Hey!" The pilot's voice rose angrily. "I didn't fly you over here to blow things up!"

Moran Healey looked up from his bag of grenades. He produced an automatic pistol, and pointed at the pilot's head. "Attend to me, Mister Parnell," he instructed. "If you think I went to the trouble of fetching this kite halfway across Ireland, and sacrificing all my gasoline, to provide you with free flights over Connemara, you're crazier than I thought you were."

"You spoke about searching for survivors—" interrupted the pilot.

"I've found my survivors," snarled Healey. "I want to turn them into non-survivors."

"Dammit!" snorted Gerald Parnell. "You'll murder no one from my airplane! I'll see to that!"

He swung his stick to one side. The plane banked away from Barley Cross, and headed towards Barra Hill.

Moran Healey saw the Fist looming ahead, and realized it would make an easier target than small whitewashed cottages.

He pushed the muzzle of his pistol into the pilot's nape. "Circle the castle," he ordered. "Or I'll put a bullet in you."

"We'll both die if you do that," choked the pilot. "Unless you can fly this thing."

"I can fly it if I have to," lied Healey. "But I need my hands free to drop bombs."

Flashes came from the roof of the castle ahead.

"They're shooting at us!" gasped the pilot.

"So now will you let me bomb them?" snarled Healey, triumph in his voice.

Gerald Parnell heaved back on the stick. The plane rose higher. "They're only shooting at us because you're dropping bombs on them."

With his free hand, Moran Healey got a grenade from the bag. He pulled out the pin with his teeth, holding the lever shut. "I wouldn't argue the point. Go back while I try to stop them."

The plane roared over the roof of the Fist. Willie Flanagan saw it appear overhead as he slotted a magazine of cannon shells into the gun's receiver.

"There he is, Eamon!" he yelled. He leaped to the ground. "Shoot!"

The plane flew into the five-hundred-knot ring of Eamon's sights as Willie's feet touched the ground. Eamon squeezed the trigger. The gun pounded a drum roll in his ears.

In the plane, the pilot saw smoke puffs outside his window. He gasped. "Christ! They're still at it! I'm not staying here!"

Moran Healey hadn't seen the shell bursts, and, anyway, he was too enraged to care about anyone's health. "Oh no, you don't!" he snarled. He pressed the pistol muzzle harder into the pilot's neck.

Gerald Parnell decided that his passenger was mad. He banked steeply, hoping to dodge the tracers and throw Healey off balance.

Healey staggered. The pistol swung off target. The grenade flew from his hand. Healey screamed, dropped the pistol, and scrabbled vainly for the bomb. Five and a half seconds later it exploded.

Eamon Toomey and Willie Flanagan saw the flash and the whisp of smoke. They watched the plane spiral towards a field of barley.

Willie thumped Eamon on the back. "Ye hit it, lad! With yer first shot!"

The plane struck the ground, and burst into flame. Several explosions shook the wreck. A column of smoke burgeoned, and drifted downwind. Eamon grinned at his fellow gunner, and pointed a finger. "That's your barley that's burning, Willie."

Willie Flanagan's smile disappeared. "Ye clumsy

bugger!" His fists flailed at the marksman. "Have ye no more sense than to ruin me crops!"

In the main street of Oughterard, Andy McGrath, one arm cuddling the turret machine gun, saw Patrick O'Meara's victim collapse. He was unaware that the man had been executed.

He heard another of Healey's men call, "That's not fair—we've surrendered!"

The villain beside him brought a hand down to his mouth, then swung the arm up again.

Sergeant McGrath recognized the movement. He had practiced it often enough himself, rifle in one hand . . . bring the grenade to the lips, grip the ring between the teeth, withdraw ring, swing back arm, release lever, throw . . .

Andy McGrath elevated the butt of the machine gun a fraction with his shoulder, and squeezed the trigger.

His target crumpled. An object dropped, rolling into the rubble. Seconds later the doorway was full of dust and flying bodies.

"Well, well," said Patrick O'Meara, mild regret in his voice. "I wonder which one of them was Healey."

Andy McGrath tipped the machine gun so that it pointed skywards. "I didn't mean to kill all of them, me lord," he apologized.

"No matter." The O'Meara sounded unperturbed. "It saved me asking each one about Kilcollum."

"Begging yer pardon, me lord," Andy McGrath hesitated. "What happened at Kilcollum?"

The Chieftain's crew heard the O'Meara clear his throat. "Nothing of importance, now," he told them. "The matter is closed."

Something in the voice warned Andy McGrath, Pete O'Malley and Curley Phelan to curb any curiosity about Kilcollum. The sergeant sought a safe topic.

"Shall we be clearing up that mess in the doorway, me lord?"

"Let them lie," said his Master. "They don't a rate decent burial. We'll go round to the hurley field, and wait for their airplane to return. I only hope General Desmond was able to cope with bombs."

The hurley ground was deserted. The shed stood silent. Patrick O'Meara waited until dusk without sighting any plane. Then the intercom crackled with his voice.

"I reckon General Desmond won his battle, too, lads." The O'Meara's tone betrayed his satisfaction. "Put a round into that shed for me, Pete, please— just out of spite."

"Load smoke, Curly," ordered Corporal O'Malley. "AP won't notice that shack."

The turret bucked under the recoil. A hole appeared in the side of Moran Healey's hangar. Perhaps the shell struck stored fuel inside. Flames licked through the smoke, as the structure caught fire.

"That's it," pronounced the Lord of Barley Cross, watching the smoke thicken and billow skywards. "Slate clean. Let's go home."

Patrick O'Meara drove with his head out of the driver's hatch, the Chieftain's headlights picking out the road before him. A fuel gauge indicated that there might just be enough diesel left in the tanks to see them home. The O'Meara didn't particularly care.

He switched on the intercom. Life must go on, even after your prime objective has been achieved.

He spoke. "Now you've re-enlisted, Andy, you'll be wanting time off for courting, I expect?"

Andy McGrath flushed in the darkness above. Was nothing sacred to the Lord of Barley Cross!

In the Name of the Father

Patrick O'Meara lay awake in his castle, thinking of Eileen O'Connor. Down below in Barley Cross, Liam McGrath lay sleepless in his cot, also thinking of Eileen O'Connor. In another cottage in the village, dark-eyed Eileen O'Connor, clutching the rag doll she had loved since she was two, slept on in blissful ignorance.

Around five, the younger man, no longer able to endure inactivity, got up and pushed wide the casement. In the half-light of dawn, O'Meara's Fist dominated the skyline. Liam made out the high flak towers floating above serrated battlements. He yawned. Having seen O'Meara's Fist framed in his bedroom window for nineteen years, Liam wearied of the marvel. Besides, like the rest of the villagers, he was privy to its infirmities—the corroded armor, the rusty rocket launchers, and the shell-less batteries. And, like most of his village contemporaries, he found it hard to imagine that that great museum piece had ever intimidated any aggressor.

He sniffed the air scented by overnight rain. This, then, was the day. He jumped at the sound of his mother's alarm in the next room, heard the bed creak as she got up. He shivered. Now would begin the long-awaited sequence of events destined to end that evening in the bedroom of the old Curry cottage, with Eileen O'Connor and himself, face to face, alone at last, and irrevocably married.

"Liam! Are you going to lie in all morning?"

He dressed quickly in his working clothes. This was going to be a day when help would have been welcome. His stepfather being on duty at the Fist meant that he and his mother would have to cope with all the household chores in addition to preparing for the wedding.

But Eileen had chosen the date purposely: Andy McGrath on duty at the Fist meant a military guard of honor to greet them outside the church.

"Liam! Will you lie abed all your wedding day?"

"Coming, Mam." He clattered downstairs, out the back door, and across the yard. First chore was pumping the top cistern full while his mother kindled the fire and cooked breakfast. Afterwards he would milk the cows, feed the pigs, carry in the turf, chop kindling, check his snares, take the mare over to Seamus Murray for shoeing, and smuggle a sucking pig across to Eileen's mother as the McGrath contribution to the wedding feast. With a bit of luck, he might even find time to give his chin an extra close scrape before he put on his Sunday suit for the ceremony.

He pumped, watching the light strengthen through the branches of the overhanging apple tree, slowly exposing the detail of O'Meara's Fist.

He spat pensively into the long grass, wondering what the O'Meara himself was doing at this very moment. Certainly, he would not be pumping water in his old work clothes—wedding day or no. Not that the old lecher had ever needed to marry—when he had merely to lift a finger to get any woman in the village. Liam switched sides on the pump handle, turning his back on O'Meara's Fist. Let the old ram lie on, probably ignorant of the news that this day the only son of Maureen McGrath was marrying the dark-eyed daughter of Tom and Biddy O'Connor. His grip tightened on the pump handle. Few people saw the old goat nowadays. There had been a time when he might have come down from the Fist to awe the reception with his presence. Liam wiped sweat from his forehead, wondering why some folk were born to rule, and others to be ruled. Although there was little sign of the Master's iron hand these days. Indeed, if gossip were true, it was over a year since he had summoned a woman to the Fist.

A spatter of drops from the overflow sprinkled his nape. He released the pump handle, loosed the clamp which attached hose to spout. Any moment now his mother would . . .

"Breakfast, Liam!"

He soused his head under the spout, then started back to the house, picking up the egg from the side of the byre where the brown hen laid each morning.

Right now, up at the Fist, Andy McGrath would no doubt be dressing the guard into line for inspection by General Desmond. There was a wonder for you: how O'Meara the Ram, self-styled Duke of Connaught, Lord of Barley Cross, Master of the Fist, and lecher supreme, succeeded in inspiring the loyalty of people like Andy McGrath and General Desmond, or, for that matter, of people like schoolmistress Celia Larkin, Kevin Murphy the vet, Doctor Denny Mallon, and other decent folk.

Maybe it had something to do with the old days when the O'Meara built his Fist atop Barra Hill, buttresssing it with armor from the warship which foundered off Clifden, and parking his tank in the driveway to the Fist on the last drop of gas. And there were legends of his fabulous exploits, like the raid on the pill warehouse in Tuam which, they say, gave Barley Cross aspirin, antibiotics and independence.

Liam sighed. Times were certainly not like that now. Just work, work, and not enough hands to go around.

His mother called. "Quit mooning out there! Come in and eat your breakfast!"

He scraped his boots on the grating at the back door and went in, placing the egg in the crook of the dresser. He said, "Does Andy know the time of the wedding?"

Maureen McGrath frowned. "Liam, I wish you would learn not to call your stepfather 'Andy.' You are not yet a grown man, and it is altogether too familiar. Could you not call him 'Da'—just to please me?" Liam sat down at the bare, scrubbed table. He mumbled through a mouthful of oatcake. "Andy is not bothered. He said I might call him what I wished, so long as I didn't call him early. He is not my real father, anyway."

"Your own father would have stood for no use of Christian names." His mother's voice shook with unaccustomed emotion. He looked up and caught her eyes sparkling angrily at him. "Flinty was a strict man," she stormed. "He'd have stood no nonsense from you!"

"Leave off, Mam," he pleaded. "Who knows what my da would have stood for? It's seventeen years since he got that arrow in his lung, fighting for the old ram up there on Barra Hill."

"Liam!" Her voice rose alarmingly. "I will not have you using words like that about the Master of the Fist."

He raised his eyebrows in astonishment. "But,

Mam—that's what everyone calls him. They say he's been to bed with nearly every woman in the village." He broke off, and bit his lip in embarrassment.

Maureen McGrath flushed. "Liam McGrath, you have been listening to prurient gossip, and much good will it do you."

"Mam," he said patiently. "I'm only repeating what has been whispered around the village since I was a gossoon. Why, half the kids have the great O'Meara beak."

"Liam!" His mother screeched. "I forbid you to discuss such things in this house. If you have finished eating, I suggest you take the mare on down to Seamus Murray, after that you give the gig a good wash. If you are going to church in style, let it at least be a clean style."

Liam stuffed the last of the oatcakes into his mouth, and rose from the table. "I'll do that right now, Mam," he said.

At the door of the smithy, Seamus Murray clapped a hot shoe to the mare's off hind foot clutched firmly between his knees and watched the smoke curl.

"Great day for you, Liam," he said.

"If I can keep my mam in a good temper it will be," Liam responded. "Why should she get so upset when I criticize the old ram up there?" He nodded at the Fist which loomed plain in the sunlight at the top of the street. "Hasn't the old despot had his way with almost every woman in Barley Cross?"

The blacksmith fished a long, triangular nail from the pocket of his apron, inserted it through a hole in the horseshoe, and hammered it home. His voice was almost inaudible. "Easy to be critical, son. The O'Meara has been lord and protector here nigh on twenty years. Before he came we were like fowls in a farmyard with the fox outside. But he disciplined us, drilled us, dragged guns half the length of Connemara behind that old tank of his, and made Barley Cross a name in the land." The smith waved towards black skeleton which lay rusting on the hump of rock in Flanagan's barley acre. "*That* didn't come down by accident. We shot it clean out of the air. They say it was the last airplane in the West of Ireland. I was there and saw it come down. We did a three-week stretch on duty in those days because the village had to be guarded constantly. Gangs used to come a-roving. And, if they thought you had anything worth stealing, by God, they were after you with guns and cudgels and knives. But we stopped 'em in Barley Cross. They learned to leave us alone."

The smith sniffed embarrassedly. In silence he snipped off the sharp end of the nail protruding from the side of the mare's hoof. "There aren't so many people around now to make trouble," he added. "You might say we no longer need the O'Meara for a protector. But, who can tell?" He straightened up, searching his pocket for a nail. "You might say we were lucky to get through in such good shape. They tell me Clifden is a ghost town, now. 'Tis a great pity. But they didn't have our luck. And, sure, 'twas the O'Meara luck, and I, for one, am glad of it. So, if he wants to play medieval monarch, I'm prepared to put up with it."

He hammered home the nail, snipping off the point, and released the mare's leg.

Liam followed him into the smithy. He watched the smith work the bellows before pushing another shoe into the glowing coals. "But, Seamus, what if it was your own wife?"

Seamus Murray turned to stare at him, his gaze level and placid. "After nearly eighteen years wed to me, Mary is not the lass to drive the O'Meara crazy with desire. Let's say the idea just doesn't trouble me."

"But when you were younger?"

The smith hooked the shoe from the coals. He spat expertly. Spittle ricocheted from the hot iron. Satisfied, he gripped the shoe with the tongs and carried it out to the waiting mare. "Let's say," he said slowly, "if anything happened, I wasn't aware of it. And, if it did, somehow Mary neglected to mention the matter."

His eyelids crinkled as he watched the hot iron bed itself into the mare's hoof. He glanced slyly at Liam. "I suppose 'tis your wedding this afternoon that has set you thinking these serious thoughts?"

Liam scowled. He cocked an eye at the menacing Fist, and drew patterns with his toe in the dirt. He set his jaw. "Nothing happens to Eileen without my say-so."

Seamus Murray smiled sourly. He began to nail on the cooling shoe. "Brave words, son. But what would you gain by standing between the Master and a woman's virginity? He could deal with you, and *then* take what he wanted."

Liam felt his resolution wavering before Murray's calm acceptance of the Master's authority. He said, "Surely the O'Meara wouldn't treat a new bride that way?"

The smith was grinning openly. "Haven't you just suggested that he treated my Mary so?" He stared quizzically at Liam for a moment, then bent back over the hoof. He rasped the clipped nail points smooth without looking up. "I shouldn't worry over much, son. Probably the Master is not even aware that you are to be married today."

He gave the hoof a final buff, then released the beast. He pushed her towards Liam with a pat on the rump. "She'll do for awhile now, Liam. Tell your mam that's the last of my good shoes. I'll be making them from scrap in future, unless the tinker finds me some more."

Liam took the mare's bridle. "Let me know when you're ready for the piglet. I'll bring it straight over. Then we'll be quits for the last two jobs."

The smith patted his shoulder. "Don't be worrying about that either, son. I'll let Andy know when we are ready for it."

Liam slid onto the mare's back. He turned her head towards home. God damn! These old ones wouldn't let you grow up. Leave it to Andy. He will settle it. Let the O'Meara have his way, he saved our lives in the past. Well, he hadn't saved Liam McGrath's life, and Liam McGrath owed him nothing. They could run the village any way they liked, but don't expect Liam McGrath to get down and bow to their pet tyrant.

His stepfather was waiting outside the front door when he got home. Andy McGrath wore his visored helmet and beribboned flak jacket. Wizened Willie Flanagan and poor Eamon Toomey stood behind him. All three carried FN rifles. Liam opened his mouth to suggest that three men were not much of a guard of honor, saw the look on his stepfather's face, and thought the better of it. He cartwheeled dexterously from the mare's back. "Hi, Andy! You're early. The wedding's not until two."

Andy McGrath's face was grim. "We'll be in time, Liam, never doubt. But first we've a little business with you." He fumbled inside his jacket, and brought out a folded sheet of paper. Pushing up his visor, he put on his spectacles and unfolded the paper. "Just so you understand, Liam, that I am carrying out orders." He cleared his throat, and began to read.

"From the Lord of Barley Cross to Liam McGrath of Killoo Farm. Take note that we intend to exercise our *droit du seigneur* with your intended wife Eileen O'Connor and that Sergeant McGrath has orders to escort her to the Fist at six of the clock this day."

Liam felt his face grow hot. "Droit . . . droit what?"

His stepfather's face was impassive. "*Droit du seigneur*, lad. It's old French. Sometimes it's called *jus primae noctis*—which is Latin for the same thing—the right of the first night. The Master intends to exercise his legal rights with your betrothed."

Liam felt the color drain from his face. A lump of ice congealed in his chest. He stammered. "The . . . the Master can't want my Eileen!"

Andy McGrath refolded the paper, then tucked it inside his jacket. He removed his spectacles and put them into a pocket. "The Master can, and the Master does."

Liam caught his stepfather's hand in sudden appeal. "But you won't let them take her away!"

Andy McGrath's gaze softened slightly. "I'm sorry, lad. I'm the one that must do the taking."

Liam clutched him. "Andy, you can't!"

His stepfather firmly removed Liam's hand. "I must warn you, son, that it is a serious offense to obstruct the Master's officers in the execution of their duty. So don't try anything foolish. You'll get your Eileen back in the morning. She won't be the first, nor will she be the last. Now I suggest you accept that your married life starts tomorrow instead of tonight. And I'll be on my way to break the news to the O'Connors."

Liam stared incredulously at his stepfather and the two-man squad awkwardly clutching their rifles. Each of those guns, by repute, held only one round because of the miserly way General Desmond released ammunition. But one bullet could settle an argument. Would they really shoot him if he tried to prevent their abduction of Eileen? In the leg, perhaps, as a warning. Willie Flanagan wa a poacher by vocation; no doubt he would prefer a noose, or the knife. But poor Eamon Toomey would do whatever he was told: he would shoot, and think afterwards.

Hot, burning tears were suddenly scalding his cheeks.

His stepfather put an arm around his shoulders. He urged him towards the doorway of the house. "Go in and talk to your mother, son. She'll listen to you. And she will tell you that what I say is the best thing to do."

Sergeant McGrath turned to Willie and Eamon. "Right, lads. To the O'Connors now, and we'll get it over with."

Eileen O'Connor opened the back door and gasped. "Liam! You know it's unlucky to be seeing me before the service!"

He tried to take her in his arms, but she held him off.

"I had to come," he panted. "My mam thinks I'm checking the snares. Has Andy been yet?"

She glanced quickly over her shoulder into the interior of the house. "You know he has. He came straight from your place."

He gripped her arms. "Do you know why he came?"

She nodded, lowering her eyes.

"Then why don't you say something?" Surely she could not remain calm, knowing the message Andy McGrath had brought. He said, "You won't let that old—?"

Eileen O'Connor drew in a deep breath. She looked him straight in the eyes. "My da says it's the law and that we must do as the law says. He says we should regard it as an honor."

He snorted bitterly. "Your da sounds like a first-class creep to me."

She glared at him. "Don't you be calling my da a creep. He did his share for Barley Cross before you were born. And you're not even old enough to stand guard at the Fist yet!"

He pulled her towards him, and again tried to embrace her. "Don't let's quarrel, Eileen. I'm not calling your da names. It's just that he is like our Andy. All the old folk act the same—as though O'Meara was God, and his slightest wish the law."

He swallowed an angry retort, and said patiently, "We'll have to get away before Andy comes."

He felt her stiffen.

"Why? Why should we go away?"

"Why? So that old lecher can't . . ."

"He's not so old, and he's not a lecher. They say he's a very civil man."

"Civil! My God!"

She drew back as far as his arms would permit. Her voice was like ice on a pool. "If I've said something foolish, Liam McGrath, please don't hesitate to point it out."

His hands trembled with the impulse to crush her to him, knowing that she would resist. He said, "Eileen, let's not quarrel over this. Do you want the O'Meara to take you up there, and . . ." He floundered helplessly, left the question hanging.

Her lips compressed into a thin, straight line, which warned him that O'Connor common sense would now prevail. "If I agreed to go with you, where would we go?"

"Why—somewhere outside the village. There's the O'Toole cabin on Kirkogue has been empty a month now."

"Because no one has wanted it since old Gabriel died there, all alone, without a soul to help him, and at the mercy of any rogue that passed that way. Who would be caring for me while you were down here working at your farm?"

"But, Eileen—I'd stay with you. I wouldn't leave you on your own. We'd start a new farm. Old Gabriel had quite a bit of pasture at the back."

Her mouth turned up at the corners. "Faith—there isn't enough soil up there to grow a week's potatoes. And the land sloping so bad you'd need a short leg to get around easy."

"Then we'll build a cottage near the village. There's plenty of stone, and I'm good with my hands."

She sighed, wagging her head in mock despair. "Liam McGrath, sometimes I think you are a great booby. How near the village would you build your cottage? Near enough, I hope, for O'Meara's law to protect us from vagabonds like the two your Andy hanged last month. But, if you seek the law's protection, don't you have to obey it, too. And the law says I go up to the Fist tonight."

She let him pull her towards him then, felt his tears wet her cheek. She stroked the back of his head. "It's not the end of the world, lad. If we lived outside Barley Cross I'd probably have been raped at twelve, and be dying from malnutrition by now. We have a good life here. No bad men. And there's Doctor Denny's hospital if you're sick. I don't want to live anywhere else. So, we take the rough with the smooth. And, if I do have to go up to the Fist, nobody outside our families need ever know. And I'm sure you'd rather I went willingly than be dragged there, kicking and screaming over something any girl outside Barley Cross would regard as a normal event, and in this specific case might even consider it an honor."

He crushed her to him, not listening, unwilling to dispute further. "Don't worry," he murmured into her hair. "I'll fix it, somehow."

She pushed back his head so that she could look into his eyes. "Liam McGrath, there'll be no fixing, somehow or anyhow! We are going to live here in Barley Cross after we are wed, and you'll do nothing to prevent it!"

"But Eileen—" he began.

"But nothing." She closed his lips with her own. "If I can put up with it, so can you. Now off you go before my mama comes to see who it is that I'm blathering with at the back door."

Mind churning, Liam stumbled blindly from the O'Connor's yard. Sunlight flashed on jewels under his eyelids. Help from someone more powerful than himself was what he needed. He lurched towards the street.

Molly Larkin filled the doorway of her father's neat cottage beside the schoolhouse. Her arms were white to the elbows with flour. She stared at him in surprise. "Why, Liam—I thought today was your—?"

"It is, Molly, it is." He felt himself coloring with embarrassment. Once upon a time he had fancied motherless Molly Larkin. No doubt she would make a fine wife—if that someone didn't mind marrying her old man as well. He said, "It's your aunt I wanted."

Celia Larkin's niece dusted flour from her hands, wiped them on her apron. "She's not at home, Liam. I believe she's up at the Fist. Would you be leaving a message?"

He backed away. There was no message he would choose prosy Molly Larkin to deliver for him. "Ah— no, thank you, Molly. 'Tisn't anything important."

Granite chippings crunched underfoot; the gate squealed as he closed it behind him.

Who else to try?

Tessie Mallon was snipping dead rose heads in her garden. She was as plump and jolly as her husband was shrivelled and sour. She slipped scissors into her apron pocket and pulled off her home-made gloves as Liam hesitated the other side of her hedge. She saw his face and showed alarm.

"The doctor is not in, Liam. Is it your mam?"

He shook his head dumbly.

"Yourself, then?"

He found his voice. "There is nobody ill, Missus Mallon, I just wanted a quick word with the doctor."

She nibbled thoughtfully at the tip of her index finger—a habit which, forty years ago, had driven the village lads crazy. "He said he'd be back in an hour or so. Should I ask him to call round at your house?"

Emotion chocked his voice. "No—no thanks. I'll catch him another time."

She held her head on one side, half smiling. "Your Eileen has already had a chat with him, if that is any help. You don't have to worry about anything."

Liam fled.

Clouds were gathering over Carn Seefin and Leckavrea. Rain would soon be pocking the surface of Lough Corrib. Endless Connemara rain. A wet afternoon for the wedding, for sure. Who else could he try? Father Con?

The old priest led him into a furniture-filled study which had not altered in fifty years, except that now the electric light no longer worked. He listened in silence to Liam's plea for help.

"Well, Liam," he said gently. "What would you have me do? Forbid the wedding?"

"Ah, no, Father." That was not the solution which Liam sought.

"What then, son? I'm too old to be trudging up Barra Hill with a shillelagh in my hand to knock piety into the O'Meara."

"But, Father, you can't condone what he's trying to do. Isn't adultery a sin for him, as well as the rest of us?"

The old priest raised his hands in gentle reproof. "No, Liam, I did not say that I condoned the O'Meara's actions. No doubt he is as much a sinner as the rest of us."

"Well—couldn't you excommunicate him, or something?"

Father Constantine smiled patiently.

"Excommunication is the Holy Father's business, son, and I haven't had word from His Holiness for many a long year."

Liam's lip protruded stubbornly. "You could at least refuse him the sacraments."

Father Con frowned. His eyes narrowed in unspoken rebuke. He said, "Liam, the church is for sinners. If the O'Meara is our biggest sinner, he must have the biggest need of it."

Liam got to his feet. "Then you can't do anything for me?"

The priest washed his hands in agitation. "My son, although it is no business of yours, because of your involvement I will tell you that I have spoken my mind frequently and forcibly to the Lord of Barley Cross. And I will tell you that, in his own eyes, his deeds are justified. Beyond that I will not go. If you are still unsatisfied, I can only recommend that you seek an interview with the O'Meara himself."

Liam shambled from the grey stone presbytery, anger mounting inside him. His resolve grew firm. No one was willing to help him defy the tyrant. The O'Meara had ruled for so long they were inured to his tyranny. He would follow Father Con's advice. An interview—but on different lines to those the priest envisaged!

Liam McGrath turned his steps towards Barra Hill. In the old, dangerous days, tradition had it, the Fist had been used as a sanctuary when the village was attacked. Certainly he remembered spending days in the castle as a child, playing in its grounds in summer. And he knew a way to get up there unobserved.

In the parlor of O'Meara's Fist, the Lord of Barley Cross caroused with his henchmen.

The O'Meara himself slumped in a frayed armchair before a smouldering turf fire, a glass of poteen on the bare boards beside him. In a chair across the hearth, Denny Mallon, MD, hunched like a shrivelled embryo, clutching his glass tightly. Kevin Murphy, the vet, and General Larry Desmond shared a broken-backed settee and a half bottle. On a stool on the pegged rug, skirt-covered knees primly tucked beneath her chin, Celia Larkin, MA, sipped a cup of herb tea brewed specially for her.

The schoolmistress put down the teacup carefully onto the saucer on the rug. "Did you have any trouble with young McGrath, Larry?"

General Desmond eased a leg over the end of the sofa. He stared reflectively into his glass. "Ah, no, Celia. Andy McGrath is a good man. He'd march off a cliff edge if I so ordered. I gave him the job of breaking the news. And Tom O'Connor's a biddable man. We'll have no trouble with either of them."

Doctor Denny Mallon stirred in the depths of the old chair. "How did the women take it? I think it's getting harder for them to accept when it hits their own kids."

The general snorted with laughter. "Bedam—I believe they are both dead keen on it. Don't they both want a grandchild to cosset? And do you think that either of them is fussy about how it is managed?"

"How about the youngsters?" persisted the schoolmistress. "Are they accepting it?"

The general looked less comfortable. "Andy tells me the lad was upset. He sent him in to talk to his mother. The girl is level-headed. She will do as Tom and Brigit tell her."

"Do you think the Master should attend the reception?"

"Ah, no. Let's keep his ugly mug out of it as much

as possible." The general grinned placatingly at the O'Meara. "I've sent down the usual gifts." He swirled the colorless fluid gently in his glass. "It's amazing the influence a bar of real, old-fashioned toilet soap has on the opinions of a nice woman. I reckon we can celebrate another eighty or ninety nuptials before we get down to the carbolic."

The O'Meara opened his eyes. He said plaintively, "Do you ever get the feeling you're invisible? All very fine for you schemers—but it's me is the fall guy." He turned to the schoolmistress. "Do we need to go through with it? After all, the lad may be . . ."

Celia Larkin interrupted him incisively. "Let it be, Pat. We get this from you every time there's a wedding. And it won't make a damned bit of difference. You'll do it if we have to hold you down."

The Master of the Fist leaned forward to pack a fresh turf at the back of the fire. "One day I'm going to disappoint you all. Ask Denny. I've been getting these pains in my chest. 'Twouldn't surprise me, if one day . . ."

Denny Mallon waved a dismissive glass. "Whisht, Pat! I'll give you a couple of pills. The exercise will do you good."

"If only you knew," sighed the O'Meara, "what I have to put up with. Coaxing them, turning my back, apologizing, listening to them cry themselves to sleep . . ."

Patrick O'Meara, ex-Grenadier Guardsman, had altered in the years since his strategic retreat in a stolen tank from the burning docks of Belfast to a more defensible position in his native Connemara. Now, discipline sat heavy on his shoulders.

"Maybe I was wrong," he groaned. "Maybe we should have gone underground."

Big Larry Desmond tilted the bottle recklessly above his glass. "If the Lord had intended us to live in burrows, He'd have given us long ears and little furry tails."

"Maybe we should have stuck to the cities?"

"*Niet!*" said Kevin Murphy, who had read Marx in his youth. "The Kelly boy took two pigs down to Galway Town last week and came back witless. The dead lie unburied in the street there, he tells me."

"You can criticize Galway Town," protested the O'Meara, "but we don't make progress either."

Celia Larkin straightened her back. "What do you expect? No one is going to invent a turf-driven airplane. Nor produce vacuum cleaners from cows' pats. But we have twenty-four children attending school. And, if you think you can claim all the credit for that, you can think again. That Kelly boy was never a ten-month child. He's their own, I'm sure."

"Then why don't they produce more children?"

She looked shocked. "It isn't for us to be prying into private matters! We interfere enough by insisting on your *droit du seigneur*." She turned to the general. "Please give that Kelly boy an escort if he has to go outside the village in future." She sighed. "God forgive me—one could almost wish he'd grow up promiscuous."

Kevin Murphy rumbled indistinctly. "Nothing wrong with that idea."

She shook her head sadly. "Kevin, your farmyard solutions won't do for us. Children are entitled to their own parents, just as parents are entitled to their own children." She removed her rimless spectacles and polished them on the hem of her skirt. "Remember the ecology freaks? Predicting what we would run out of—oil, coal, gas, living room, fresh air. They never thought we'd run out of people first."

Denny Mallon exhaled clouds of smoke. "I thought the dark-skinned races might have done better. But their crops are letting them down. Something to do with radiation affecting bacteria and viruses, which in turn affect the plants. I caught a broadcast from Athlone years ago—when we had the radio," he added apologetically.

Celia Larkin's lips tightened. "If it *is* the ultraviolet. If those clever professors were so sure, why wasn't something done when they first discovered what was happening?"

Denny Mallon sucked imperturbably on his pipe. "The ozone layer never stopped *all* the ultraviolet. Can anyone know how much radiation it takes to cripple a gene?"

Kevin Murphy scratched his scalp. "Sure—'tis a statistical thing. Genes are getting hit by radiation all the time. Suddenly, for some reason, the percentage of hits tips the scales from acceptability to calamity."

General Desmond reached again for the bottle. "Statistics be dammed—it's our cloudy Connemara skies that I'm grateful for."

Kevin Murphy accepted the bottle from the general. He said, "The beasts seem to hold their own. Maybe it *is* Larry's clouds, or maybe they are not as sensitive as us. But we're getting enough births to keep the herds and flocks going." He grinned at the Lord of Barley Cross. "Be grateful I don't require your services in *my* department."

Celia Larkin frowned. "That's enough of your lewd talk, Kevin. If we can hold on long enough, Barley Cross might start producing radiation-resistant kids. Or the ozone layer might repair itself." The childless spinster pulled out a frayed handkerchief and blew her nose loudly. Sunlight glinted on her spectacles as she raised her head. "But, in any case, I can go to my grave hoping that, if there's the faintest chance of things improving in the years to come, we simpletons in Barley Cross will have helped to supply some of the hands and heads that will be needed to get this sorrowing planet progressing again."

There was silence for a moment.

Then General Desmond put down his glass and said, "Amen to that."

"Amen," mumbled veterinary surgeon Kevin Murphy, scowling at no one in particular.

"Amen," whispered Denny Mallon, MD, staring into the empty bowl of his pipe.

The Lord of Barley Cross got to his feet. He consulted the old wind-up watch he had adopted since batteries ran out. "Well, madame and gentlemen, if anything is going to happen, it'll be soon. There's only an hour to the wedding. If you'll excuse me, I'd better be getting a bath and a shave. Can't let the future Missus McGrath see me in this state." He jerked a thumb at the bellrope. "Ring for Michael if you want another bottle."

"*You* shout, if you want us," said the general.

The Lord of Barley Cross pushed stockinged feet into slippers and shuffled towards the door. He paused to stare sourly at his henchmen. "If only I hadn't promised Celia twenty years ago—" He sighed. "You'll be flogging the O'Meara along until he drops, I suppose."

The doctor's eyes gleamed puckishly. "We might let you off the hook when you're eighty."

A metal arm on the wall moved from the vertical to the horizontal, causing a bell to tinkle. The general reached out and reset it.

"There's your signal, Pat."

The O'Meara shrugged. "I'll be off then to face the music."

He opened the door of his bedroom and went in. An arm encircled his neck, another his chest. The tip of a knife pricked his shirt front.

"Easy now, son," he grunted, tugging at both arms, striving to maintain his balance.

"You have until I count ten to promise not to

touch Eileen O'Connor tonight," whispered a voice in his ear. "And no noise, or you'll get an arrow in your lung like my da did."

"Your da? Is it you, Liam?"

"Don't waste time. I'm counting."

The two men swayed silently as the O'Meara tried to free himself from Liam's clutch. The Master of the Fist panted, "If I raise my voice, you're dead."

The arm about his neck tensed. A voice sobbed in his ear. "Not before you, old ram. Shout if you want."

The O'Meara's voice was hoarse. "And if I promise?"

Liam's grip relaxed slightly. "I'll let you live."

"I promise."

Liam released him, and they stood panting. The Master of the Fist shuffled over to the bed, and sat down on the coverlet. He waved towards a chair.

"Sit down a moment."

Liam tucked the knife into its sheath. He moved warily across the room, amazed at the ease with which he had achieved his object.

The O'Meara dabbed his face and neck with a grubby pillow. "I wondered if you'd show up." He unbuttoned his shirt, revealing the fine mesh of chain mail beneath. "I put on my wedding garment, just in case." The O'Meara ran a palm over the links. "Picked it up years ago at a fine house in Westport. It has been useful." He rubbed his neck wryly. "You have a stronger left arm than I anticipated."

Liam's mouth sagged open. "You expected me?"

The O'Meara reached over to his bedside table, opened a drawer, and got out a large revolver. He pointed the gun at Liam, and closed the drawer with his free hand.

"Now, son," he said. "The tables are turned. Never rely on a promise extracted under duress."

Liam stirred, silent with shock, hands gripping the sides of the chair.

"I shouldn't budge, if I were you," the O'Meara cautioned. "Not without first getting my permission." He turned the chamber of the gun with his thumb. "This thing is fully loaded. Not like the guards' rifles. That's policy, in case you manage to steal one of them. It limits the number of pot shots anyone can take at me."

Liam found his voice. "Why did you expect me?"

The O'Meara tugged his shirt from his trousers. "I don't make much of a target from the bottom of the hill. Most bridegrooms elect for a personal call. And, since all of you know the secret path through the spinney, I leave my window catch off. It's as good as a carrot, and saves a deal of reglazing."

He laid the gun on the coverlet. "You'll excuse me undressing," he said. "I've got to shave and take a bath." He used both hands to pull off his shirt, then bent down to remove his slippers and socks. "If you think you can beat me to it—go ahead," he invited. "But I warn you, I don't need to count up to ten before I kill a man. And, no matter who gets who, the sound of a shot will bring those fellers out there running. If that happens, the man to watch is Larry Desmond— he's a killer."

Liam felt the moisture filling his eyes. "You—you *bastard*!"

"Ah, no!" The O'Meara seemed genuinely surprised. "It's you that is the bastard."

Liam blinked furiously. "Don't call me a bastard. I'm not planning to sleep with *your* wife."

The O'Meara tossed his socks into a corner. He picked up the gun, and clicked the chamber round thoughtfully.

"I have no wife with whom you might sleep, Liam. And a bastard is precisely what you are. Your mother was not married to your father."

Liam quivered, as though an electric current galvanized his limbs. "Put the gun away, and I'll shows you how I feel about that statement."

The O'Meara laughed. "Liam—poor old Flinty Hagan couldn't have fathered you. He lost the necessary equipment during a raid on Oughterard before he was married. We all kept quiet about it because he was a sensitive man, and we thought a great deal of him."

Liam's lips trembled. The old goat was trying to provoke him, but he wouldn't give him the satisfaction of seeing him lose his temper. He said, "Then why did my mother agree to marry Flinty?"

The O'Meara sat silent for a moment, then seemed to come to a decision.

"Well now, Liam. We seemed to have arrived at what you might call the moment of truth. You have asked me a question which I would rather not answer. If you insist, I'm afraid we must escalate our discussion to a more formal level."

Liam let his lip curl scornfully. "Don't fence with me. Let's have a straight word out of you."

The O'Meara nodded in agreement. "So be it, son. Up to this moment you could have walked out of this room any time you wanted, and no hard feelings on my part. Now, as I warned you, you've promoted our chat to a really serious plane—that is, namely, your examination for informed citizenship. Some lads never learn about this test. Others avoid it by not challenging my *droit du seigneur*. But you have dived in head first. So now I'm going to provide you with information you may not have realized you were asking for. Your response, after due consideration, will govern whether you leave this room vertically or horizontally—and remember *I* am the judge.

"Here goes. You mam married Flinty Hagan because Barley Cross needed children, and at the time Flinty was the only available bachelor."

"But you said Flinty couldn't—"

"Don't interrupt, son, or I might make a hasty decision. Just listen. So far as I know, I am the only man in Barley Cross who can father a child. The reason goes back a long way, and there isn't anything we can do about it. Informed adults in the village are aware of this and have accepted the solution which the people out there in my parlor thought up. The solution is that I engender the children in Barley Cross, but their legal fathers get the credit.

"That, briefly, is how our village has managed to remain a living, functioning community, with enough people around to keep it going. Now, Liam, if you wish to graduate into a useful citizen of Barley Cross, you must accept our solution, *and* keep quiet about it. That doesn't mean you can't talk it over with your Eileen. But it does mean you don't discuss it in front of the children. Because the way a child grows up governs how he or she acts when they are adult. And we want the children of Barley Cross to believe that the world is a sane and happy place where everyone gets his own daddy and mammy. And we hope that the child will be able to adjust to our madhouse when it's old enough to understand. It also means that you don't gab about it in the village or do anything which might inadvertently destroy the illusion we have built up so painstakingly. And it means that your Eileen comes up here tonight, like every other Barley Cross bride in the last twenty years."

The O'Meara paused, rubbing his jaw reflectively. "Those are the facts. Don't go shouting for help. No one is going to rush in and save you from the crazy O'Meara. Those gentlemen outside have an idea that you might be in here. And they realize that I am making a reasonable attempt to dispel any objection you may hold to the way the village is run. What they do not know are my methods of persuasion. But it has all happened before, and they have confidence in me."

The O'Meara straightened his back. He raised his arm. The gun pointed at Liam's breastbone.

"You may have qualms about accepting our solution. Your views on putative incest, for instance may not correspond with ours. The subject is not open for debate. You may walk from this room a responsible adult, or you may be carried out a dead juvenile. Now, sir—how do you say?"

Liam's eyes had been growing wider and wider. "But, if Flinty Hagan wasn't my father . . . ?"

"Keep going," urged the O'Meara. "You are getting warm."

Liam McGrath fingered his own hooked nose, as if he had just become aware of it. He eyed the similar protuberance on the face of the elderly man sitting barefoot and shirtless on the bed. Suddenly he grinned.

"Put up the gun, Da, or you'll have me late. An informed citizen ought to be on time for his own wedding."

A Cure For Croup

The sound of a tolling bell woke Liam McGrath. He nudged his sleeping wife.

"Hear that racket, Eileen!"

Eileen McGrath stirred in her sleep. She had been up half the night nursing their one year old son through an attack of croup, and she was in no mood for conversation.

Liam frowned at the bell's clamor. It could only be the village church bell, which Father Con never permitted to be sounded as a tocsin.

Eileen's eyes opened wide. "What time is it?"

Liam leaned across her to consult the ancient wind-up alarm his mother had given them as a wedding present.

"Only half five. Do you think there's something wrong?"

She said drowsily, "Sounds like a death knell to me."

He swung his legs out of bed. The Curry cottage clung to the root of Kirkogue mountain, a cockstride out of Barley Cross. From his bedroom window Liam could see along the village's one and only main street. He peered through the curtains. Figures moved on the distant roadway.

And the bell tolled.

He grabbed his trousers from the chair back, and put a leg into them.

Eileen raised herself on one elbow. "Where are you going?"

He buckled his belt. "I'm off to see what's happened. It may be an emergency."

She sighed. "Don't wake Tommy. I've only just got him off."

Liam nodded. Their son's harsh breathing and racking cough had demanded the village doctor's attention the previous night. Liam could hear stertorous respiration from the next room. He tiptoed downstairs, lifted his jacket from the newel post, and slipped out into the morning light.

Seamus Murray stood at the door of his forge. The smith's face was unduly solemn. He seemed not to notice Liam's presence.

Liam shook the smith's arm. "What's happened, man? What's the bell for?"

Seamus's mouth opened and closed, like a fish in a jar. Then the words gushed out. "The O'Meara's dead! They found him at the foot of the stairs when the guard went in to report the 'all clear' this morning. He'd had a heart attack."

Liam stared, brain refusing to accept the news. Patrick O'Meara, Lord of Barley Cross, Master of the Fist, the focus of village life for as long as Liam could remember, *dead*? It was like hearing the church clock had vanished.

He said stupidly, "How come they found him so early?"

Seamus Murray shot him a pitying look. "The Master always wanted a report as soon as it grew light enough to see the O'Toole cabin. We've reported at that time for years—though I doubt a lad of your age would appreciate why."

Liam knew why. He had suffered the saga of Barley Cross versus the Rest of Ireland ever since he had been old enough to pay attention.

He ignored Murray's dig. "So who found him?"

The smith scanned the road. Liam's face appeared to be the last thing he wanted to look at. "Christ, man—how should I know? I don't stand guard at the Fist any more. Does it matter? We've lost our protector—the man who kept us from death and destruction in the years gone by—and all *you* want to know is who found him!"

All Barley Cross went to the funeral, which was customary. But many a wife shed more than customary tears for the deceased. Patrick O'Meara, the ram of Barra Hill, had left no widow to mourn his passing, but in a very real way he had been a father to the community, and many of the women had peculiarly fond memories of him.

The O'Meara's henchmen met in the parlor of the Fist as soon as the obsequies were done.

General Larry Desmond drained a tumbler of poteen with scant regard for its potency. He wiped the back of his hand across his mouth, then set the empty glass on the carpet between his feet. "Well," he said. "We're in a pickle now."

At the other end of the broken-backed settee, Kevin Murphy, the vet, stared gloomily into his own glass. "God dammit!" he muttered. "I loved that bloody man. Why could it not have happened to one of us instead?"

Celia Larkin, schoolmistress and spinster, sipped a cup of herb tea brewed especially for her by Michael, the O'Meara's servant. Neglected runnels in her face powder showed where the tears had flowed. She sniffed. "Maybe it's the Lord's judgement on our presumption. Father Con ranted about it often enough."

Denny Mallon, dwarfed in the great, shiny armchair, sucked at an empty pipe. "Father Con's views on delegated procreation don't necessarily reflect those of our Maker. Think about Judah's advice to Onan in Genesis. And, anyway, this is no time to be questioning tenets. But for Patrick O'Meara, Barley Cross would be a futureless dormitory by now. I can't imagine even Father Con would want that."

General Desmond refilled his glass from the bottle on the floor. "Dinny, ye are overly pessimistic as usual. A few of us here still have a kick or two left in us. Point is—where are we going to find a man to father the next generation of kids in Barley Cross?"

"The child of the Kellys—" began Celia Larkin.

Kevin Murphy grunted. "Christ, Celia, he's only ten or eleven years old. We're surely not dependent on adolescent precocity to—"

General Desmond choked over his drink. "God love us! Let the little fellow grow up first! We're not even sure he's fertile. The Kelly's never had any more kids."

Celia Larkin compressed prim lips. "You misunderstand me, gentlemen. It was the father I had in mind. And my idea was for it to be done surgically. Presumably the way Kevin achieves it with his beasts."

Kevin Murphy jerked upright. "Hold on, now! I'm no gynecologist. Better ask Denny here about that kind of maneuver."

Doctor Denny Mallon lowered his pipe. "The Kelly boy might be a possibility in a year or two—if he *is* his father's son. But Con Kelly never managed another child. As for artificial insemination, I have neither the equipment nor the skill—and no wish to employ them either. We have discussed this notion before, and rejected it. We agreed, if I rightly recall, that women are not cattle, and, anyway, to go in now for clinical insemination would explode our carefully nurtured fiction that the husbands of Barley Cross are the fathers of their children. No, my friends, what we need is a new *seigneur* to exercise his *droits*."

General Desmond's eyes narrowed in sudden suspicion. He glared at the doctor. "Just what have ye hidden up your sleeve, Dinny lad?"

Denny Mallon picked at the charred bowl of his pipe with a black thumbnail. He closed his eyes, as though weighing a doubtful course. Then he shook his head.

"It's not ethical to betray a patient's confidence."

"Denny!" squealed Celia Larkin.

"But, if you were to give me your word—"

"Christ, man! Yes, yes!" interrupted Kevin Murphy.

Denny Mallon turned raised eyebrows on the general and the schoolmistress. "You, too? Both of you?"

"God, man! Give up! Yes!"

"Anything, Denny. Just tell us!"

The doctor tapped his pipe on the heel of his hand. His listeners strained forward to catch the soft-spoken words.

"Eileen McGrath tells me she's missed her menses for the second month in succession. I think she's pregnant of her second child!"

Larry Desmond's breath came out in a low whistle. "Young Liam McGrath?"

Denny Mallon nodded. "Who else?"

Celia Larkin's eyes flashed behind her rimless spectacles. "What exactly does that mean, Denny—you're the expert."

Denny Mallon grimaced. "It could mean that our dear Patrick passed on his fertility to Liam McGrath— for which mercy I would be grateful. Or it could be that our ozone layer is repairing itself since we stopped assaulting it with fluorocarbons—which is unlikely. Alternatively, it could be that some of our children are developing an immunity to heavy ultraviolet doses. And that would be the best answer of all."

"But you don't know which?"

Denny Mallon shrugged. "Only time will tell. Meantime, I think we should make full use of young McGrath."

Kevin Murphy said, "Will he oblige?"

"Give me a chance to ask him!"

Celia Larkin pounced. "You'll do it, then?"

The doctor grimaced. "Looks like I've got the job."

The general snorted. "And it looks like we'll have to get ourselves an interim government."

Kevin Murphy looked doubtful. "D'you think they'll take orders from us?"

"They'll take orders from Larry," the schoolmistress said firmly. "He still runs the army. And he can delegate duties to us. It'll work 'til we get a new Master."

Denny Mallon got out his pouch, and poked his pipe bowl into it. He said, "I have to visit the Curry cottage tomorrow. The McGrath infant is not well, and I have a theory to check. I'll find an opportunity to talk to Liam." He rolled up the pouch, and slipped it back into his pocket. "But we've got to offer him everything—Lord of Barley Cross, Master of the Fist, the lot—or it won't work. He must replace Patrick in every way. Anything less would confuse the village."

The vet grunted doubtfully. "I'm not sure the village will accept him."

Larry Desmond drained his glass. "I'll guarantee the army's acceptance."

Celia Larkin shot him an acid glance. "And *I* the schoolchildren."

Kevin Murphy said, "But how can we justify his taking the O'Meara's place? He's no more than a boy. They're used to an adult tyrant like we built Pat into."

The general chuckled. "Those in the know won't need any justification other than his fertility."

"But the others? The Toomey's, the Flanagans—?"

"If Pat had only left a will nominating young McGrath . . ." Denny Mallon began pensively.

Celia Larkin sniffed disparagingly. "That would be too good to be true."

The doctor fumbled inside his jacket for one of the last ball points in Barley Cross. "Get us a bit a paper, Celia. I'll write one out that'll meet the bill."

The following afternoon, Doctor Denny Mallon found Liam McGrath's donkey standing by a peat stack on the main road out of the village. The doctor rested an arm on the animal's rump, and waited. Liam came round from behind the stack, arms full of turves.

Denny Mallon waved a salute. "God bless the work, Liam. 'Tis a soft day we're having." He shielded his pipe bowl from the drizzle, and struck a home-made match."

Liam pitched his turves into the panniers borne by the donkey. "Are you looking for me, doctor?" His voice was sharp with anxiety. "You're not worried about our Tommy?"

Denny Mallon puffed smoke into the moist air. "I want another look at him, Liam. And maybe take a sputum sample. But nothing to worry about. I want a quiet word with you first."

Liam's face set hard. "About what, Doctor? Is there something wrong with my son? If there is, there's nothing you can't say in front of my wife."

Denny Mallon cocked an eye at the white cottage perched on the toe of the mountain. Up there, pre-sumably, Eileen McGrath went about her wifely du-ties. The top of Kirkogue was lost in mist. The nearest house in Barley Cross was a drizzle-masked shape. Doctor and youth might have been the only tenants of a nebulous, rain-soaked, peaty landscape. Which was the way Denny Mallon had planned it.

He said, "Well now, Liam—I wouldn't be too sure of making such a pronouncement meself. What if I was to say I'm here on an errand for General Desmond?"

"Like what?" Liam demanded guardedly. "I'm not old enough to serve at the Fist, yet. And if someone wants help with a job, he don't have to get the general to order me to—"

"Now . . . now!" soothed the doctor. "No one is complaining about you, son. And the only person seeking your help is the general himself."

Liam frowned. "What can I do for him?"

Denny Mallon put away his pipe. Home grown herbs didn't burn well in damp weather. He said, "I believe you had an interview with the O'Meara when you got married?"

Liam McGrath grinned at the memory. That particular day, he reckoned, Liam McGrath grew up. "The Master told you about it, did he?"

Denny Mallon turned up his jacket collar, and dug his hands into his pockets. "Let's say I had his confidence. Did he happen to let you in on a certain secret, about which I would be reluctant to expand in unselected company?"

Liam's grin disappeared. "If you mean, do I know who fathered our Tommy—yes."

"*Ah!*" Denny Mallon's hobgoblin face creased in what Liam recognized as a grin of satisfaction. "But *who* fathered your *second* child?"

Liam goggled at the doctor. "Eileen is really going to have another?"

"I'm her doctor, aren't I?"

Liam was abruptly babbling nonsense. He rolled down his shirt sleeves, and pulled a scrap of tarpaulin from the top of the peat stack. "Come on, doctor—let's be off. Thanks for the news. Eileen suspected she might be—"

Denny Mallon raised a damp hand. "Hold on, now, Liam. You've not heard the general's message yet."

Liam pulled the tarpaulin round his shoulders, gripping the donkey's rope. "Make it quick, doctor. Can't we talk on the way?"

Denny Mallon shrugged. "I'll put it bluntly, son. You're aware of precisely what our recent Master's most important service to the village was. And I've just told you that you've fathered your second child. Well, since your Tommy will be the only child in the village with a sibling—"

Liam frowned. "A *sibling*?"

"A brother or sister."

"Oh!" Liam's mouth made a circle. He said guardedly, "And so?"

"So you are the only male in the Barley Cross capable of taking over from the O'Meara. Because you are the only one who has inherited his peculiar talent."

Liam glanced nervously towards the cottage on Kirkogue. "What are you trying to tell me, Doctor?"

Denny Mallon inhaled like a man prepared to plunge into icy water. Inwardly he berated Celia Larkin for lumbering him with this pest of a job. He said, "Our recent Master has nominated you in his will to be his successor. And, since all the kids in Barley Cross are his children, you have as good a claim as any to the title. The general has charged me to invite you to take up your new role immediately."

After what seemed to be several hour's thought, Liam said, "He can't ask me to do that, Doctor!"

Doctor Denny Mallon shrugged. "He can, Liam. Haven't I just done it for him?"

"But what would folk in the village say?"

The doctor shrugged again. "You might have to put up with some comment. Even the O'Meara was criticized. You can't expect to please everybody. But you'd have General Desmond behind you."

Liam flicked another glance at the cottage on Kirkogue. "What if I have to—you know . . ."

"That would be your own problem, son."

Liam squared his shoulders. "And if I refuse?"

Denny Mallon stared impassively from beneath drizzle bedewed eyebrows. "Then Barley Cross goes down the drain."

Liam grumbled. "It's not fair to expect me to—"

The doctor's face was sphinx-like. "Who told you life is supposed to be fair? Do you imagine Pat O'Meara enjoyed playing a libidinous tyrant? Sometimes there's a need to subordinate personal inclinations to the wishes of the community!"

"I'm not sure the community wants me to—"

The wizened, bent figure seemed to swell. "I'm not just talking about Barley Cross. There are bigger communities."

Liam said weakly, "Can I talk to Eileen first?"

"That might be the best idea," agreed the doctor. "And I'll postpone my sick call to a more propitious moment."

Eileen McGrath said, "If you think I'll agree to your taking over from the ram of Barley Cross, you've another think coming, my lad."

"But Eileen! Didn't you tell me, once, that the O'Meara was a civil man, and that it was an honor to be chosen for his *droit du seigneur?*"

"You and the O'Meara are two different people," his wife pointed out. "The O'Meara had no wife to object to his shenanigans. And you do!"

"But wouldn't you like to be First Lady of Barley Cross—and live up at the Fist?"

Eileen McGrath's honest face grew sober. "I suppose any woman would say yes to that—although there's a great deal needs doing to that barn of a place before I'd hang my hat in the hall."

"Well then—"

"There's no 'well then,' " she affirmed decisively. "One wife is enough for any man. And one wife is all you're going to have."

Liam found Father Con shining brasses in the church. The priest had aged in the short time since Liam's wedding. He now walked with a stoop, frequently clutching his side.

"Well, Liam," he greeted. "You've come to help me with these dratted brasses, no doubt?"

Liam grinned. He was fond of the old priest. He picked up a rag and a candlestick. "If you like, Father. Actually I called for a bit of advice." He told the priest of the general's proposal.

" 'Twould be a fine promotion for you."

"It would be . . ." Liam hesitated. How aware was Father Con of the motive prompting the O'Meara's promiscuity? One had to be discreet.

"But you're bothered about certain aspects of the job?" added the priest.

Liam let out a sigh. "That's about it, Father."

"Hmm." The priest put down the portable lavabo he had been polishing, and squatted in a pew. "I think we discussed this matter before? And I refused to condemn our late Master's conduct—much to your dismay?"

Liam nodded. "That's true."

The priest sighed. "Well, Liam, if you decide to take on the O'Meara's job, I might also refuse to condemn *your* conduct. One day you may discover that there are higher loyalties than those between husband and wife." The priest thoughtfully examined the bowl he held. "Jack Ketch is not necessarily guilty of murder when he carries out the state's decrees. Nor the mother of theft when she steals to feed hungry children. So our late Master might have been innocent of adultery when he exercised his seigneural rights—for surely our fine school would be empty of scholars, and our church empty of sinners, had he not done so." The old man rested his head on the wood of the pew. " 'Tis a problem that's given me scant peace these last few years. And I'm no nearer the solution now than I was at the start."

"Perhaps if you appealed to someone higher?" Liam suggested diplomatically.

The priest snorted with derision. " 'Twould be a marvellous day that I hear from a superior, Liam—supposing there are any of them still living. And remember—they, too, would be only men, with men's limping insight into ethical matters. Sometimes 'tis better to pray, and take your answers on trust. Desperate situations demand desperate remedies. And Barley Cross's situation is surely desperate."

Liam put down the polishing rag. "Are you telling me it's okay for me to take on the O'Meara's job, Father Con?"

The priest grimaced. "If you wanted it, and I said 'no,' would you take any more notice of me, than you would if you didn't want it, and I said 'yes'?"

Liam felt bewildered. Father Con could be pretty vague when he didn't want to come right out with something. "I suppose you're right, Father," he agreed.

"Suppose?" The old man jerked his head up angrily. "Is that the best you can say? Consider, Liam, who is there to give *me* comfort and advice. Who can give me absolution for *my* sins? Do you think you are the only soul in Barley Cross with a problem? On this matter of the Master's succession you must be guided by your own conscience, and make your own decision. The day of dogmatic religion is over. Soon you won't even have *this* remnant of Mother Church to guide your footsteps."

Liam sidled towards the church entrance. Father Con with the miseries was a person to avoid. They both needed someone cheerful to talk to. Someone like—Liam clamped his hands. Of course! Eileen's mam. Muttering "I'll have to think about it, Father," he slipped out through the porch, into the sunshine, and was off, running.

Brigit O'Connor was in her kitchen, floury to the elbows over a batch of soda bread. She said, "Mister O'Conner is down at the mill. He'll be making a new blade for Mick McGuire's water wheel. Did you want him badly?"

Liam's father-in-law, being a joiner by trade, was often called on to fix bits of Barley Cross's machinery. Liam got on well enough with him, but he would not deny that he had half-hoped to find his mother-in-law alone. He said, "No sweat, mam-in-law—I'd just as soon bring my troubles to you."

Dumpy Brigit O'Connor beamed fondly at Liam. She had always cherished a soft spot for Maureen McGrath's lad. "Will I be making you a cup of tea?" she asked. "While you tell me what's bugging you."

Liam hoisted himself onto a corner of the table. He swung his legs for a moment, in thought. His mother-in-law might not be as well informed as Father Con. He said, "Doctor Denny says the O'Meara has left a will naming me as the next Master, and General Desmond has asked me to take over."

"Well now . . ." Brigit O'Connor hefted, one-handed, a steaming, black, iron kettle from the stove top. She poured boiling water into a dented aluminum teapot. "That would be a great step up for you, Liam."

His legs stopped swinging. "You wouldn't mind, mam-in-law?"

She stirred the pot vigorously. "Indeed, no! Wouldn't you make as good a Master as the O'Meara, after you've had a bit of practice?"

Liam sneaked off the corner from a loaf cooling under a towel. He poped the bread into his mouth. "I wish Eileen felt that way."

His mother-in-law studied him with bright button eyes. "Does she not fancy living up at the Fist?"

"It's not that." Liam hesitated. The Master's habits were not supposed to be discussed, although his deeds were public knowledge. "There's an aspect of the job she's not keen on."

Brigit O'Connor's eyes gleamed—possibly with the memory of a night at the Fist a bride was supposed to endure with fortitude. "You mean the O'Meara's bedroom antics?"

Liam nodded. Somehow his mother-in-law always understood. "I don't think Eileen is too happy about me doing that sort of thing."

Brigit O'Connor poured out two mugs of herb brew. She pushed one towards Liam. "Well, surely the sexy bits are optional? You don't *have* to do it, do you?"

He grimaced. "I'm not so sure. Doctor Denny says the village brides will expect it, because it's tradition. And Brege O'Malley gets married in a fortnight, so the question would crop up straight away."

Brigit O'Connor lodged her elbows on the table to study her son-in-law. Liam McGrath was a good lad: nothing prurient about him. But if being Lord of Barley Cross meant he had to take each village bride to bed on her wedding night, then Liam would do it conscientiously. "I wonder why the Master picked on you," she murmured.

He grinned with embarrassment. "I dunno." He glanced slyly at her. "Perhaps because Eileen is pregnant again."

Brigit O'Connor's eyes opened wide. "Liam! You clever boy!" She darted round the table, and hugged him. "I'll have a word with our Eileen for you. Meantime . . ." She stood back to smile at her reflection in a mirror on the sideboard. Mother of the First Lady of Barley Cross! That would shake them. And no harm done if some of the dignity rubbed off onto Biddy O'Connor. She said, "Is there any way I can get a glimpse inside the Fist? So I can tell Eileen what it will be like up there."

Liam said, "I'll have a word with Doctor Denny."

General Desmond ushered Brigit O'Connor through the door at the end of the landing. "It'll be twenty years since you saw the inside of this room, won't it, Biddy?" he asked, smiling.

Brigit O'Connor gave the general the gimlet eye. Eighteen years ago she had been bright-eyed Brigit Callaghan on the eve of her wedding night. She remembered the bedroom well enough, and the man who had awaited her there. She said, "That's quite enough from you, General Desmond. What passed between me and the O'Meara that night is no business of yours, or anyone else's."

General Desmond feigned alarm, and backed off.

Bright O'Connor stared about the room with grim nostalgia. Same old wooden bed. Same old yellow roses on the wallpaper. Same view of treetops from the window overhung with ivy to render easy clandestine entry and exit. Same worn carpet edged by bare boards. She sighed. For all his tyrant's power, Patrick O'Meara had never looked after himself properly. She gave the general a quick, belligerent glance. "If you want my opinion, Larry Desmond, the place is a pigsty. Typical bachelor's pad. Sure, you wouldn't get me living up here for all the tea in Chiny. And you'll not get our Eileen so easy."

The general's smile faded. "What's to do then, Biddy? Between you and me, it's essential we get young Liam installed up here as Master. And the sooner the better."

Brigit O'Connor planted knuckles on her hips. "Then you'd better throw out every last stick of furniture and scrap of carpet in the house. Get some women up to scrub the place from top to bottom.

Repaint every bit of woodwork. New curtains at every window. Then fill the house with furniture a woman could be proud of."

Larry Desmond rubbed his jaw in thought. "Denny said you'd give me good advice."

She laughed harshly. "It don't take a clarryvoyant to spot a dirty dump. I'm ashamed to think you let the poor divil live and die in this midden."

Larry Desmond studied the carpet. For once his assurance seemed to have deserted him. At length he muttered, "You loved him too, Biddy?"

She sniffed. "Didn't we all? D'you think we'd have put up with his antics for a minute if we hadn't?"

Larry Desmond sighed. "That maybe explains a thing or two. I'll let Denny Mallon know what you recommend. It'll mean mounting a raid for the first time in years, but we'll have to get furniture from somewhere."

The expedition had the village lads hopping with excitement. Reared on the stories of the glorious days, they saw an opportunity for adventure. They pleaded with the general to be let come. Straws drawn from a cup decided who got the hard greased rifles resurrected for the occasion. And the general insisted on personally leading the raid.

Liam watched them march away, slit-eyed with envy. Thirty men, all armed, and the three horse drawn carts for the loot.

Eileen came to stand beside him. "And why isn't me bold bucko going with them?"

He grunted bitterly. "General Desmond says he daren't risk me getting killed."

Eileen McGrath pursed her lips. Liam guessed she was perversely pleased with his answer. She said, "But you haven't told him you'll be the next Lord of Barley Cross?"

Liam shrugged. "I don't have to, love. The O'Meara

left a will naming me. The general posted it outside church this morning. As far as he's concerned, I am the next master."

She said quickly, "Where are they off to?"

He slumped against the door jamb. "There are some fine houses outside Oughterard. They are seeking some new furniture for the Fist."

"And who's going to live there when it's all dolled up?"

Liam studied the boggy landscape, face mutinous. "No one, if you won't agree to me being the Master."

Her voice rose. "Liam McGrath—"

He turned his face away. "Forget it, Eileen. If you don't want it, neither do I."

Little Tommy had another attack the following day. Liam went down to the doctor for a bottle. He seized the opportunity for a quiet chat.

"How long d'you think the raid will take?"

Denny Mallon corked a small sample of his croup mixture, and stuck one of his precious labels on the bottle. He handed it to Liam. "Depends on how fast they are at furniture removing. Remember now, tell your Eileen—one teaspoonful only, when the little fellow starts to breathe hard."

Liam took the bottle. He said, "I'm afraid they are wasting their time. Eileen won't hear of me being Master."

Denny Mallon got out his pipe, and polished the bowl on his sleeve. "Does she know why the general wants you?"

Liam shrugged. "If she knows, she doesn't care. No way do I get to have seigneural rights with the future brides of Barley Cross!"

The doctor grinned. "I'm not sure that I'd agree to it either, in her place. D'you think the Fist might tempt her, when we've got it done up?"

Liam rolled his eyes. "She'll be tempted, all right.

But no way will she put up with me doing what the Master is supposed to do."

Denny Mallon stared at his pipe. "Maybe she'll have to be let into the secret. I'll be wanting a chat with her soon about the baby. I think we have an allergy on our hands. But I need to make a few more tests before I'm sure."

Liam looked startled. "Can an allergy cause croup?"

The doctor lodged the cold pipe in the corner of his mouth. "Indeed they can, son. But so many things can set them off. I'm trying to pin down the hapten or allergen responsible."

"And if you find out, we could do something about it?"

Denny Mallon nodded. "That's the general idea."

The raiding party came home the following day. The village turned out *en masse* to welcome its warriors. General Desmond led the parade, feet first, on a cart piled high with booty, one leg wrapped in bandages.

Celia Larkin stood beside Denny Mallon. "What's the old fool done now?"

"Looks like he got himself shot in the leg." The doctor waved a greeting as the cart bearing Larry Desmond went past. "I hope he doesn't want the damn thing lopped off."

"He must have found someone livelier than he expected."

The doctor sniffed. "Maybe geriatrics with a kick in 'em are not confined to Barley Cross."

"Don't be snide," chided the schoolmistress.

It took the rest of the week to clear out, clean up, and refurnish the Fist. The village's temporary government met at the weekend in a splendidly furbished parlor. General Larry Desmond, crutch by his feet on the new carpet, said, "Since I posted that notice proclaiming young McGrath as Master everybody is asking when will he take over. His wife can't ignore that."

Celia Larkin, primly perched on a brocade tuffet, said, "That's your trouble, Larry Desmond. You should have married again. You can't understand what a woman feels about a husband's fidelity."

General Desmond suppressed a sharp retort to the effect that the schoolmistress, being a spinster, wouldn't know any more about marriage than a widower. Instead, he said, "She can't put young McGrath's fidelity before the future of Barley Cross!"

Kevin Murphy ran a palm caressingly over the pile on the arm of the settee. "I've known animals to refuse to breed when taken from their mates."

The general's eyebrows went up. "Are you telling me we've wasted our time? And me with a dozen slugs in me leg!"

Denny Mallon waved his pipe. "You've done your part well enough, Larry. I think it's now time for diplomacy. Let me have a chat with Liam's wife. Maybe I can talk her 'round to our way of thinking."

That same day, Eileen McGrath got a note from the doctor, asking her to bring the child in for an inoculation. The doctor also made other preparations.

As they walked down to the village, Eileen said to Liam, "I hope you are not expecting me to traipse all the way out to Killoo Farm to visit your mam as well? It's bad enough having to bring Tommy out to the doctor."

Liam said, "We can go straight back home after we've seen him, if you want. I was hoping we might leave Tommy with your mam while we take a squint at the Fist. I hear they've done marvels with it."

She lifted a corner of the shawl covering her son's face. The infant snored peacefully. She said, "I'd like to see it, too. My mam thinks I ought to let you accept the Master's job, so we can move up there. She says they've made it into a real palace."

He said, "Let's do that first. We can call at the doctors afterwards."

Brigit O'Connor got to her feet as they entered her living room. She curtsied to Liam. "Come in, me lord. I'll take the little fellow."

Eileen stared, dumbfounded at her mother. "Mam —you *bowed* to Liam!"

Her mother puffed out a pouter pigeon bosom. "And why not? Isn't he our new lord? I always bowed to the O'Meara."

"But—" Eileen stared from her husband to her mother. "I haven't agreed—"

Brigit O'Connor laughed shortly. "My girl, 'tisn't you that appoints our lord and master. We have the O'Meara's word as to who's to succeed him."

Tom O'Connor entered from the kitchen, a saw in his hands. He halted, pulling off his cap. "Good day to ye, sir. Hullo Eileen, me lady."

She opened her eyes wide. "But, da—!"

Her father said hurriedly, "I'll make a brew of tay." He vanished back into the kitchen.

Eileen stamped her foot. "I don't want to be the First Lady of Barley Cross!"

Her mother shrugged. "Ye're the only person in the village who feels that way."

Later, they walked up to the Fist. Villagers stepped out of their path. Men doffed caps, or saluted. Women bowed or curtsied. Eileen grew redder and redder. She murmured, "I can't stand much more of this."

Liam gripped her hand. "It isn't far now."

Just beyond the O'Meara's old tank, now blooming with bindweed and woodbine, a voice called, " 'Tenshun!"

The members of the Fist guard stiffened.

Sergeant Andy McGrath bellowed, "Present arms!"

Rifles came smartly to the fore. Liam's stepfather came to the salute.

Liam muttered embarrassedly, "Thank you, sergeant." Other salutes and curtsies might be part of an elaborate legpull, but Andy McGrath took his job too seriously to act the fool on duty.

General Desmond one-footed towards them across the forecourt. He sketched a left-handed salute for Liam, and addressed Eileen. "Excuse me not bowing, me lady, I'm still in a bit of a state. May I conduct ye 'round your new home?"

"But it's not—" Eileen began. "I haven't . . ." She let the words trail off. General Desmond was stumping ahead of them, running on about the recent raid and how a spry septuagenarian had got him in a shotgun's sights before he could take cover.

They passed through the newly oiled and polished doorway into the Master's parlor. Candles flickered in a shimmering chandelier overhead. Glass gleamed from a glistening oak sideboard. Underfoot the carpet was as soft as a field of spring grass.

Michael, the O'Meara's man, appeared. He still wore his grubby flyaway collar and stained green waistcoat, but his hands were spotless. He said, "Can I get you some refreshment, sir? Madame?"

Eileen stared at him, unable to speak. "Some tea?" Liam suggested. A good stiff jolt from the poteen bottle would have been more to his taste, but Eileen held firm views on alcohol.

"Very good, me lord." Michael turned on his heel.

"Perhaps we could take it in the library?" suggested the general. "This way, me lady."

He opened a door on the left. Liam saw a room lined with more books than he had ever imagined. Denny Mallon, chest heaving from a hurried dash up to the Fist, got to his feet.

"Good day, me lord, me lady."

He pulled out chairs for them.

"I'll leave ye a moment," said the general. "While I make sure Michael knows where to bring the tay."

They sat down with the doctor. He placed both hands on the baize covered table. "Well, sir, madame —how do you like your new home?"

"But Doctor Denny!" Eileen's face was scarlet. "I haven't agreed to move up here. We only came for a look."

"But sure. It's all been done up specially for you and our new Master." Denny Mallon's voice was gentle, persuasive. "And doesn't the whole village want you living up here? It hasn't been the same without a Lord of Barley Cross domiciled at the Fist. So the sooner you move in the happier we'll all be."

Eileen's lip grew stubborn. "If we move in, you mustn't expect Liam to exercise his droits or whatever when that O'Malley girl gets married next week."

"But, my lady—he may be expected to do just that."

"Expected or not, I'm not having adultery in my house."

Denny Mallon seemed to shrivel even smaller. Perhaps he saw a carefully constructed edifice crumbling despite his bravest efforts.

"My lady—could you tolerate it elsewhere? Out of sight?"

Eileen McGrath's mouth set firm. "Indeed I could not, doctor. And you've no cause to be tempting me so. What's so important about these rights of the Master? They're just a tradition we could very well do without."

"But we really can't, my dear." Doctor Denny Mallon was suddenly down on his knees before Eileen McGrath. "I beg of you, my lady. Let your husband inherit his title and duties. For without him we are doomed. While the O'Meara lived we could hope. But now he is gone and we have only Liam."

Eileen McGrath whimpered. The sight of Doctor

Denny Mallon, a pillar of the community, on his knees before her, pleading, seemed to unnerve her. She grasped his hands and tugged. "Doctor Denny, stop! You mustn't kneel to me. It isn't dignified. Please get up!"

Denny Mallon resisted, head bowed. "My lady Eileen—if I get up without securing your consent to our wishes, all the work of the last twenty years will have been wasted. Will it help persuade you if I get the general, the vet and the schoolmistress to kneel here beside me?"

Eileen McGrath's voice broke in a sob. "Doctor Denny, please get up. It isn't fit that you should act like this. The O'Meara wasn't worth it. Everyone knows he was an old lecher with an appetite for virgins—"

"Eileen!" Liam was shouting. "You are talking about your real father!"

She paused. Her hand flew to her mouth, her eyes suddenly frightened.

Liam lowered his voice. "Listen to the doctor, love. He's trying to tell you something dreadfully important. Patrick O'Meara was Master here because only he could father children. No one else in Barley Cross—or the whole world so far as we know—was able to do that. And now the doctor thinks I've inherited the Master's fertility. So General Desmond has asked me to take over."

Eileen's eyes grew round. "You mean the O'Meara did it out of duty?"

"My lady—" Denny Mallon interrupted urgently, "let me tell you about two villages. One is a backward place dominated by a medieval type of tyrant and his clique of sycophants. This tyrant's father debauched every bride in the village on her wedding night on the pretext of exercising his *droit du seigneur*. And the tyrant's son hopes to pursue the same lustful course despite the protests of good folk like yourself.

"The other village is the only place I know of where babies are suckled, infants play in the street, and children go to school as they used to do the world over. Moreover, it's a place where married couples can hope to have children of their own to love and cherish. In fact, it's a village where the inhabitants can look forward to the future."

The doctor bit his lip, and lowered his head.

"Both these communities exist because of a fortuitous arrangement of one man's genes, and the determination of people to practice self-deception on a heroic scale—because they are both aspects of the same place, and it depends only on your prejudices which one you choose to inhabit. Because, my dear, they are both the same place, and you may live in either, depending on your beliefs. I, silly old fool that I am, happen to think we live in the village with a future."

"Doctor Denny!" Eileen tugged at his wrists, her lips trembling. "Please get up, and say no more. Liam will do it, and I'll try to see things your way."

One hand on the table, Denny Mallon got awkwardly to his feet. There was no triumph in his face. His eyes were solemn. He said, "Thank you, Eileen McGrath, for finding the courage to make the right decision."

She was dabbing her eyes. "Hadn't we better be getting down to your surgery to see about inoculating our Tommy?"

A ghost of a smile flickered at the corners of the doctor's mouth. "Sure that won't be necessary now, my lady. I've ascertained that the little fellow's croup is an allergic reaction to fossil pollen grains blowing off the peat stacks below your cottage. I was going to suggest you move away from that neighborhood to give him a chance. But now I don't need to. Up here at the Fist, away from those stacked turves, he should be all right."

Eileen McGrath smiled, her eyes veiled. "What a wise suggestion, doctor. It will certainly do for a reason to explain why I changed my mind, should anyone ask."

Denny Mallon nodded knowingly. "It might at that, my lady."

Liam McGrath, Lord of Barley Cross, attended his first meeting with the caucus the following Saturday morning. Neat in his best clothes, he entered the parlor through his private door.

General Desmond and the vet, Kevin Murphy, sat at each end of the plush new settee, a bottle of poteen and the general's crutch on the floor between them. Celia Larkin, the schoolmistress, perched on a dainty tuffet, sipping tea in silence. An armchair which matched the settee for luxury almost swallowed the shriveled form of Doctor Denny Mallon. And, on the other side of the fireplace, an old sagging chair, arms and back shiny from use, stood empty.

General Desmond cocked a casual thumb at the empty seat. "That used to be the O'Meara's. We've kept it specially for you, son, so you'll know your place. Now, about the O'Malley girl's wedding. We've decided you'd better get down there early and show your face—"

Liam slipped obediently into the Master's chair. He nodded, listening carefully to his instructions from the real Masters of Barley Cross.

Liam McGrath knew his place.

A Test for Tyrants

Liam McGrath lay beside his sleeping wife, trying to plan. Already dawn brightened the corners of the bedroom. In a few hours, Father Con would be saying the words to make Brege O'Malley wife of Christie Kennedy—and thus pose a problem for the New Lord of Barley Cross.

Liam shifted restlessly. What would the O'Meara have done about it? Liam recalled very clearly what the previous Master had done after his, Liam's, wedding. But the O'Meara had ruled Barley Cross for longer than Liam could remember, and Liam, fresh to the job, could not hope to match such expertise.

At six o'clock he reached a decision, and got up. He dressed without disturbing Eileen, and slipped out of the Fist by the bedroom window and the secret path through the kitchen garden.

At the foot of the hill, he turned toward the river, making for a lonely cabin which stood just off the track leading to McGuire's mill. It was light enough to see that he had the road to himself. A raw wind blew, promising rain. Typical Connemara wedding day, Liam reflected.

The cabin was in darkness. He rapped, not loudly, but persistently. A light flickered behind the curtains, a bolt rasped, the door opened an inch.

"It's me, Liam," he hissed. "I need your help, Katy."

He heard a sigh of exasperation. "Liam McGrath— you may be our new Master, but it doesn't give you the right to get an honest whore out of bed at six in the morning!"

"Let me in," he pleaded. "I've got to talk to you."

He caught a giggle. "Well, so long as it's only talk you want . . ."

A chain rasped, and the door opened wide enough to admit him. Kate Monaghen, in curlers and a red flannel nightie, peered at him in the lamp light. "You'll be getting a worse name than the O'Meara," she warned. "*He* abstained from commercial fornication."

Liam closed the door behind him. "No one saw me, Katy." He shrugged off the overcoat he had draped over his shoulders. "I put this on to alter my appearance."

She set the oil lamp on a table. "If you think that old rag will hide our new Master—"

He sat down, breathing heavily. "Can't be helped, Katy. I had to see you. I need your help."

She said, "I'll put the kettle on. We'll have a sup of tay while you tell me your troubles."

As she poured, he blurted, "Brege O'Malley gets wed today. And I've got to do my *droit du seigneur* thing with her tonight."

"Droyt du what?"

He explained.

She raised her eyebrows. "Sure, that shouldn't be a difficult job for a fine upstanding young felly like yourself."

He sighed, seeing suddenly a vision of Brege O'Malley. Saint Brege the Ice Maiden, they had christened her as children. Twelve months younger than Liam, she, Christie Kennedy, and the other educable infants of Barley Cross at that time, had squeezed together into the too-small desks of Celia Larkin's one-room school. Brege, even then, had affected piety—wearing below-the-knee skirts, aping the habits sartorial and moral of the nuns she claimed she would have joined, had there been a convent handy.

"Well?" It was Katy, bringing him back to the present.

He lifted his head. Now that he needed to stay awake it was a job to keep his eyes open. He began diffidently, "I—er—" The trouble was, Katy Monaghen might be one of those Barley Cross citizens, like his stepfather, who accepted all they were told about the Master. He floundered on. "I don't know how much you know about the Master's responsibilities—?"

A furrow appeared between her eyes. "I know enough to agree that you ought to get on with your droyts, if that's what's mithering you."

Katy would, of course. Being a harlot, a droyt or two would be neither here nor there to her. He sighed. "It ain't that, Katy. It's what Christie Kennedy will want to do about it."

"Bugger Christie Kennedy," she snapped. "Just get your guards to throw him out if he shows up."

Liam shook his head. "That would only make things worse. I'll have to let him into the Fist, and face him on my own . . . try to talk him out of killing me."

Her eyes opened wide. "Would he try to do that?"

Liam shrugged. "I tried to kill the O'Meara when I got wed."

She said briskly, "Then you must kill Christie first."

Liam groaned. "That's not on. If I took a life each

time I tried to start one, it wouldn't be much benefit to Barley Cross, would it?"

She nibbled her lip, studying him in silence. "So that's the reason why the O'Meara bedded every bride in Barley Cross? Well, bloody well! And what can I do to help you?"

Liam raised his eyes, face haggard. "Has Christie ever visited you . . . in your professional capacity?"

Kate Monoghen regarded the Master archly. "Liam McGrath—would you be asking me to break my hypocritic oath? Sure all me business is confidential."

His lip trembled. "Knock it off, Katy. I'm serious."

She whispered, "And what if Christie Kennedy did come to see me?"

"I—I could threaten to tell his wife."

She stared at him, incredulous. "Glory be to God! And on his wedding day, too! And ye the Lord of the village, who should be setting us all a good example!"

"You don't understand, Katy," he pleaded. "It's only because I'm Master that I have to blackmail him."

She eyed him narrowly. "And just where would I come in?"

Liam peered around the edge of the curtain into the brightening daylight, as if half afraid that an eavesdropper crouched outside. He said, "I want you to come up to the Fist for the day."

She laughed bitterly. "And what would your wife say? She knows what I am. Sure, she wouldn't let me past her front door."

He wanted to contradict her, but he knew it would be a waste of time. All Barley Cross knew that Kate Monaghen was a loose woman. The women tolerated her, as they tolerated the lewdness of the Master, in grim silence. His Eileen would probably slam the door in Kate's face.

He mumbled. "My wife won't be there. She's taking the baby and herself off to her mam's for the

weekend. So that, officially, she won't know what
goes on at the Fist."

"Oh? And what does go on at the Fist?"

He moaned. "Christ, Katy—don't you understand?
I've got to take Brege O'Malley to bed, and try to get
her in the family way. And Christie Kennedy will
probably climb in through my bedroom window and
do his damnedest to stop me."

She nodded thoughtfully. "I see. And, just as he's
going to stick a knife into your pelt, I bust out of the
wardrobe crying: 'Halt, Christie Kennedy! Or I'll
tell yer new wife all about the antics you got up to
with me last summer?' "

"Something like that," he agreed lamely. "It's the
best I can think of. The O'Meara would have had a
smarter way of doing it, but I'm not the O'Meara."

"And thank God for that!" Her eyes flashed angrily. "The O'Meara would never have taken me into
his confidence. I may not set a shining example in
the village—but I'm as loyal a citizen as any of em!"

He said startled, "Then you'll come?"

She flourished a fist. "Just tell me how to get past
those damn guards of yours."

General Desmond was hovering in the hall when
Liam returned. "Where've ye been, me lord?" he
demanded brusquely. "Ye're supposed to be at the
church by nine o'clock."

"I've been attending to the Master's business,"
Liam retorted, concealing his awe of fierce Larry
Desmond, still unsure how far he might venture
with the old soldier.

"I've an honor guard picked for your escort," the
general continued, as if Liam had not spoken. "Two
of our smartest men, and a corporal to carry the
presents and deliver the summons. We're sending
the bride a tablet of soap and a bottle of perfume,
and the same to her ma. It's more than usual, but we
want to build you up as a generous tyrant."

"So pleased—" Liam began.

"And Michael has pressed your uniform."

Liam's ears twitched. "Uniform? I have no uniform."

The general smiled genially. "The O'Meara used to wear his old Grenadier Guards outfit at functions. If we pad the chest out a bit it'll fit you good enough."

"But I've never been in the army," Liam protested. "I'm not even old enough to serve at the Fist."

"Ach, away with ye!" The general waved a carefree hand. "What's the use of being Master if ye can't bend the rules occasionally. Ye've to look impressive, today."

Liam took a deep breath, knees quivering. It was now or never. Unless he intended to knuckle under to Larry Desmond for the rest of his life. "No uniform," he stated firmly. "Positively no uniform. I'll wear my best suit, if you like. But no uniform."

General Desmond's white eyebrows bristled. "Now listen here, young Liam—"

"*Master!*" Liam corrected, holding his lips firm. "Master of the Fist and Lord of Barley Cross."

General Desmond looked straight at him, as if seeing Liam for the very first time.

Liam stared back, without speaking.

The general seemed to shrink. "Okay, me lord," he conceded. "No uniform. Your best suit will do nicely. And, would ye condescend to attend at the reception after? Ye need only stay for the meal and a couple of dances."

"I'll do that," Liam agreed. "I'll even wear some kind of badge or chain of office, if you can dream one up."

Larry Desmond brightened. "Now there's an idea." He rummaged in his pockets. "Pat used to wear an old medallion around his neck. I was keeping it as a souvenir." He pulled the hand from a pocket, and offered Liam a chain. "Perhaps ye'd—?"

Liam took the chain. He examined the disc attached to it. One side of the medal bore the figure of Saint Christopher, the other the words P. O'MEARA, KILCOLLUM, CONNEMARA. Liam slipped the chain over his head. "I'll call it my chain of office."

"Thank you," said Larry Desmond. "Maybe ye'll make a dacent Master after all."

Liam arrived purposely late, and lingered at the back of the church. He was not keen on meeting Father Con's accusing eyes over the head of the bride he intended to force into adultery before the day was out.

Later, at the reception, he found himself given a seat of honor beside the bride's mother, and was obliged to attempt polite conversation with Ma O'Malley.

She leaned confidentially towards him. "Will ye be sending for our Brege tonight, me lord?"

He pondered the tone of her voice. Was she hoping he'd say "Yes"? Women were mysterious creatures. Since his accession he had discovered more mild-looking, middle-aged matrons who secretly approved of the O'Meara's carnal excesses than he could have imagined. He murmured, "My corporal has the summons in his pocket. Will Brege be willing?"

Madame O'Malley eyed him coquettishly. "Don't be worrying about our Brege, me lord. I'll see she's willing. And, if she ain't, dammit if I don't come up to the Fist meself in her place!"

Liam tried not to blush. He sneaked a glance along the table. Brege's father, Pete O'Malley was busy tucking into the turkey. Liam whispered, "I hope you don't let Mister O'Malley hear remarks like that. Not that you wouldn't be welcome," he added gallantly. "But it's Brege's turn this time."

When Franky Finnegan struck up a waltz on his fiddle, Liam found the nerve to plunge into the prancing throng, his arms around his hostess. Ma

O'Malley danced enthusiastically, as if determined not to waste an instant of glory in the new Master's embrace. Liam sweated, counting beats under his breath, accommodating his stance to the O'Malley figure.

Two dances, Larry Desmond had stipulated. The next one, then, had to be with the bride. As Franky finished with a flourish, Liam released his partner and glanced around the floor.

The new bride stood momentarily alone, her husband making for the bar. Liam excused himself, and headed towards opportunity. Franky struck up again, and he led the Ice Maiden, unexpectedly gorgeous in long white satin, onto the floor.

She murmured, "So kind of you to come, me lord. And thank you for the presents."

Since fine quality toilet soap and French perfume had not been available in Barley Cross for years, except on those occasions when the Master showed his generosity, Liam reckoned she meant it. He cracked a grin. "Liam's the name, Brege."

She pouted. "But you're our Master, too."

"And still Liam McGrath," he countered. "I hope I haven't changed."

She smiled nervously, then nodded at the medallion. "Would that be your chain of office?"

He flicked it with his thumb. "It belonged to the O'Meara. General Desmond thinks I should wear it."

"Then it is to show us you are the Master!"

He was getting fed up with the way people harped on about it. He said curtly, "If you like."

She lowered her head, her voice almost inaudible. "Does that mean you'll be sending for me tonight?"

In his confusion he trod on her foot. God! Was the Ice Maiden seeking a call to the Fist? He opened, then shut his mouth. Couldn't ask questions like that. In a carefully neutral voice he asked, "Did you not get the summons yet?"

She shook her head, mute, waiting for him to invite her personally. He couldn't speak. His tongue was swollen and dry. He scanned the crowd, seeking the corporal. When was the man supposed to deliver the summons anyway? Had he forgotten it? And everyone wanting to know. The reception was turning into a bloody shambles. Liam choked, flushed, then managed to say, "Excuse me—got to see my corporal about something."

He released her, cast aside manners and propriety, and pushed blindly off the dance floor. Damn everything! He couldn't face Brege's mute curiosity. He ran from the hall, ignoring the startled glances of other guests, heading for the Fist, hating Brege, hating General bloody Desmond, and most of all, hating himself.

He found the general in his parlor, with Kevin Murphy, the vet. The general waved cheerily. "You survived the ordeal, then, me lord?"

Liam held tight on to his temper. "Just when is that corporal supposed to hand over the summons?"

The general frowned in thought. "I told him to hang on until the 'do' had quietened a bit. Lot of people who aren't relatives leave early. Didn't want to upset too many who might not appreciate your emulating the O'Meara."

"Oh!" Liam's anger drained away. As usual, the general had acted for the best. He said, "Well he was still hanging on to it when I left, and the O'Malley women are going nuts waiting. I got the impression that Brege expects to be summoned. Her mam is all for it."

The general nodded. "Just as well. If the young lady should refuse, ye could clap her parents in jail until she changed her mind. We did that once, Kevin—do ye recall?"

Kevin Murphy nodded. "Divil a bit of trouble in Barley Cross after that incident. Might be a good idea to throw somebody into the cooler right now. 'Twould establish Liam's authority for sure."

The general rubbed his chin reflectively. "Young Kennedy might be a suitable candidate. It'd keep him out of the way, too." Larry Desmond appraised Liam. "We can't maintain a permanent guard on your bedroom, unfortunately. It would mean telling them too much. But if you have any trouble with young Kennedy, Kevin and I will be standing by. Just ring for Michael, and we'll come running."

Liam hid his embarrassment. Thank goodness he had kept his feelings about the general to himself. He murmured, "Thank you, gentlemen. I'll keep you in mind."

A cool breeze wafted through the open window. Liam sat by the bed, one hand gripping the O'Meara's revolver concealed beneath the counterpane. Christie Kennedy must surely have heard the news by now. Michael had reported the honor guard's return over half an hour ago. Was Christie shirking it? He had always been a bit of a blowhard at school. But when your wife's honor was at stake . . !

Something whizzed past Liam's head to strike the wall behind him. He turned in astonishment. The feathered butt of an arrow projected from the wallpaper. He swiveled back to discover Christie Kennedy astride his window sill, a stretched bow in his hands, and an arrow lined up with Liam's breast bone.

"Right, you bastard!" Christie gritted, swaying.

For a brief moment Liam considered—and rejected —the response the O'Meara might have made to that epithet. But both he and Christie were bastards. And Christie, drunk, was probably immune to that sort of reasoning.

Liam moved to face him, coughing to hide the

clink of the chain mail he wore under his shirt. "What do you want, Christie?"

Christie Kennedy's lip lifted in a sneer. "Only your signature on a bit of paper which says you cancel the summons your bloody corporal just gave my Brege."

Liam pondered. Christie's attention had to be diverted while he got the gun out. No arrow could penetrate his medieval underwear—but what if Christie aimed for the head? He needed outside help. Liam called softly, "Katy!"

The door to his private bathroom opened, and Katy Monaghen sauntered into the bedroom. She wore a brassiere and briefs of red satin. Black suspenders supported black stockings which left on display the top four inches of her creamy thighs. A red satin rosette decorated the garter above her right knee.

"Hi, Christie!" she called.

"Jesus!" The arrow tip wavered. Liam had the gun out instantly, but it wasn't necessary.

Christie said thickly, "What the hell are *you* doing here?"

Kate Monaghen smiled sweetly. "I'm protecting our Master from the attentions of ardent young hooligans like you."

"And drop that bow, or I'll blow your head off," Liam added.

Christie lowered the bow, as though in a dream, not even looking at Liam. "Why are you dressed like that, Katy?"

She minced towards the window, and took the weapon from Christie's nerveless fingers.

"Come on in!" Liam urged. "We want to talk to you."

Dazedly, Christie got his other leg over the sill.

Kate said, "I thought it might remind you of old times, honey."

Christie dragged the heel of his thumb across his forehead, his eyes on Kate's plump bottom as she stooped to prop his bow in a corner. "Jasus!" he muttered. "I've drunk too much."

"Is that where you got the nerve from?" Liam asked.

Kate flashed him an angry glance. "Cut that out, Liam. And put the gun away. It won't be necessary."

She turned back to Christie. "Ye're all worked up about Liam's droyt doo seenyer, aren't you, honey? Would ye sooner he ignored Brege? Especially when every bride in the village since the year dot has been honored by a summons to the Master's bed."

"If you call it an honor," Christie mumbled slackly.

"Here, hold on!" Kate's voice rose in protest. "Is that what you thought when you visited me last summer?"

"Ah—no!" Christie showed confusion. "That was different. I mean—I paid you."

"Oh!" Kate registered surprise. "You mean, if Liam gives Brege money, everything will be all right?"

"No, I—I didn't mean that." Christie's eyes rolled wildly. "You're getting me confused, Katy."

She sat down beside him on the window ledge. "Sure, 'tis yerself is responsible, Christie boy." She addressed Liam. "Could ye lend us a spare bedroom— and a bottle? The lad here is worn out with excitement. He could use a lie down. I might even keep him company."

Christie looked owlishly at Liam. "Do *you* think it's an honor?"

Liam gazed back levelly, conscious that the day hung in the balance. He said, "I wouldn't do it unless I thought so." Suddenly inspired—since he hadn't spoken to Christie's mother— he added, "Just ask your mam what she thinks of it."

Christie's face sobered momentarily. "Can't figure

it out. My old lady is all for it. She told me not to do anything daft."

Kate slipped a bare arm around his neck. "And ye're not going to, honey, are ye? Not when your mam says ye mustn't."

Liam pushed the revolver into his belt. "Wait here," he ordered. "I'll see if there's a bed made up." If he rang for Michael he'd have Larry Desmond and Kevin Murphy charging in to the rescue. He jerked a thumb at the fine inlaid cabinet across the room. "There's a bottle and glasses in there, Katy. Would you offer our guest a drink?"

General Desmond wagged his head in reluctant approbation. "I dunno how ye've done it, me lord, but ye seem to have pulled it off."

Liam grinned with embarrassment. He *had* thought of fetching Kate Monaghen in the first place. He said, "It was Katy who did it, really."

Kevin Murphy's glass clicked against the bottle. "And with luck, she'll keep him quiet all night."

Larry Desmond laughed. "It's a change from the way Pat would have worked it. Kind of ironic, if Christie is giving Kate a tumble in one room while Liam—"

"That'll do!" warned the vet. "If Celia were here you wouldn't dare talk like that." He grinned. "Still and all, young Christie won't want to shout too loud in the morning about what's happened." He raised his glass. "Glory be, Larry—I think we've picked a winner!"

Larry Desmond smiled sourly. "Let's wait and see how he copes with the Ice Maiden. I reckon she'll be a harder nut to crack."

Liam closed the bedroom door behind them. The house was quiet. Brege Kennedy still wore her wedding dress. She stood silent in the center of the room, not looking at the turned-down bed, nor at the flowers in the vase on the dresser.

Liam rubbed his hands together nervously. "Would you like a drink, Brege?"

She shot him a pleading glance. "You know I don't touch strong liquor, me lord."

He blinked. "It don't have to be spirits. I could wake Michael to make us a sup of tay."

She said, "I think I would like that."

He rang for the servant, then motioned to one of the well-padded armchairs. "Sit down, Brege. Make yourself comfortable."

They sat in silence until Michael appeared. Then in silence again until he reappeared with teapot, milk jug, sugar basin, cups and saucers on a silver salver. When he had gone, Liam cleared his throat. He stammered, "Look—look Brege—this is no easier for me than it is for you." It crept into his mind, then, that if they didn't do it, no one would be any the wiser. And it would save both of them a deal of grief. And, of course, it would be cheating.

Brege gave him an angry look. "Then why insist on having me here?"

He was taken aback. "Hasn't your mam told you?"

She lowered her face, staring at her hands on her lap. "Me mam said I ought to come. She thinks it's an honor."

"Is that all she told you?" Liam was beginning to realize just how well the secret of Barley Cross was kept.

Brege frowned. "What else should she have said? That you'll put her and me da in jail if I don't do what you want?"

"Ah—no, Brege. It's something more serious than that." Liam hesitated. It appeared to be his prerogative who got let into the secret. He said, "I'd better tell you, Brege. I am the only fertile man in the village. If we don't do it tonight, you'll—you'll never have any children. And if every bride refused to go to bed with me, in fifty years or so, Barley Cross would be a mausoleum."

She was staring wildly at him. "But Liam—it's a sin! We'd be committing adultery!"

He winced. Hadn't he known Saint Brege would come up with something like that! He said, desperate, "If you weren't really married, we wouldn't. I don't want to cast doubts on your marriage, but if a man isn't able to consummate it, there's no marriage. Ask Father Con."

She bridled. "I can't talk to Father Con about that kind of thing. Anyway, it's only if a fellow knows beforehand that he's infertile that the marriage is invalid."

Liam said gently, "And we don't want to find that out, do we? So if you do what I ask tonight, any child you might have could just as easy be Christie's."

She turned towards him impulsively. Tears were trickling down her cheeks. "Is it the truth you're telling me, Liam McGrath?"

"So help me, God." Liam crossed himself. "It's all a plan my counselors cooked up, years ago. If your mam and my mam hadn't gone along with it, neither you nor me would be here upsetting each other."

"But why must it be you?" she pleaded. "Why not my Christie?"

He shrugged uncomfortably. "It just so happens that Eileen is having another child. Tommy may have been the O'Meara's, but this second one has to be mine. It seems that I, out of all the lads in Barley Cross, have inherited the O'Meara's fertility."

She sniffed. "What does your Eileen think of it?"

"She ain't too happy," he admitted. "But she's agreed to put up with it for the same reasons everybody else has."

Brege dabbed her eyes with the scrap of linen. "Do we do it just the once?"

"So far as I know," he said gently. "If you don't conceive, it's just your bad luck."

She hid her face in the handkerchief. "I'm shy, Liam. I've never done it before."

He sighed with relief. He was over the hurdle. It was now just a matter of patience and understanding. Barley Cross would never know its luck. He said gently, "I'll show you how."

She took a quick sip of cold tea. "Could we have the light out, please . . ?"

The ruling caucus met in Liam's parlor the following day. Brege Kennedy was safely away to the new house which her husband's da had built for her—and where she would find her new husband snoring in bed. Kate Monaghen was safely back in her cottage down the mill lane, richer by a tablet of toilet soap and a bottle of French perfume. And Liam McGrath was hoping that his Eileen would not be too curious about the events of the previous night when she returned from her mam's.

Liam straightened his hair, and entered the parlor.

General Desmond looked up. "Ah, Liam—ye've come to report success, I hope?"

Kevin Murphy said drily, "By the smirk on his face, I should imagine that he has."

Liam said, keeping his voice even, "I did what was required."

"Hark now!" The general lifted a finger. "Has he, or hasn't he?"

Doctor Denny Mallon removed an empty pipe from his mouth. "The Master has just told us he has, general."

The general waged the finger. "But not in so many words, Doctor. What if he and our Ice Maiden decided to fool us all, and pretend they've done it? We'd never know, would we?"

Liam glanced from one to the other. Obviously

they had been discussing the possibility that he would cheat.

Celia Larkin looked up from her knitting. "Are you accusing our new Master of lying, Larry Desmond?"

The general's jaw dropped—histrionically, Liam suspected.

"I never said so," he protested. "I'd just prefer a more positive assurance than he has given us so far."

The schoolmistress lowered her knitting. "If you're wanting a blow by blow description of the exploit, you'll have to manage without my presence."

"Ah no, Celia." Denny Mallon waved his pipe. "That won't be necessary. If Liam says the job's done, then done it is."

"Hold on, now!" Kevin Murphy sat up straight. "If the job's been done, then surely Liam can tell us something that would prove he's handing us the truth. Something maybe Denny, here, could confirm. Has the lady a mole on her person, for instance?"

Four pairs of eyes turned on Liam. He shifted his feet uneasily. "She insisted on the light going out," he protested.

General Desmond cackled harshly. "Wouldn't ye know there'd be a snag? I had a feeling that the Christie victory was a flash in the pan."

"That's quite enough, Larry Desmond," snapped the schoolmistress. "You agreed to his being made Master. If you trusted him then, why can't you trust him now?"

Why not indeed. Liam agreed silently. But then the general hadn't been faced by a tyro tyrant refusing to wear a uniform until yesterday. And when puppets don't work properly you lose faith in them.

"Enough!" Denny Mallon exploded. "Let the Master be!" He turned to Liam. "Tell them, son!"

Liam gazed pleadingly at the doctor. "But it's *her* secret. Brege will never forgive me if I let it out."

"Tell us what?" demanded the general. "Have you two been cooking something up between you?"

"Tell them!" thundered the doctor. "They'll never be satisfied until they know. And—" Denny Mallon glowered round the room, daring anyone to contradict him. "—anything said at this meeting is as inviolate as the confessional."

Liam blew heavily. So much for promises made in the dark. Poor Ice Maiden! Sacrificed on the altar of the Master's probity.

Reluctantly he told them what Doctor Denny already knew, and had kept secret for years.

"Brege Kennedy isn't pious, nor cold, nor shy—like we thought. She has a deformity she doesn't want anyone to know about. She has knock knees."

The Wedding March

The entire population of Barley Cross attended the funeral, apart from the guards up at the Fist, Sally Corcoran who was in labor attended by Doctor Denny Mallon, acting midwife, and . . . the Fintan Dooleys.

Kevin Murphy, slouching along beside the Lord of Barley Cross on the way back from the cemetery, said, "I wonder what's up with Finty? He was five years at the Fist in the old days, and always very close to the general."

Liam McGrath scarcely heard him. General Desmond's death monopolized his thoughts. Could anyone have stopped the general drinking? Larry Desmond had been a forceful character, and not the easiest of citizens to get on with, but his loss would be a hard blow to the village. Someone had to be persuaded to take his place.

Celia Larkin, back bent a little, trudged at the Master's other elbow. She said to the vet, "Didn't Finty take over the Curry cottage after Liam moved out?"

Kevin Murphy nodded. "Indeed he did. He tried the O'Toole place before that, but it was tumbling down round his ears."

Liam came back to the present. He beckoned one of the uniformed pallbearers. "Seamus, nip up to Kirkogue and see if anything's wrong with Finty Dooley or his wife."

Watching the soldier hurry away, Kevin Murphy said, "Have ye anyone in mind for the general's job, me lord? 'Twill have to be filled, ye know. Five years of peace since ye went up the hill don't mean we can relax our vigilance."

Liam sighed. Why hadn't General Desmond nominated his successor! He asked, "Who's next in rank?"

Kevin Murphy scratched his head. "Sure it would be Andy McGrath—your stepfather, me lord. I did hear Larry made him a major, or suchlike."

Liam kicked the flints in the road. "If I appointed Andy, would they think it was . . ?"

"Nepotism?" supplied Celia Larkin. "Liam, as Lord of Barley Cross you have a perfect right to appoint whom you wish as our general."

Liam grimaced. His stepfather was a good citizen, cheerfully accepting the Master's rule—even on doctrines like *droit du seigneur*—without question. Such docility would hardly be an asset in a general. He said, "It isn't the legality which bothers me, Celia. It's Andy. With all due respect—he ain't exactly brilliant, if you follow my meaning."

Celia Larkin frowned over her spectacles. "Your step da is a good, reliable man. He would make a fine general."

Liam blinked. An unexpected vote for his stepfather! He shot a glance at the vet. "Andy McGrath suit you, Kevin?"

Kevin Murphy rubbed a bristly chin. "We don't need brilliance. Andy is a cautious man. I reckon he could do the job."

Liam masked his surprise. Apparently no one shared his opinion of his stepfather. He said, "Okay, I'll have a word with Doctor Denny. Then I'll see Andy."

The vet wagged his head in admiration. "See what I mean, Celia? They instill cautiousness in the McGraths."

Liam located the doctor at the Corcoran cottage. Denny Mallon held a squawking bundle.

Sally Corcoran smirked from the bed. "Good morning, me lord."

Liam kept an impassive face. Sally's husband Charlie was sure to be somewhere around the house. Liam didn't want to irk him with undue familiarity towards his wife—even though they all knew that the bundle in Doctor Denny's arms had nothing to do with Charlie, and everything to do with Liam.

Denny Mallon laughed jovially. He thrust the child at its mother. "Take her, Sally. Another Barley Cross citizen. Another step on our road to the future."

Straightfaced, Liam said, "Congratulations, Sally. I'll send down a present when I get home. Meanwhile . . ." He pulled a shiny medallion from his pocket, and tucked it into the infant's bindings. The trinkets were part of a hoard he had discovered at the Fist, relics of a long-forgotten papal visit, metamorphosed into a successful gimmick since the mothers had begun looking for them. He kissed the baby's head. Pity it was a girl. Maybe his next would be a boy.

He strolled down the Corcoran's path with the doctor. Denny Mallon said, "Andy will do nicely for general. But, consider Liam, he will be, *ex officio*, a member of the council."

Liam blinked. The idea hadn't entered his mind. Andy McGrath would never have the nerve to argue with the Lord of Barley Cross, despite Liam being his stepson. Liam said, "So what do we do about it?"

Denny Mallon chuckled. "Ah, get along and ask

him, son. We never educated Larry. We may have better luck with your step da."

Liam paused at the Corcoran's gate. Seamus Gallagher pelted down the street towards them.

"Me lord—" Seamus gasped for breath.

"Take your time, man," urged the doctor.

"Me lord—Finty Dooley is lying up at the Curry cottage with an arrow through his leg, and the Missus Dooley is gone!"

The counselors assembled in Liam's parlor. The new general sat stiffly at Larry Desmond's end of the settee, eyeing askance the bottle of poteen on the carpet at the other.

Kevin Murphy, seated above the bottle, slopped a tot into a glass. "Here, Andy. Don't act so formal. We're very easy here. First names and all that, if ye've a mind. Knock this back, and tell us what ye've done about the Dooley's."

General Andy McGrath held the glass like an unexploded bomb. He said, "I have sent a three-man patrol up Kirkogue with instructions to track down whoever abducted Claire Dooley, and if it's possible, to bring her back." He paused, forehead shiny. "I have also sent a couple of lads with a litter to bring Finty down. They'll have to go slow coming back, but I expect them here inside the half hour."

Denny Mallon clapped. "Good man! Will they be giving us a shout when they arrive?"

The general nodded. "I told them to report straight to the guard at the gate."

Celia Larkin put down her knitting. "Why only three men to track those villains, Andy?"

The general studied his glass for a moment. "Well, Celia, those raiders didn't try to kill Finty. An arrow through the leg shouldn't be fatal. I guess they just wanted to run off with his wife. Now my men are armed with automatic rifles, and they've plenty of bullets. No bow-and-arrow outfit could stand up to them. But I've told them to report back without engaging if they find themselves seriously outnumbered."

Kevin Murphy glanced swiftly around the company. "The villains must be hard up for women to take Finty's wife. Sure, Claire Dooley is no chicken—"

"That's enough of that!" snapped the schoolteacher.

Kevin Murphy coughed with sudden embarrassment. He thumped the arm of the settee. "Can't fault your logic, General."

"Thank you." Andy McGrath turned gravely towards Liam. "Are my dispositions satisfactory to the Master?"

Liam bit off a tart comment directed at the vet. Andy would have to learn to discount Kevin Murphy's comments, especially after the poteen bottle had gone round. He said, "Have the men supplies with them?"

Andy McGrath came to attention, still seated. "Four days food, me lord. Plus fodder for the horses."

Horses, too? Liam glowed inside. And all fixed up within half an hour of being appointed general! Maybe they had made a good choice in Andy. He said, gravely, "Thank you, Andy. Will you keep me informed of progress?"

Andy McGrath relaxed a hair's breadth. "As soon as I have anything to report, me lord."

Liam scanned his counselors. "Anything else?"

Denny Mallon cleared his throat. "There's this matter of Father Con—"

Celia Larkin interrupted sharply. "There's no problem with Father Con."

The doctor raised a hand. "Let me speak, Celia. Father Con is getting old. I don't count on us having him with us much longer. Young Adrian Walsh has been helping him—in church as well as in the presbytery. The lad is keen. I wouldn't mind him being our next shepherd. He could start taking over from Father—"

The schoolmistress's voice was icy. "There is no way Father Con can make Adrian Walsh into a priest. That's a bishop's job. Young Adrian mustn't be given any wrong ideas."

Liam held his tongue. He had heard a whisper about Adrian Walsh and Sean O'Rourke's daughter. Maybe Adrian had his sights set on targets other than the priesthood. Just let the lad get himself hitched to Rita O'Rourke, and Liam McGrath would sharp make a father of him!

The doctor stared at the schoolmistress, hands spread. "But in an emergency?"

Celia Larkin's voice rose higher. "What emergency? We still have the Father with us, haven't we? Tom O'Conner is making him a wheelchair. I have the children running his errands. We can go to him for a while, instead of him coming to us."

Kevin Murphy said, "What Dinny means is that maybe the good Lord would overlook a small infraction—"

Celia Larkin's voice became painfully shrill. "You've been listening to that *celidh*-dancing set, haven't you? Well, you just tell them that we don't make the rules. And if there are any infractions, we won't be making them either. If, eventually, we have to do without Father Con, then that is just what we shall do."

"Moreover," Liam interjected, feeling it time the subject was aired, "bearing in mind our current surplus of girls, we can't afford to let Adrian stay celibate. He should get married as soon as he's old enough. Unless—" Liam turned to the schoolmistress. "Do you think we might be permitted a married clergy? I believe they used to have them in Europe."

Celia Larkin snorted like a horse. "Those priests that got a dispensation were married before they took Holy Orders. And they never afterwards lived with their wives."

Kevin Murphy wagged his head in mock distress. "Such a waste!"

The schoolmistress glared at him. "And Father Con hasn't the authority to give that sort of dispensation either!"

Doctor Denny Mallon sighed. "No further business, me lord."

"In that case—" Liam began.

The door behind him opened. His servant Michael sidled in. The man bowed to the company. "Word from the gate, sirs and madame. They have Finty Dooley below on a litter."

Fintan Dooley winced as the doctor drew a stitch tight. Kevin Murphy sloshed more poteen into Finty's cup. "Swally that down, lad, and ye won't feel a damn thing."

Finty said, "The pain ain't so bad, Kevin. Me whole leg is gone numb."

Andy McGrath leaned over the table. "Did you see any of them?"

Finty winced as the needle again punctured his flesh. "Sure, there was three or four of them, Andy. One of the buggers kicked at me door while the others hid out of sight. When I came out a young felly with a ginger beard put the bolt through me pin."

The incredible words rang in Liam's head. "How young was the fellow?" he demanded.

"Eighteen—nineteen?" Finty shrugged. "I reckon none of them was over twenty. If I could only have reached me shotgun—"

Liam met Doctor Denny's gaze over Finty's head. *Eighteen? Nineteen?* Liam was twenty-five. And, like the rest of Barley Cross's younger generation, he had been sired by the village's previous Master.

Denny Mallon shaped a word. "How?"

Liam turned back to Finty. "You sure about their ages?"

Finty groaned. "Would I tell you a lie, me lord?"

Liam shivered with hope. Was there, somewhere close enough for raiders to be based, another village like Barley Cross? A village with someone capable of fathering children? The desire to find another to share his burden almost overwhelmed him. He gripped the doctor's shoulder. "Denny—what if they've got their own O'Meara?"

Denny Mallon had gone pale. He put down his needle, closed his eyes, and bowed his head. "Dear God," he muttered. "Let it be so."

Kevin Murphy, refilling Finty's glass, echoed, "Amen!"

Finty was put to bed, singing.

The counselors reconvened.

"Andy—you mustn't hurt any of those young men," Celia Larkin declared. "Their lives are too valuable to risk in vengeance. Someone should go after that patrol you sent, and tell them so."

Kevin Murphy's eyes gleamed. "Ye mean it's okay to pot at an old man like Finty, but not at young rascals who'd as soon put a bolt through ye? Sure, that's a quare old point of view."

General McGrath got to his feet. "With your permission, me lord. I'll despatch a messenger with fresh orders."

The vet intervened. "What sort of orders, Andy?"

The general turned fractionally towards the other end of the settee. "To refrain from attacking those young men, whatever the provocation. To stay out of sight, and trail them to their base. And to report back as soon as they know where that base is."

Liam nodded. Andy McGrath could be trusted to make the right moves. But steps would have to be taken to contact this other village. And it would have to be done the right way. *His* way. The council would want to discuss and argue about methods. But, on this subject, Liam wanted no argument. If

there was a fertile male alive within reach of Barley
Cross, Liam wanted to find him. And, if necessary,
Denny, Kevin and Celia would have to be stam-
peded. He said, "Orders approved, General. And
here are a few more. I want half a dozen of our
marriageable young ladies informed that they have
three days to fix up their trousseaux and be ready to
move. I want the biggest cart you can find converted
into a mobile home with enough bedrooms for the
brides, myself and a chaperone. I want an escort of
soldiers, armed with automatic weapons." He turned
to Celia. "And I want a fancy rigout made for myself
and my two children—something royalty might wear,
velvet, lace and stuff. Can I leave that to you?"

They stared at him as if had gone mad.

He stared back, offering no excuses. This plan,
which he had thought up since hearing Finty Dooley's
report, was not subject to their veto. Let them think
what they pleased.

Celia Larkin said, hesitant, "*Velvet*, Liam?"

He glared at her. "Cut up my curtains if you have
to."

"Timber for something that big?" mumbled Kevin
Murphy.

So timber was scarce in Connemara! Lima scowled
at the vet. "Pull down a house for it. There's plenty
empty."

"What if we can't find six girls willing to do as you
ask," Denny Mallon queried.

Liam smiled grimly. "Just let drop that there might
be a husband for them in the deal. They'll be willing
enough."

"You plan an expedition?" prompted the doctor.

Liam hid his relief. At least Denny didn't oppose
the project he envisaged. He said, "We'll have to
make friends with these people who raided the
Dooleys. We can't let them think we're enemies."
He paused. "What if *all* their menfolk are fertile?"

Kevin Murphy looked shocked. "Christ! I'd invite a few of them to imigrate to Barley Cross!"

Denny Mallon grunted. " 'Twould be a fine thing for our future."

Liam pounced. "So it's worth any effort we make. And my expedition might pull it off. I will want Celia along to look after the girls. Andy can command the escort. You and Kevin stay here, in charge."

Kevin Murphy snorted. "An armed escort and Celia? That don't sound very friendly to me."

Liam blessed him for the joke. The vet could be thorny over anything not to his liking. He said, "We have to be able to look after ourselves in case they don't want to be friends with us. But I think Andy summed them up right—those lads were looking for wives."

The vet pulled his lip. "Reckon I go along with that, me lord. We must make an attempt to fraternize with them. I'll sort out a matched team to pull this mobile house for you. Praise be we're over the ploughing!"

Doctor Denny thumbed the bowl of his empty pipe, eyes reflective. "I'm not keen on your children going."

Liam felt a stab of guilt. Trust Denny to pinpoint the weak spot. But the presence of two genuine children might just swing the deal he planned. And who else's kids dare he risk? He said, "Nor me, Denny. But they're living proof of what's on offer."

"You envisage exchanging your services for theirs?"

"Something like that. If they've only one stag they'll be just as keen for fresh blood as we are."

"And if they have more than one?"

"I have the girls."

The doctor shrugged. "I'm glad Eileen is your wife, and not mine." Liam winced. He could imagine Eileen's only too predictable reaction to his taking the children on a wildcat expedition. He said ruefully, "That's what you pay me for, isn't it?"

Doctor Denny sighed. "God help us all! Sometimes I wonder if it's all worth it." Ceclia Larkin sent her tuffet skating backwards. "You men! You're all the same. You're short of guts. If Liam's plan will help the village it's our duty to back him up."

Liam saw his stepfather flinch. The Larkin contempt was a novel experience for the general. Andy McGrath said stiffly, "I'll get the carpenters on the job immediately, me lord. And trust me, you'll have an escort fit for a prince."

Liam got up. He'd had enough discussion. "That'll be fine, Andy. With luck, we'll overawe those raiders."

Kevin Murphy placed the bottle of poteen, untouched, on the table. "By Christ, Liam—ye might do just that!"

The mobile home was ready in four days. On the first day Eileen had refused to speak to Liam. On the second he had retaliated with a similar silence. On the third she had demanded a place on the expedition, and Liam had ordered his bedroom extended. On the fourth, Tom O'Connor put the final nail into the woodwork, and let loose the painters. That evening, Liam surveyed the great green and white contraption which somehow reminded him of a picture of Noah's Ark he had seen in a schoolbook.

The O'Connor oeuvre was mind-boggling. Cantilevered out on each side of the cart on which it rested until the wheels were lost under the overhang; a row of glazed and curtained windows along each side; a red-tiled, peaked roof from which projected a stovepipe chimney—nothing like it had ever have been seen in Connemara before. Was this what he asked Andy to build? Six horses would scarcely budge it!

Liam choked on a laugh. If this didn't overawe the raider folk, nothing would.

General McGrath's scouts returned on the fifth day, and Liam learned where he was going.

"Achill Island?" mused Denny Mallon. " 'Tis a bleak and draughty place."

"And it'll take a week to get there in your pantechnicon," the vet commented. "Presuming ye can get it through the mountains."

Liam watched Michael carefully folding his new outfit. He said, "We'll skirt the mountains, Kevin. Achill won't run away."

Achill Island is reached via a bridge over the Atlantic Ocean. At the sight of the viaduct spanning the Sound, Liam halted his caravanserai. The bridge appeared unguarded, but then, that was how he would have arranged it to appear had he been an Achill Islander.

Magnificent in his parlor curtains, Liam flung his reins to General McGrath. "Stay here," he ordered. "I'm going ahead with the kids. It's worth the risk if it saves us being ambushed."

Andy McGrath's face grew hard. Liam was forgetting that the kids were also his grandchildren. He said "Liam—"

Liam's mouth set in a firm line. "*Please* . . . da?"

The general tossed Liam's reins to a nearby soldier. He swung his horse's head around. "I'll get them for you."

The Lord of Barley Cross approached the bridge to Achill in dead silence, heart thumping, a child on each hand. Behind him, his cohorts watched, anxious.

A flash of sunlit metal on at the far end of the bridge caught his eye. Someone flexing a bow?

He called loudly, "Would you shoot at children, then?"

A wild-looking youth wearing a sealskin jacket and trews stepped into sight, bow cocked. He shouted back, "Halt, then—and state yer business!"

Liam halted. He noted that the youth was clean-shaven. At least he wasn't the trigger-happy hooligan who had pinked Finty Dooley. He called, "We've come to trade."

"What sort of trade?"

"Women—seeing as you are so short of them."

The youth's face grew suspicious. "What do you know about us being short of women?"

"Enough to offer you a deal."

The voice stayed wary, but the bow was lowered. "What kind of a deal?"

Liam knew the islander was hooked. He spread his arms wide. "Let me talk to your leader. I'm not armed."

"What's in yonder wagon?"

Liam grinned. "My trade goods—with an armed escort."

The youth beckoned other ruffians out of concealment. He conferred with them. Then he called, "You and the kids can come over, but the rest of your mob and *that*—" he indicated the juggernaut, "—stays on your side of the bridge."

Liam shrugged. Inwardly he was far from displeased. He didn't want Andy and Celia fussing around until he'd had a chance to sort things out with this youth's boss. He faced his troops, and made "Stay where you are" gestures. Then, clutching his children's hands, he went over the bridge.

There was a pony and trap concealed in the bushes on the far side. The youth motioned Liam and the children into it. One of the ruffians climbed onto the driver's seat. They set off. The others followed on horseback.

The youth drove no more than a mile before turning in at a stone gateway. A gravel drive brought them to the forecourt of a house. The trap halted. Liam saw figures in brown habits working in the gardens around the house, tonsured heads bent over hoes and rakes.

He said, "Is your leader a monk?"

The youth ignored him. The other vaulted from his horse, and entered the house. He reappeared with a tall, elderly man who wore an ankle-length purple habit. A crucifix hung on his breast. A purple biretta perched on his head.

Liam had seen pictures of bishops. He knew what to do. He got down from his trap, bent a knee, and kissed the ring on the man's gnarled finger. "My lord bishop," he said.

"Get up, son," responded the man. "And call me Zbigniev."

The cleric didn't sound like a foreigner. "You *are* a bishop?" Liam asked, wondering if he had made a mistake.

"For longer than I care to remember," Zbigneiv answered. "But not of your country, my son. The riots of long ago caught me here on a fishing holiday, and I was never able to go home. Now, tell me what you want."

Liam tugged his velvet tunic straight, wondering if he looked as big a fool as he felt. This was no Achill Island yokel to be dazzled by a show of finery. Any prelate whose conscience permitted him to lead a band of raiders wouldn't impress easily. He said, "I'm Liam McGrath, the Lord of the village your men visited last week. I've come to take Missus Dooley back home."

"Missus?" Zbigniev's intonation mimicked Liam's. He swung on the two youths. "The woman you took was married?"

"*Is* married," Liam corrected. "We patched her old man up."

Liam's captors shifted uneasily. "We didn't know, yer grace. And there wasn't much time for discussion."

Zbigniev frowned. "This is no matter for levity, Dominic. We may be tragically short of women, but—"

The bishop's voice faltered. His mouth opened like a cod on a slab. He had just seen the children in the trap. He turned inquiringly to Liam. "How?"

"Mine, your grace. Like your people, we still produce children in Barley Cross."

Zbigniev ignored his response. He rushed towards the trap, arms outstretched to embrace the two infants. "Glory to God! Are they not a wonderful sight!" He stood, arms around them. "Surely, Liam, you did not bring these precious mites along just to impress me?"

It was uncomfortably near the truth. Liam lowered his gaze. "I wanted to demonstrate our peaceful intentions, my lord. I have soldiers back there, but they are only to protect my—er—merchandise."

"And what is your merchandise?"

Liam took a breath. Bishop Zbigniev might have progressive ideas about banditry and still hold old-fashioned notions on sex. But the nettle had to be grasped. He said bluntly, "I have six young ladies back there, your grace. Each is willing to marry one of your young men—on one condition."

"Oh? Pray continue. What condition?"

Was the bishop hiding a smile? Liam rushed on. "First, I want Claire Dooley back. Second—" Liam hesitated. This was a bishop he was propositioning. It came out in a rush. "—I want six rapes committed in Barley Cross."

Zbigniev frowned. "Rapes? That is a harsh word, my son."

Liam stood his ground. "You may describe it how you like, my lord. But I want six pregnancies in exchange for six wives."

Zbigniev raised his eyebrows. "And how may one guarantee even one pregnancy?"

Liam flushed. "You know what I mean, your grace. As far as I know, apart from your village and mine, the whole country is childless. I know where Barley Cross's children come from. And I take it that you are aware how it is managed in yours. I'm offering you a straight swap—six pregnancies for six brides."

Reluctantly Zbigniev released his hold on Liam's children. He turned a regretful face. "My son, I'm afraid you are a little late with your proposal."

Too late? They had come with the minimum of delay!

Zbigniev bowed his head. "Rory MacCormick perished at sea fifteen years ago. He was the last man on Achill to father a child."

Liam felt his hopes draining away. What rotten luck! A generation too late! There was no deal he could do with the bishop. And no fresh blood in Barley Cross—unless? He faced the bishop squarely. "Is there a chance some of your young men might have inherited their father's fertility?"

Zbigniev shook his head. "I have no proof so far, my son. Indeed, I can only guess which of our youths had Rory for a father. Not all matters are confided to the clergy, you know. All I know is that, since Rory drowned, there have been no more births in Achill. We have a dozen unwed young men aged from fifteen to twenty-five—and any one of them might be the man you need."

Liam toed the gravel, mind churning. Fat chance of another miracle like him! It was like chasing a rainbow. Still—he had promised to find husbands for his maidens. He said, "Half a deal is better than no deal at all, my lord. With your permission, I'll bring on my dancing girls."

They parked the juggernaut in the center of the village at the foot of Slievemore. Surf boomed against the nearby cliffs. Seabirds shrieked. The sun shone. Barley Cross and Achill Island citizens mingled under the beaming gaze of Bishop Zbigniev. Claire Dooley was produced unharmed, and given into the care of Eileen McGrath and Celia Larkin. The woman clutched at them as though they were lost relatives. "How's Finty?" she demanded.

"Och, he'll live," Celia responded. "Doctor Denny

put a few tucks into his hide." She dropped a knee to Zbigniev. "Your grace, I suggest you get your eligible bachelors into our caravan, and we let them socialize with our young ladies. Those who don't come out, you can marry."

The bishop stared hard at Celia. "And you are?"

"Celia Larkin. Schoolmistress and chaperone."

He nodded sagely. "And you were privy to Liam's plan?"

She colored. "I was, your grace. And I make no apology. If the good lord had not wanted us to survive, he wouldn't have let us even think up the idea."

Zbigniev winced. "Such charming sophistry. I am sorry there is no way I can make up for our inability to strike a bargain."

Celia Larkin smiled grimly. "Oh, but there is a way, my lord . . ."

Later, Liam said to Dominic, "We've spare cottages in Barley Cross if you want to come back with us. But we've little use for fishermen or seal hunters. And any of your spare bachelors can visit us if they fancy their chances of getting a wife. But there are no more girls willing to leave the village."

Dominic slid an arm around a blushing Kathleen Mulroon. "We'll be returning with you, me lord." He grinned slyly. "We might even insist on ye having yer droyts if we don't have no luck on our own."

The council met again in the Master's parlor.

Kevin Murphy swirled poteen in his glass. " 'Twas a valiant try, Liam. Pity we didn't think of it fifteen years ago."

"Ach—times were different then." Denny Mallon stuffed dried grass into his pipe bowl. "Sure, two miles outside the village was a war zone. We'd have never risked the journey."

"And it wasn't all a dead loss," Andy McGrath

pointed out. "We got four new citizens out of it, and each of them has already volunteered for Fist duty."

Liam said, "And there's a faint hope we might have another O'Meara among them."

The vet tipped poteen recklessly down his throat. "I'd be glad if we have. This village is getting just a wee bit inbred."

Celia Larkin glowered over her tea cup. "No harm if the stock is good. Think of racehorses."

Kevin Murphy snorted. "It's people we're raising, Celia—not bloodstock!"

She grinned triumphantly. "I'm glad you've reminded me." She jerked the tasseled rope which summoned Michael.

He appeared. "More tay, is it, Miss Larkin?"

"No, Michael. Bring in the lad."

Michael shuffled out, to reappear leading a blushing Adrian Walsh. The boy must have been waiting out in the yard. He wore a heavy jacket. A muffler swaddled his neck.

Celia Larkin cooed at him. "Tell the gentlemen what happened to you on Achill."

Liam blinked. Adrian Walsh on Achill? That was news.

The schoolmistress seemed to read his thoughts. "Do you think I'd leave him here at the mercies of those two?" She nodded at the doctor and the vet. "God knows what follies they'd be teaching him." She turned to the youth. "Go on—speak up, Adrian!"

Adrian began, hesitant. "I—Miss Larkin smuggled me onto the cart-house the night before we left for Achill. I stayed in her bedroom. When we got to Achill, she brought me out to meet the bishop felly. He made me lay face down on the ground. Then he put his hands on me head."

"Who did this to ye?" Kevin Murphy demanded.

"The felly with the purple robe and the crucifix."

"And for why would he do all that?" pursued the vet.

"Show him, Adrian," Celia Larkin instructed.

Adrian Walsh opened his coat, and pulled off his scarf, revealing a frayed and over-large dog collar encircling his scrawny neck.

Doctor Mallon dropped his pipe. "Holy Mother of God—what have they done at you, son?"

Celia Larkin smirked. "Bishop Zbigniev ordained him. And he's promised to ordain any more lads I send to Achill."

Kevin Murphy groaned. "Jesus! Now we'll be over-run with clergy!" Celia Larkin gave him a basilisk stare. "Any more remarks like that and I'll send girls instead!"

The vet flourished his glass. "Boy priests! Sure ye know we were hoping Adrian could take over in time, but this is too much. We're slipping back into the Middle Ages. Does your bishop, by any chance, wear chain mail and carry a sword?"

"Adrian," Denny Mallon intervened, "you are scarcely fourteen years old. Do you think you'll be able to do Father Con's job in Barley Cross?"

The boy turned grave eyes on the doctor. "Not yet, Mister Mallon. But Father can teach me what I need to know. And I'm legally ordained. So, when he gets too old . . ."

The youth fell silent.

Liam considered. The boy was no fool. Celia Larkin, it seemed, could teach her fellow counselors a trick or two. They couldn't argue with a *fait accompli*. Neither Denny, nor Kevin, nor Andy would have had the initiative to talk Bishop Zbigneiv into ordaining the lad. Let Celia have her triumph. It would be unfair to spoil it with complaints about the lad's youth.

Liam smiled with wicked joy. "I reckon Adrian will manage if we give him time enough."

He stood, dismissing them and further comment.

Finty Dooley was waiting in the hall. Finty had a

bandaged leg, and leaned on a stick. He said, "I just wanted to say thank ye, me lord, for getting me old woman back."

Liam flushed with pleasure. Gratitude was rare, and pleasant to experience. He said, "Sure, Finty, I was only doing my duty."

Finty fiddled with his cap. "Just the same, me lord, Missus Dooley is grateful to be out of the clutches of them crazy Achill lads and their fake bishop."

Liam's heart missed a beat. He stared cautiously around. Adrian and the others had dispersed. No one else could have heard Finty's words. He leaned forward to hiss, "*Fake* bishop?"

Finty looked embarrassed. "Sure, 'tis what they told the missus. He's a failed priest what came up from Blarney early on in the troubles. He's no more a foreigner than ye are. They took him in at the monastery. They reckon he's harmless, apart from his delusions. But the Achill lads pretend he runs the village. They let him think he's their leader."

Liam said quickly, "Has Missus Dooley said anything about this to anybody else?"

Finty squirmed. "Sure, she didn't like to open her mouth, sir. Not with Miss Celia being so taken with the felly."

Liam grabbed his coat from the hall stand. He gripped Finty's arm none too gently. "We're going for a walk up Kirkogue. I want a word with your missus. Then I'll have to find Dominic and his pals."

Limping fast to keep up with the Master, Finty gasped. "What's the hurry, me lord?"

Liam's face was pale. Hurry wasn't the word. At that moment he could have done with being in five different places at once. He said, "Finty, no one else must ever hear what you've just told me. Neither from you nor your wife." He glared at the puzzled Finty. "So help me—if you breathe a word about

Bishop Zbigniev to anyone, I'll have you shot out of the cannon of that tank on Barra Hill. And the same goes for Missus Dooley."

Finty's jaw dropped. "What—what's the matter, me lord?"

Liam halted to give Finty his undivided attention. "Listen carefully. That man Zbigniev was a bishop up to five minutes ago. And, as far as I'm concerned, he still is a bishop. I never heard what you told me about him. He's made young Walsh into a priest for us, and Adrian is going to stay made. Those lads from Achill can learn to keep their mouths shut, or face my displeasure. In a few years, when Father Con is gone, Barley Cross will be looking for someone to solemnize its marriages, hear its confessions, visit its sick, christen its children, say its Masses, and bury its dead. Well, by God, I'm going to see that Father Adrian Walsh is here to do it. And, if the good lord don't agree, he can take it out of my hide."

Liam tramped on. Finty Dooley panted after him, overawed by the Master's vehemence. But Liam had forgotten him. The Lord of Barley Cross was busy with his thoughts. His village had had a tumultous past. It looked as though it could expect a stormy future!

Crown of Thorns

Angry voices outside his dining room window disturbed the peace of Liam McGrath's breakfast. The Fist was usually quiet at this hour, apart from the racket the birds made. He got up to peer out of the casement.

Four young men stood on his doorstep, disputing with Eamon Toomey, who was guard for the day. Liam recognized the men as the Achill Island Irregulars now enlisted in the troop which guarded the Fist. Eamon Toomey faced them, his rifle at the high port.

Liam hesitated. Sometimes poor Eamon took his duties too ardently. Should the Lord of Barley Cross intervene? Eamon's rifle held only one bullet, but one bullet could do serious damage if it went off.

He heard Eamon's stolid tones. "You know you lads ain't supposed to be up here when you're off duty."

Dominic Nunan, always leader of the Achill immigrants, shouted loud enough to be heard indoors, "We want a word with the Master!"

Eamon stood unmoved. "I told you—the Master don't see no one without an appointment."

"Ah, come on, Eamon!" Nunan's voice was persuasive. "He'll see me. It won't take but a minute. It's important."

Eamon's tone was stubborn. "The Master is having his breakfast."

"I don't mind waiting."

Liam heard a rifle being cocked. "This is your last warning—"

It was time to intervene. Liam leaned out of the window. "What's the trouble, Dominic?"

Nunan tugged off his cap. "Can I have a word with you, me lord?"

Liam didn't quite trust the young islander. The immigrants had proved to be a wild bunch, and Dominic Nunan the wildest. Nunan had jeered at Liam's request for a conspiracy of silence regarding Bishop Zbigniev of Achill, neither promising, nor refusing, to keep silent. Liam was still unhappy about the incident. For, if Zbigniev's episcopacy was a fraud, so also was his ordination of young Adrian Walsh. And, if young Adrian's orders were invalid, Barley Cross would be priestless when Father Con died. Liam refused to contemplate the prospect. The village needed someone to marry its brides, comfort its sick, and bury its dead. And, if a handful of citizens, Nunan among them, could be persuaded to keep their mouths shut, there would be no danger of the secret leaking out. Liam sighed. He pitied Kathleen Mulroom, the girl Nunan had married. Several unmarried girls remained in the village, but no more husbands had been sought in Achill. In some ways Liam was not sorry. He said, "Speak up then, Dominic, I'm listening."

Nunan twisted his cap like a bashful gossoon. Liam

was not deceived. Dominic Nunan was as bashful as a gin trap.

The islander said, "It's kind of private, me lord. If I could come inside for a minute?"

Liam caught Eamon Toomey's eye. "Let him in, Eamon. Put him in the parlor. I'll be along in a tic."

The Achill islander got up out of Denny Mallon's chair when Liam entered the room. Nunan's eyes gleamed like those of a wild animal venturing onto cultivated ground. "I wanted to be the first to tell you the news, me lord." Nunan cocked his head to leer at the Lord of Barley Cross. "Doctor Denny says my Kathleen is pregnant."

Liam stood, stiff with shock. Kathleen Nunan was one of the few young wives in the village with whom he had not exercised his *droit du seigneur*. She had married Nunan on Achill in a ceremony conducted by Bishop Zbigniev, and Liam had not been sure if his droit extended as far as the island. Well, now that didn't matter. Kathleen Nunan pregnant meant there was another male in Barley Cross who could father children, and Liam McGrath no longer carried the burden alone.

Liam's smile was genuine. "That's great news. Congratulations, Dominic."

Nunan smirked. "I guessed you'd be pleased, me lord, seeing as children are kind of hard to come by. But it sets us a problem."

Liam raised his eyebrows. "What sort of problem?"

Nunan fiddled with his cap. "I know it's meant to be a secret about how kids are conceived in Barley Cross. But if you want me to spread my genes around—how am I going to manage it?"

Liam's heart missed a beat. For almost a year, since the expedition to Achill, he and his councillors had prayed that one of islander Rory MacCormick's bastards might prove fertile. But they hadn't considered how to spread those new genes, should their hopes be fulfilled. Now this youth was dropping the problem right in his lap!

"Well, I can't go about raping the village wives like you can," Nunan pointed out. "I'd get shot, or Kathleen would divorce me. But, if you was to abdicate in my favor—?"

The word echoed in Liam's mind, like a highwayman's challenge. *Abdicate!* He kept his face expressionless. This Achill hooligan had thought it through, and come up with a novel, but logical, solution.

He temporized. "Do you think you could manage the Master's job?"

"I could try."

"Do you fancy being Master?"

Nunan stroked the plush back of the settee. "Reckon I might get used to it."

"What does Kathleen—your wife think about it?"

"Och—we haven't discussed it yet. But she knows about this droyt lark of yours. I reckon she'd get used to me having it off around the village, like you do."

Liam compressed his lips. Nunan's blunt vernacular left him feeling disturbed and old-fashioned. What to do? He dared not ignore the youth's suggestion. Doctor Denny Mallon was forever harping on about the need for new genes. If Nunan could provide them, the doctor was going to grab him with both hands. But the Achill youth couldn't be let go at it like a bull in a field. There were conventions. This thinking should have been done months ago. He would have to talk to the doctor.

He said, "Give me a couple of days, Dominic. We'll work something out."

Dominic Nunan put on his cap. His humility had vanished. He grinned. "Okay, me lord. I can spare you a couple of days."

Liam let it pass. The fellow held all the cards.

Barley Cross's ruling caucus assembled in Liam's

parlor that afternoon. Liam told them of the morning's visitor, and of Nunan's ambition.

Doctor Denny Mallon shifted uneasily in his chair. "Young Dominic's telling the truth. I examined his wife this morning. She's pregnant all right."

Four pairs of eyes turned towards Liam McGrath. He flushed. "Don't ask me what to do about it. I got you here so we could talk things over."

Denny Mallon sucked an empty pipe. "Dominic's suggestion has merit. We do need his genes. But he can't donate them like Liam does unless he has Liam's authority."

General Andy McGrath coughed to catch the meeting's attention. "The village wouldn't like that. Liam was chosen by the O'Meara himself to succeed him as Master. Who's going to choose this fellow?"

Kevin Murphy at the other end of the settee to the general studied a bottle of poteen on the floor by his foot. Voice gently mocking, he said, "Andy, let me explain. We counselors chose Liam. And we chose him because he was the only male in the village who could do for us what the O'Meara had been doing for years. Do I have to spell it out further for ye?"

Andy McGrath colored. "Ah, no, Kevin. I appreciate what you are getting at. But there are a lot of folk in the village that aren't so sophisticated as us council members. We've got to bear them in mind."

"I wonder!" Celia Larkin lowered her knitting. "Still, it would be safer to proceed on Andy's premise. Could we apoint this young man to be deputy to the Master?"

Kevin Murphy choked on a cough.

The schoolmistress eyed the vet coldly. "There is nothing humorous in my proposal, Kevin. Most rulers have deputies."

The vet got his face straight. "No offence, Cee. I appreciate your point. But no ruler that I ever read about would have delegated our Liam's particular droit."

Denny Mallon waved a pipe stem. "How about us having two Masters? A sort of duumvirate? There are Roman precedents."

The vet's voice had an edge like a scythe. "Denny, as Andy has pointed out, we are not dealing with sophisticated Romans. The village wouldn't stand for nonsense like that."

The doctor opened a grubby pouch. He pushed dried grasses into his pipe bowl. "Nonsense or not, Kevin, we need the fellow's blood. Half our genetic pool has been contributed by Liam or Patrick O'Meara, and it ain't healthy. You know the fruits of inbreeding. We are building up a load of trouble for ourselves. We need what Dominic can provide. And he's already told us on what terms he'd be willing to provide it. "No offense, Liam. But this is something I've prayed for since the world went sterile. We can't afford to turn Nunan down."

The Lord of Barley Cross straightened in his battered armchair. Why contest the obvious. Dominic Nunan had to have the Master's position if he were to do the Master's job.

It hurt, but Liam said it. "I'll resign if you wish, Denny."

Denny Mallon puffed out a smoke screen which hid a rueful grimace. "It's an idea, Liam—if the village will accept it. An abdication in favor of young Dominic on health grounds?"

Kevin Murphy nodded gravely. "Until the Achill felly has done his duty a few times—then we can bring Liam back."

Liam shook his head. The doctor and the vet were fools. "You won't get away with that, Kevin. Nunan's not the sort of fellow you can push about. Once he's Master, he'll stay Master.

The vet reached down for the bottle. "No need to

let him in on our plans. Let him worry about what hits him when it happens."

Celia Larkin's needles flashed in the sunlight. "What health grounds? Liam is as fit as a fiddle."

Liam felt obliged to show enthusiasm. "I'll catch anything you like," he volunteered. "Measles? Mumps?" He hid the irritation in his voice. Sometimes, listening to the four of them, you could believe he wasn't even present.

"It would have to be something that got him off Barra Hill," reasoned the vet.

"Like altitude sickness?" Celia Larkin suggested drily.

Denny Mallon lowered his pipe. "Is that supposed to be a joke, Celia? I didn't expect levity from you. I'll have to think up something suitable. A nervous breakdown would do. We only want him *hors de combat* until a few children have been born with a different set of chromosomes."

Celia Larkin peered over her spectacles. "And who will promulgate the news to the populace?"

The doctor waved his pipe. "Sure, that'll be done by Liam himself. The Master must announce his own abdication, *and* name his successor."

Celia Larkin put down her knitting. "And who's going to persuade the people that Dominic Nunan is fit to be our Lord and Master?"

Denny Mallon shifted uncomfortably. "Sure, they'll accept Liam's fiat on that matter."

Celia Larkin kept her gaze fixed on the doctor. "Why? The fellow doesn't belong to the village. He's an immigrant from Achill. Why should they accept him?"

"Jasus, Celia—" Kevin put down his glass, splashing the carpet. "—hasn't Dinny just said? The Master will choose him, and they'll accept the Master's decision."

The schoolteacher's needles began clicking again.

"I doubt it. I very much doubt it. But, if that's the best you men can think up, we'll have to try it."

Liam felt his gorge rising. This cold-hearted crew were planning his removal as if he were a piece of furniture. He said, "Do I announce the abdication from a phony sickbed? Swathed in bandages? Waving a crutch? And, incidently, where do I live after my abdication? The Dooleys have our old cottage."

The vet stooped to top up his glass. "Ye could move into Nunan's place. Surely the felly won't need two homes!"

Andy McGrath coughed. "We'll take you in, Liam. Your mam would be pleased to have you back."

Liam scowled at his stepfather. No doubt Andy was thinking of the fun he'd have with his grandchildren. Four to a room they'd be sleeping! He got up, anger choking him. He glared at them. "Just a bloody stud bull for you, that's all I've ever been! And now you no longer need my services, you're not worried what happens to me. Well, thank you for nothing! Just decide what illness I'm to catch, and let me know. I'll try not to disappoint you."

He ran from the room.

The vet stared at the doctor and the schoolmistress. "The Master seems a wee bit touchy today."

Celia Larkin rolled her knitting around the needles. "Wouldn't you be—rejected in favor of a hooligan from Achill? And we didn't even give him a vote of thanks for all he's done!"

Denny Mallon seemed to shrivel, sinking even deeper into his plush armchair. He puffed hard on a dying pipe. "Let it be! We've a couple of marriages scheduled for this summer. Liam should be glad of a vacation."

He sat alone at the breakfast table. Michael, stained waistcoat concealed by a green baize apron, hovered, steaming teapot in hand. The servant said, "I'm sorry to hear the news, me lord."

Liam kept his face down, concentrating on eggs and rashers. "Does everyone know about it, Michael?"

His man poured tea, then placed the pot on a silver trivet, and pulled a cosy over it. "Your letter of resignation is posted at the gate, sir. And there's a copy on the smithy wall, and another on the church board."

Liam gulped. It had all happened so quickly. One day he was Master, the next he had notice to quit. Celia must have produced his instrument of abdication. Denny Mallon's and the vet's scribbles were illegible. How had he ever fooled himself into thinking he could dominate those three!

"May I say, me lord," Michael added, "the parlor, kitchen and garden staffs have all asked me to convey their sympathy with your illness, and their regrets at your departure."

"Thank you, Michael." Liam put down his fork. The servant didn't deserve the lie his counselors had manufactured for him. "Doctor Denny says it may cure itself in time, but I've got to rest. If I carry on as Master, he guarantees me a nervous breakdown."

"That would be a pity, sir."

"Dominic Nunan will make a good Master," Liam forced out the words. "He is young. He'll have no favorites, since he is new to the village. And I'm sure he has our welfare at heart. Didn't he choose to become a citizen? Hasn't he volunteered for Fist duty?"

"I'm sure you're right, sir." Michael brushed crumbs from the tablecloth. "Will me lady be down soon?"

Liam met the man's troubled eyes. "She has gone to my mam's already, with the children. She won't be coming back."

"I see, sir. And her things? Shall I be after packing them?"

"She has taken all she wants. The Nunans can have what's left."

"Very good, me lord . . . sir?" Micheal hovered, like a butterfly over a flowerbed. "Would it be possible for me to come with ye, me lord? I could serve ye down below, just like I've done up here."

Liam swallowed a lump which hadn't come from eating breakfast. "There's no room at my mam's, Michael. She can hardly fit the four of us in."

"I understand, sir." Michael's lip trembled. "May I add a personal comment, sir? Ye've been a good master to me. It's been like serving the late O'Meara over again. I shall miss ye."

Liam pushed away his plate. Food had lost its appeal. He got up. "I'll start putting my things together, Michael, then I'll be off. No use hanging on until the new man arrives." He held out a hand. "You won't see me up here again. Look after my successor."

Micheal took his hand, solemn faced. "I'll try, me lord."

Liam found a smile. "It's Liam now—not 'my lord,' Michael."

"Yes, sir, Liam. Thank ye, me lord."

Liam fled, before he lost control.

Short-sleeved and sweaty, plain Liam McGrath pushed the potato fork into the soil to unearth another clutch of early Arrans. It was his job to lift the praties while his stepfather stayed up at the Fist supervising modifications required by the new Master.

A shadow fell across the tines of the fork. Liam looked up. A figure sat on a horse on the path bordering the potato field. Liam shaded his eyes, and recognized the new Lord of Barley Cross. He stuck the fork upright, and went towards the path. "Were you wanting me, Dominic?"

The man on horseback scowled down at him. "I

was. And the title is 'Lord' or 'Master.' Take your pick."

Liam wiped earthy hands on his overalls, concealing the hurt. "I see, my lord. Point taken. What can I do for you?"

Dominic Nunan gestured with his thumb. "You can get up to that bloody Fist and warn those servants of mine that there'll be trouble if they don't mend their ways."

Liam hid his surprise. What villainy was Michael up to? He said, "What are they doing, my lord?"

Dominic flicked at the flies with his riding crop, lips twisted in a sneer. "Damned hot down here in the fields. Don't know how you put up with it, man."

Liam ignored the barb. "The servants?" he prompted. "What are they getting up to?"

The horse moved restlessly, and the Lord of Barley Cross jerked hard on the bridle. "It's not what they're doing. It's what they are *not* doing. Cold food. Bed's not made. Towels not changed. Can't hear the bell when I ring. No cleaning done. Sudden shortage of decent drink. Chatting with the guards when they should be working. I could go on for hours."

Liam kept his face straight. "Why not get a new lot of servants?"

"Tried. No one will come."

Liam shrugged. "I don't know what I can do about it, my lord. I have no authority up at the Fist, as you know. They'd take no notice of me."

Dominic Nunan's face reddened. "You mean you refuse to go up there? You know they'll do anything you ask."

Liam grimaced. "Since I abdicated, I have no power over them."

"If I order you up to the Fist will you talk to them?"

Liam shook his head. "No, my lord. Your authority don't cover me that far. If you want me up there against my will, you'd better send your soldiers."

The new lord of Barley Cross jerked his horse's head 'round, and flicked its rump. "Right—we'll see about that!"

General Andy McGrath came home with a frown. He found his stepson bagging potatoes in the barn.

"What have you been saying to the new master? He came back in a rare old state."

Liam tied the neck of the sack. "He came down here seeking help, but he got none from me. He's the fellow with the power now. Seems that Michael and the staff are giving him the runaround, and he can't cope with it. Well, if he can't control his own household, he's not fit to run the village."

Andy McGrath sighed. "Michael's lot are giving him a rough ride."

Liam shoveled potatoes into another sack. "Then let him sort them out himself. We all have problems. But we don't go shouting for help without first trying to sort them out for ourselves."

Andy McGrath picked up a potato, rubbed the dirt from it, and sniffed the skin. "Dominic's been having trouble for a fortnight. He's not had a warm meal, nor a good night's sleep in that time. Kathleen is threatening to go home to her mam. A cat yowled outside their window most of last night. There was no hot water this morning because the gardener forgot to stoke the furnace before he went home."

Liam grinned. "Jasus—they're murdering him!"

Andy McGrath didn't smile. He tossed the potato back into Liam's sack. "They'll push him too far. He ordered me to come down here for you, today—with an escort."

Liam stopped shoveling spuds. "What did you say to him?"

"I told him he couldn't order that sort of thing

unless you had committed an offense. He said you *had* committed an offense by refusing to help him. I talked him out of it, but he wasn't happy."

Liam leaned the shovel against the barn wall. "Maybe you didn't pick a winner this time, Andy."

His stepfather scratched his head. "Lord love us, son—I didn't pick him in the first place. 'Twas Dinny and Kevin thought it up between them, they being so obsessed with the idea of getting new blood into the village. They never considered what kind of fellow they were getting it from. For meself, I never trusted that Achill scoundrel. But Dinny and Kevin were keen, so I went along with them."

Liam's grin was lopsided. "They caught Celia that way, I think." He pulled off his shirt, and headed for the pump. "But she cooperated a bit harder than you did." He stuck his head under the pump. His stepfather worked the handle while he soused himself. "Writing out those copies of my resignation!" Liam dried himself on an empty sack. Then he clapped his stepfather on the back. "Come on in to supper, da. Let Dominic look for solutions without our help."

Andy McGrath had been gone an hour the following morning when four horsemen galloped up the lane to Killoo Farm. Liam, in the potato field, recognized the ex-Achill Islanders, led by the new Master.

He shouldered the fork, and trudged along the furrow to meet Dominic Nunan.

The new master scarcely gave him time to get within earshot.

"Liam McGrath," he shouted. "I have decided that you are an unsettling influence in Barley Cross. I hereby proclaim you *persona non grata,* and I give you an hour to quit the village."

Liam almost dropped the fork in his astonishment. "You're joking, Dominic!"

Nunan's face twisted in anger. "I've told you how to address me. And I don't joke."

Liam weighed the odds. One man with a potato fork against four horsemen carrying automatic rifles. Not that it would come to shooting, but he would have liked a go at their loud-mouth boss, if he could have banked on the other three not interfering.

From the side of his eye, Liam saw Eileen come to the farmhouse door with the children. He drew closer to Nunan, lowering his voice. "Where am I supposed to go?"

The new master towered over him, face white. "To hell, if you like. I don't care, so long as you get out of Barley Cross."

"An hour doesn't give me much time."

"It's all you're getting. I could walk the length of your bloody village in five minutes."

"And if I refuse to go?"

"We'll burn your house down—and any house you go to for shelter."

"I have a wife and two children."

"Take them with you. You'll be glad of their company."

Nunan's face loomed over Liam, like a hateful gargoyle. He choked. "Dominic, you're a pure bastard. Just give me the chance, and I'll—"

Dominic Nunan jeered. "Go on! It's a crime to threaten the Master. Say it, and I'll clap you in jail until people forget you ever lived."

Liam waited until he could see the man clearly. "Can I take anything with me?"

The new master's eye roved the farmyard, lighting on a handcart employed to transport small loads to market. "You can take what you can fit on that cart, and no more."

"But I'll need food, clothes, beds, a tent . . ."

Nunan laughed. "Your problem, man. I've just solved mine. I'll leave Peadar here to keep an eye on you. I've other matters to see to. But I'll be along in an hour to see the back of you."

Liam watched three horsemen gallop down the track to the main road. He contemplated disobedience. But it was Andy McGrath's home that Nunan threatened to burn. How would Andy react to the new master's threat? It wasn't fair to put him to the test. Andy McGrath had always respected authority. Dominic Nunan had been legally proclaimed Lord of Barley Cross, and Liam McGrath was a nobody. Liam sighed. He would leave the farm sooner than embarrass his stepfather.

He trudged back to the farmhouse. Eileen waited at the door. He said, "I'm sorry, alanna, I seem to have mucked things up. I've got to leave the village. We'd better start packing my things."

She picked up the younger child. "*Your* things?"

He ran his hands through the curls of the elder one. "You can stay here. Nunan's not banishing you."

Eileen's mouth set in the stubborn O'Connor line. "Where you go, lad, I go too. And the children."

He knew better than to argue. He took her arm. "So be it. Let's pack."

He became aware of a figure at his side. Peadar Fahey, the islander who had married Nora Kelly, said, "I ain't happy with this, Liam. I think Dominic's gone too far. But he'll have me blood if I don't see ye off the premises. Can I give ye a lift in any way?"

Liam was about to reject the olive branch, when Eileen thrust past him. She held out her younger child. "If you'll just mind the kids, Peadar—"

The ex-Lord of Barley Cross trundled his loaded handcart towards the main road. His wife walked beside him. His two children perched precariously atop a pile of blankets, clothes, pots and pans, folding chairs and a picnic table, towels and nappies. and a basket of food. Astonished faces were pressed to windows when they reached the village.

At the smithy, where a copy of Liam's abdication

notice decorated the wall, Seamus Murray came to the door of the forge. Eyes crinkling in the light, he wiped his hands on a leather apron, then waved. "Where are you off to, lad, with your bits and pieces all piled on a barrow?"

Liam let down the cart legs onto the road. He waited to get his breath. "I have to leave the village, Seamus. The new master has banished me."

The blacksmith leaned against his door frame, and got a clay pipe from his pocket. "And what have you been doing, to upset the new chap?"

Liam shrugged. "I guess he doesn't care to have his predecessor hanging around reminding folks of other times."

Seamus Murray found a pouch, and thumbed dried grass into the bowl of his pipe. "Didn't think you'd knuckle under to that sort of nonsense."

Liam got a fresh grip on the cart handles. "He threatened to burn down my da's home if I didn't leave—and he'll burn any place I go to in the village. He gave me an hour to get out."

Seamus Murray stuffed the pipe, unlit, back into his pocket. He gripped the ear of an urchin lingering by the smithy door. "Run and tell Missus Murray that I want her here quick. Tell her to put on a warm coat, and to bring mine too."

The child fled on his errand.

The blacksmith advanced into the roadway. With a sweep of his hand, he removed Liam from his place between the cart shafts. "Out of the way, my lord." Then he took Liam's place, and stood waiting.

Liam gasped, "Seamus—you mustn't! I have to . . ."

Mary Murray came hurrying down the path from the house adjoining the smithy. She wore her best black gabardine, and carried a jacket for her husband. The smith took the jacket, donned it, then picked up the shafts.

"Which way, me lord?"

Liam couldn't find words. He pointed down the street.

Seamus Murray began to push the cart. His wife linked an arm through Eileen McGrath's, and fell in beside her. The urchin who had run the smith's errand was off like a hare.

Sally Corcoran stood in her doorway nursing the child born the day of General Desmond's funeral. Her husband gaped over her shoulder. He called, "What's going on then, Seamus?"

The blacksmith put up a hand to steady one of Liam's children. "Sure, aren't I just giving an old friend a lift to quit the village?"

Charlie Corcoran's eyes bulged. "Quit the village— Liam?"

The smith nodded. "Aye. On the new fellow's orders."

"And who's minding the forge?"

Seamus Murray spat. "Sod the forge. I may not be coming back either."

Charlie Corcoran grabbed two coats from behind his front door. He pushed his wife and child into the path, pulling the door shut behind him. "Would ye mind if we came along with ye?"

Seamus Murray heaved the cart into motion. "Sure, and you'd be welcome, lad."

Charlie Corcoran, his wife and child, formed up behind Eileen McGrath and Mary Murray.

Tom and Biddy O'Connor were waiting at the gate with Liam's mother. Tom shouted, "Hi, Liam! Weren't we just thinking of a stroll ourselves!" He fell in beside his daughter. Brigit O'Connor pushed an arm through Liam's, and said, "Ye didn't think, now, ye could walk out on yer old ma-in-law?"

Maureen McGrath said, eyes glinting, "I can't think what Andy is at, letting them push you around. If I'd been there, I'd have given that fellow a piece of my mind."

Liam grimaced through moisture which unaccountably glistened in his eyes. At least he wasn't going alone into exile.

The new curate, his too large collar chafing his ears, waited at the church gate. Father Con sat patiently in the wheelchair Tom O'Connor had built for him. As the blacksmith rumbled abreast with Liam's handcart, the apprentice priest piped, "Not too fast, now, Mister Murray. Father Con grumbles if I shake him."

Villagers were emerging from every door. Liam acknowledged the salutes of the Kennedys, the O'Malleys, The Flanagans, Franky Finnegan with his fiddle . . . suddenly, it seemed, the entire population of Barley Cross had decided to follow its ex-Master into exile.

At the end of the street, where the road forked for Barra Hill and the Fist, Seamus lowered the legs of the cart. Down the hill came a gentleman wearing a hard hat and a green baize apron showing under his shiny black topcoat. A crowd of women and a couple of soldiers trooped behind him. Eamon Toomey and Sean O'Rourke carried their rifles slung, muzzle down.

Michael halted before his ex-Master. He raised his billycock. "Me lord, Liam, with your permission, I will take my place among your friends."

Before Liam could speak, Eamon Toomey presented himself, and came to a quivering salute. "Beg to report, sir," he began, using the formula drilled into him years back by Sergeant McGrath, "I have relinquished me post up there. I don't find it palatable no longer. Would ye care to reassign me to something a whit more agreeable?"

Liam began to feel dazed. He said, "I don't have any place to reassign you to, Eamon. The new master has banished me from Barley Cross completely."

Eamon Toomey remained at attention. "Sure we

all know that, sir. Could I not act as yer personal bodyguard?"

Liam sighed. Eamon Toomey's loyalty shone as bright as any displayed by the people behind him. He said, "If you want to, Eamon. Go ahead, you are my bodyguard."

By now, several of the more mature citizens had siezed the opportunity to rest their bones on the stone wall flanking the Fist road.

Liam, noting them, said, "Can we spare a few minutes, here, Seamus?"

The blacksmith lowered the cart, put his bottom on a shaft, and hoisted a small McGrath onto his shoulders. " 'Tis as good a spot as any to settle the future of Barley Cross, me lord. Let's wait here 'til the new fellow comes down to see what all the shindig is about."

"That's not what I meant—" Liam began. But it was too late.

Franky Finnegan struck up a jig on his fiddle. A space was cleared in the center of the road for two of Celia Larkin's pupils to exhibit their skill at covering the buckle. On the far verge, several men got down in a circle while one of them dealt hands for poker.

Liam gave up. Barley Cross had its own way of handling emergencies.

The counselors were next out of the Fist. The crowd fell silent at the sight of them. Led by wizened Denny Mallon, they descended Barra Hill. The doctor paused at the tank guarding the Fist approach, and, in a gesture of irritation, struck one of his few remaining sulphur matches on its rusty flank.

Liam heard his comments.

"Damn the fellow!" The doctor puffing out the smoke redolent of a grass fire. "The impertinence of sacking us!"

Kevin Murphy got to windward of the pipe. "Buggers as bright as him don't need advice. I'd have sacked him one meself, had I been twenty years younger!"

Celia Larkin flourished her knitting, her spectacles awry. "So much for your new master. God dammit—I wouldn't give him house room!"

Liam grinned. The counselors seemed to have fallen out with Dominic Nunan.

Kevin Murphy made a rude gesture up the hill. "Banishing our Liam and threatening to bring an army from Achill! By God, Andy McGrath will show him, when he learns what's happened."

Celia Larkin grasped his arm. "There'll be no fighting if I can help it."

The vet shook her off. "Would ye not try to stop him setting up a harem?"

"He didn't exactly say a harem."

The vet shrugged. "We all know what he meant. Didn't Michael say he had Maeve Molloy in his bed last night against her will?"

Doctor Denny's mouth set firm. "We'll have to do something about him." He raised his spectacles to inspect the crowd in the road. "What's everyone doing here?"

Ceila Larkin gripped the hand of her niece, who had run to greet her. "Sure the village is showing better sense than we did." She laughed humourlessly. "I warned you they wouldn't like our fancy tyrant."

Kevin Murphy eyed the crowd below. "Somehow or other, I have the strongest feeling that I should be elsewhere at this moment."

The schoolteacher eyed him sourly. "That's about the only sensible thought you've had in a fortnight. I would imagine that we're not very popular in the village right now."

Denny Mallon spluttered with indignation. "Well, I've done nothing to be ashamed of."

Celia turned her sour gaze on him. "You've only put a devil on horseback—that's all!"

The devil arrived during Franky Finnegan's encore. The new master and his three retainers swept down Barra Hill like the Four Horsemen of the Apocalypse.

The fiddle died. The dancing ceased. The card game broke up. Some of the more timid citizens got down behind the wall on which they had been sitting.

Dominic Nunan reined in his horse a yard from Liam's group. His voice was curt. "What bloody game is on?"

People shrank back, letting the old master face the new.

Liam said softly, mildly, "I am leaving Barley Cross, as you ordered."

Dominic Nunan snarled. "I didn't order you to take the whole village with you!"

Liam spread his hands. "I didn't tell anyone to come with me."

Nunan raised his quirt, and struck. "Well you can bloody well tell someone to go back!"

Liam stood, arms down by his sides, fists clenched, a red weal on his cheek. "I can't tell anyone to do anything. I'm not the Master."

Dominic Nunan grinned evilly. "By Christ, if you don't, I'll tell them something that'll upset you and your gang of religious hypocrites. That should move you fast enough!"

Liam guessed he referred to Adrian Walsh's not-so-holy orders. He murmured, "I have your promise on that matter, my lord."

The new master laughed. "By Christ—you have nothing at all!" He stood up in his stirrups. "Listen to me, citizens of Barley Cross! I'll tell you how Liam McGrath has been fooling you. That lad of—"

Liam hurtled forward, grabbed a leg, and heaved. Dominic Nunan came sideways off the horse, clutched Liam and brought him down. They rolled in the dust.

"Damn you, let me speak!" The new master's words expired in a gurgle as Liam got him by the throat.

"Keep quiet," Liam panted, "or you die!"

The crowd formed a ring around the combatants, watching fascinated as their old and new ruler thrashed on the tarmac.

Liam released the pressure on Nunan's throat slightly. "Are you going to keep quiet?"

Dominic Nunan dropped an arm down to his fisherman's boot, and came up with a seal-skinner's knife in his fist.

He grunted, "You asked for this, McGrath!"

The knife struck Liam in the thigh. He spasmed, losing his grip on the Achill man's throat. Nunan raised his arm for a lethal stab. Liam grabbed his wrist. They rolled over and over, leaving a trail of blood on the tarmac.

Liam couldn't hold the blade off much longer. His leg had gone numb. His shoulder ached from the bruising he had got when Nunan knocked him down.

The new master of Barley Cross forced the knife lower. "Die, you bastard," he screamed.

Desperately, Liam shouted, "Eamon!"

From somewhere came the crack of a rifle shot. A cavity opened in the side of Dominic Nunan's head, spraying Liam with blood. Nunan's body went limp. The knife clattered onto the tarmac.

Liam pushed the corpse off him. He staggered to his feet. The world was spinning. He gripped his wounded leg with one hand, and wiped bits of Dominic Nunan from his face with the other.

"Holy Mother of God! This disgraceful exhibition would never have been allowed in the O'Meara's day!"

Liam peered through a mist of sweat. The voice was Father Con's. The old priest was so blind and deaf, he couldn't possibly appreciate what had happened. But the words rang like an accusation. Liam croaked. "Nor will it be allowed in McGrath's day from now on, Father!" He addressed the villagers. "Thank you for your concern. You must go home now. There is nothing more you can do here."

They buried the mortal remains of Dominic Nunan that afternoon. Many of the villagers stayed away. Father Walsh officiated, his piping treble faltering over the words of the burial service.

Then Liam went back to the Fist.

The weather turned cool on the morrow. A mist hid Leckavrea and Lough Corrib. Liam settled a turf on the parlor fire with the sole of the boot on his good leg, ignoring the assembled counselors. Would the villagers have followed him so cheerfully in a drizzle like today's?

Michael set bottle and glasses on the floor by Kevin Murphy, and withdrew.

Liam turned to face them. Time, it was, to come to terms with them. Their days of bullying the Master were over and done. "Well?" he challenged.

Doctor Denny Mallon steepled his fingers, not quite avoiding Liam's eye. "Seems we are back at square one, more's the pity."

Kevin Murphy grunted as he reached for the bottle. "In my opinion, we're well rid of the fellow."

Celia Larkin's needles clicked like castanets. "I don't agree. We mishandled the whole situation, and we ought to be ashamed of ourselves. We have lost a fertile man we should have treasured."

General McGrath coughed. "It ain't so bad as that. There's Katy Nunan's child to be. And, from what I hear, Dominic had his way with a few of the kitchen staff. There may be hope for us there, too."

Liam could hardly believe his ears. His stepfather was beginning to sound like the other three. He said, voice heavy with sarcasm, "Don't any of you want to know what I think?"

Kevin Murphy spilled poteen onto the carpet.

Denny Mallon lost his pouch down the side of the cushion, and had to search for it. Celia Larkin dropped a stitch, and knitted on, hoping she could locate it later.

General McGrath was the first to find his voice. "Sure, Liam, me lord, we'd be glad to have your opinion."

Liam eased the bandaged leg out in front of him, feeling a savage delight in exhibiting his wound. He raised his stick. "This is no opinion. This is a firm decision. So listen. We lost Dominic Nunan through your incompetence—and my foolishness in putting up with it! From now on, I'll listen to you, but, if I don't like what I hear, I'm ignoring you. And, if you don't care for that, you can get yourselves another Master."

Doctor Denny found his pouch, and his courage. "I think you are overreacting, Liam. Anyone can slip up."

Liam felt like striking the man. "Slip up? The biggest boob anyone will ever make in the whole wide world, and you call it a slip up? Why couldn't you let the fellow have his harem? Instead of disagreeing, and getting sacked? It would have been another way of solving our problem. The Master of the Fist is supposed to be a tyrant. We could have put up with a genuine despot for a year or two. I was prepared to go into exile, wasn't I?"

"The village would never have let you go alone."

Liam sighed. "How long do you think they would have stayed with me once it started raining? They wanted a confrontation with Dominic, and you stirred him up to provide them with one."

Kevin Murphy spread his hands. "Okay, me lord. We were stupid. On behalf of Dinny, Cee and meself, I apologize. Andy was out back at the time, supervising Dominic's new fortifications, so he's just an ordinary fool, and not a super idiot like the rest of us."

Liam lowered his stick. He felt tired. The leg had begun to throb. "Okay," he admitted. "We were all fools. I shouldn't have shouted for Eamon. But I never dreamed he would shoot to kill."

The vet looked up. " 'Twasn't Eamon who shot him. That fool was still fiddling with his gun when the Nunan felly was killed."

"Not Eamon?" Liam searched their faces. "Then who—?"

" 'Twas Paedar Fahey. Him that married Nora Kelly."

"And I've made him sergeant, for saving your life," added Andy McGrath.

Liam choked. Promoting a fool for an act of idiocy! "By God, if I was his general, I'd have had him shot!"

Celia Larkin said placidly, "Don't let on about that to Paedar. He thinks you're wonderful. As far as that lad is concerned, you've inherited all the old O'Meara charm."

"Though there's little evidence of it today," added the doctor.

Liam blinked. One apology, and their short-lived penitence was gone. There was no way he would ever reform this crew. For good or ill, they, along with Larry Desmond and Patrick O'Meara, had supervised the fortunes of Barley Cross for the last thirty years, and they now regarded it as their God-given right. Could Liam McGrath manage without them? Perhaps his stepfather had summed things up accurately. There was Kathleen Nunan's child to look forward to and cherish. And maybe a couple more kids out of the kitchen staff, if rumors were to be believed. He could organize another expedition. Not to Achill. Perhaps out Sligo way. See if any other villages had a Nunan, or McGrath, or an O'Meara. Barley Cross might be luckier next time.

He shook his head. "What beats me is—no one

asked after my health while I was deposed. And me supposed to be heading for a nervous breakdown."

Doctor Denny Mallon sniffed. "Ye've still a thing or two to learn, Liam. On serious matters, such as the Master's health, we have to take the village into our confidence—in a roundabout way, sort of."

Liam frowned at the doctor. Denny Mallon sounded far too cocky. They were already trying to manipulate him. "What do you mean? In a roundabout way?"

The doctor scooped up a pipeful of dried grasses. "Sure, Michael doesn't miss a thing that goes on in here—and we wouldn't have it otherwise."

Liam gaped at him. Michael? His quiet man-for-all-seasons in collusion with this cunning lot? Did he crouch, ear-to-door during their discussions? With Denny Mallon's tacit approval? And then retail it to selected confidants in the village?

Liam clutched the arms of his shabby armchair, seeking the feel of something solid. Was there anything in this community of Barley Cross which was as simple as it appeared on the surface?

Faintly he heard the doctor's voice. "Don't worry too much about it, Liam. Remember, we all play for the same team!"

Against his will, Liam began to grin.

A Deal in Poteen

Doctor Denny Mallon met Liam McGrath on the plank bridge below Mcguire's mill, for what the doctor had described as a private chat.

Denny Mallon kicked loose gravel from the boards into the water below. He said, "I fear we are in trouble, Liam."

The Lord of Barley Cross gazed over the bald pate of his counselor. He watched the mill wheel revolve below the sluice, and, within the sluice, saw the glint of the copper worm through which Mick McGuire, miller and distiller, produced his superior brand of poteen.

Privately, Liam doubted if the village of Barley Cross would ever be out of trouble. He said, "What is it this time, Denny?"

The doctor peered both ways along the bridge. Voice almost drowned by the roar of the water, he whispered, "It's Father Adrian. The young fool has fallen in love with Rita O'Rourke."

Rita was the sixteen-year-old daughter of Sean and

Peggy O'Rourke. Sean was one of Liam's more dependable guards at the Fist. Rita, as far as Liam's knowledge went, was a nice, unprecocious girl who wouldn't go curate chasing just for fun.

He spat reflectively into the stream below. "So? Lots of people fall in love. I managed it myself, once. It's no crime."

Denny Mallon made a face. "It is, if you're a priest. And it makes you want to get married."

Liam caught his breath. Then he laughed. "Well, there's no one to marry our Adrian, now that Father Con's up in the churchyard. And that's one job Adrian can't do for himself. He'll have to settle for living in sin."

Denny Mallon got out his pipe. "I wish you would take things seriously. Rita won't agree to anything that's not official and above board."

Liam swung round on his counselor. "Rita should have more sense—wanting to marry a priest! Don't she know the rules?"

Denny Mallon looked away. "I guess we all know the rules, Liam. But, sometimes, there's a case for bending them."

Liam turned his back on the water wheel to lodge his elbows on the bridge rail. "Well, I can't give Adrian dispensation to marry. Celia would have my hide for it—even if Adrian would accept my authority in clerical matters."

The doctor got his pipe going. "I think you should call a meeting to discuss the matter. We might be able to back Celia into a corner, and get her to accept a compromise."

Liam snorted. "Celia Larkin compromise? She'd see young Adrian unfrocked before she'd agree to anything irregular." Liam discreetly crossed his fingers as he spoke. Only Liam McGrath and a select few knew that Father Adrian Walsh's ordination was invalid, and wouldn't stand scrutiny. Thank God schoolmistress Larkin was not one of the few! He added, "In any case, if I gave him permission to marry, who would do the job?"

Denny Mallon hunched over the bridge rail, face gloomy. "What about that bishop fellow on Achill who made Adrian a priest?"

Liam's face became equally gloomy. "You mean Zbigniev? Young Fahey went back to the island to see his mam, a month back. He tells me the bishop fell off a cliff while he was out after gulls' eggs. They never found the body."

The doctor went rigid. "That's torn it!"

Liam stared at him. "I don't see why you're so worried. Young Adrian knew what he was about when he decided to apprentice himself to Father Con."

The doctor shrugged. "Young lads don't foresee everything. If Adrian can't marry Rita, he's going to chuck his hand in."

Liam's eyes widened. Any development which deprived the village of its pastor threatened the future of Barley Cross. And the future of Barley Cross was Liam's concern. He said, "Adrian can't do that! Who's going to marry our brides, and hear our confessions, if he won't?"

"Now you are beginning to see sense," approved the doctor. "If you'll listen to me, I have an idea . . ."

Liam McGrath, Lord of Barley Cross and Master of the Fist, sat with his henchmen in the parlor of his fortress atop Barra Hill.

Michael, his servant, set a tray bearing silver teapot, sugar bowl, cream jug, and a cup and saucer, on the carpet beside Celia Larkin. At Kevin Murphy's end of the settee, he set a newly opened bottle of poteen and two glasses. At the opposite end of the couch, General Andy McGrath studied a sheet of paper through a pair of rimless spectacles looted from an optician in Tuam.

Michael withdrew. The meeting came to order.

"The way I see it," Celia Larkin said promptly, "we should write to the Pope for permission."

Liam marveled. Twelve months ago, Celia Larkin would never have considered the possibility of a priest marrying, papal permission or no.

"Don't be daft, Cee," admonished Kevin Murphy. "How in heaven's name would we get a letter to the Holy Father, when Galway City and Sligo are about as far as anyone has traveled for years?"

Celia Larkin poured herself tea. The letter-to-the-Pope gambit was not to be taken seriously, and they all knew it. But Celia Larkin had to establish her position from the outset. "Very well," she conceded. "We must find at least a bishop to dispense Father Adrian. I'll not settle for less."

"You, I deduce, are advocating another expedition?" Denny Mallon asked politely.

Celia Larkin's cup clattered against its saucer. Her nerve was not what it had been. Once, she would have eaten these three men for breakfast. "Something of that nature," she admitted. "All the bishops in Ireland can't be dead yet. We must find one that's still kicking." She turned towards Liam. "Would you not agree, my lord?"

Liam, who had completed plans with the doctor in anticipation of just such a demand from the school-mistress, nodded. "I go along with that, Celia." He glanced at his stepfather. "If the general can spare him, I'd like to send Sergeant Fahey and three men on a reconnaissance. Traveling light, they could reach Dublin and get back in a week. And I wouldn't expect any trouble on the way. Most of the survivors outside Barley Cross will be too old for rape and pillage by now."

" 'Twould be no bad thing if they did run into trouble," the vet commented. "Sure, I'd not feel quite so lonely if I knew there was another village in the land with people young enough to be interested in a bit of villainy!"

"Amen to that," said Denny Mallon piously. "You might ask your recce team to look out for kids as well as a bishop."

"I'll do that," Liam agreed. "Perhaps you'd ask Father Adrian to step up to the Fist when it's convenient, and I'll put him in the picture."

Celia Larkin put down her cup with a crash. "And perhaps *you'd* step down to the church to see him, Liam. You are not quite God yet!"

"As you wish, Celia," agreed the Lord of Barley Cross meekly.

They dispatched Sergeant Paedar Fahey on reconnaissance the following morning. With him went Padraig O'Hare and Col Kavanagh, his two fellow Achill Islanders, and Rita's father, Sean. Since all three Achill men were privy to the secret of Father Adrian's spurious ordination, and since Sean O'Rourke would have a vested interest in getting his daughter wed, Liam felt he could not have picked a better team.

The party trotted off on four of the village's strongest horses, leading another beast loaded with supplies and equipment. In Sergeant Fahey's breast pocket lay a letter addressed to Father Adrian Walsh of Barley Cross. Letter and contents were Denny Mallon's brainchild, the writing Liam's, disguised.

The missive conveyed an episcopal blessing to Father Walsh, and the information that permission for his marriage had been granted and that, moreover, Father Walsh and Rita O'Rourke had been married *in absentia* by the undersigned bishop, who was now too old and frail to contemplate traveling to Barley Cross to perform the ceremony there, and may the Lord's blessing be on the happy couple.

That, doctor and master had agreed, should do the trick.

Sergeant Fahey's instructions were succinct. He and his party were to travel around for a few days, and then return to Barley Cross with a signature on the letter.

Paedar Fahey, who boasted of saving the Master's life, and who now displayed a continuing interest in the welfare of the Lord of Barley Cross, had said, "Whose signature, me lord?"

Liam McGrath knew his man. Bluntly, he had said, "I don't give a damn who you get to sign it, so long as it comes back with someone's moniker on it. If Father Adrian won't carry on as our shepherd without being able to get legally into bed with Rita O'Rourke, then, by all that's holy—or unholy—I'm getting him the permission he requires."

Paedar Fahey had patted his breast pocket. "Don't worry, me lord. I understand. The end justifies the means."

"God help us all, I hope so," said the Lord of Barley Cross.

The presbytery had not altered in appearance since Father Con's day. The same dusty furniture filled the same dusty hall. Barley Cross's new pastor apparently preferred stasis to change.

Adrian Walsh let Liam in, and led him to the parlor. He said, "What can I do for you, my lord?"

Liam said, "Is there anyone else in the house?"

Father Adrian shook his head. "The Missus Mooney who looks after me goes home by six to avoid gossip." He smiled. "No one thinks we might get tempted in the daytime."

Liam grinned in return. Walsh had been an over-serious youth. He seemed to have found a sense of humor from somewhere. Liam perched on a dusty settee. The lad had filled out in the last year or two. From a skinny youth, he had grown into a tall, raw-boned young man, whose wrists and ankles projected too far for elegance from the cassock he had inherited.

Liam said, "That's what I came to talk about. This matter of you and Rita O'Rourke."

The young cleric's face clouded over. "You have been talking to the doctor, my lord?"

Liam squirmed on the cushions. "Look," he said. "Let's go off the record. Drop this 'my lord' stuff. I'm Liam, you're 'Adrian.' And no one else is listening. Do you want to tell me anything about yourself and Rita?"

The younger man shrugged. "What is there to say? We love each other, and we want to get married. But who's to marry us?" Adrian Walsh sounded desperate.

Liam held up a hand. "Hold on, now. If I can get you permission to wed from a bishop, will you agree to soldier on here in Barley Cross as our pastor?"

Adrian Walsh looked down his long O'Meara nose. "What sort of permission?"

Liam realized with a pang, that he and the young cleric were actually half brothers, since they both shared Patrick O'Meara as their real father. The thought gave him confidence. He said, "Contradict me if I'm wrong, but isn't there such a thing as marriage by proxy? Recognized by the church, I mean?"

Adrian Walsh hesitated. "I'm no expert in theology, but I believe I've heard of something like that. The couple are obligated to get married properly afterwards, before a priest."

Liam held his breath. "Well—if I can get you legally married without you actually being at the ceremony—would that satisfy your scruples?"

Adrian Walsh looked unhappy. "To tell you the truth, Liam, since Father Con died, my scruples are well nigh atrophied. I'm just about ready to chuck the job in."

Liam was astonished by the note of desperation in the youth's voice. He said, "But if I can get you married, won't that make things okay?"

Adrian Walsh sat down on a hard chair. "Will it, Liam? And who's going to forgive me for breaking my priestly vows, if I marry? Where do I turn for absolution?"

Liam sat rigid. He hadn't considered that aspect of the problem. Father Adrian might shrive every penitent in Barley Cross, but there was no one in the village to shrive Adrian Walsh.

"Jasus!" he breathed. "You are in a spot!"

The young priest dropped his head onto his hands. Voice cracking, he sobbed, "And I don't see any way out of it."

Disturbed, Liam leaned forward. "You got something on your conscience, Adrian?"

The young man looked up, face haggard. "Not yet. But I soon will have, won't I?"

Liam grabbed the youth's hands in an attempt to reassure him. "Not if I can help it, you won't. Now, stop worrying. I didn't realize how Father Con's death would affect you."

Liam left the Presbytery, and headed for the O'Rourke cottage. Too late, now, to recall Paedar Fahey. Paedar would have to be sent out again with instructions to find a cleric prepared to salve Adrian Walsh's conscience. Actually, there could be little to salve. Since Adrian's Holy Orders were a fiction, there was nothing for him to recant. But the youth didn't know his ordination was invalid, and couldn't be told without upsetting the rest of Barley Cross's population. Had the O'Meara faced problems like this? A pity, it was, that the days of hedge-priests were gone. But Paedar Fahey could be trusted to find someone who would look and act enough like a priest to satisfy poor Adrian.

Peggy O'Rourke opened the door to Liam. She

dropped him a curtsy. "Sure, himself is away on your errands, me lord."

Liam got a foot inside the jamb. "It's you I want to talk to. Missus O'Rourke—before I seek a word with your Rita. Can I come in?"

Flushing at the honor of a visit from the Lord of Barley Cross, Peggy O'Rourke pulled the door wide. "Ye're welcome, me lord. Come in. I was just about to peg out some washing, but it can wait."

Liam settled himself on a chair, eyeing the steam billowing from the kitchen doorway. "Go ahead and finish the job," he urged. "I can wait, too."

Peggy O'Rourke beamed. "Thank ye, me lord. I wouldn't want to miss this bit of fine weather we're having. I'll be done in a few minutes. There's a drop in the bottle on the sideboard."

Liam waited, content. Get the wife on your side, and the battle was half won. When Rita's mother returned, he said, "I suppose you know about Rita and Father Adrian?"

Peggy O'Rourke fiddled with the strings of her pinafore, and avoided his eyes.

"It can't be helped," Liam reassured her. "Kids are kids, and we have to help them as much as we can."

Ma O'Rourke beamed. It was like the sun coming out.

"So I've sent your man off with the others to find a bishop who will release Father Adrian from his vow of celibacy. Then Adrian and Rita can get married. If we do manage to find a bishop willing to help us, do you think your lass will go along with the arrangement?"

"Will Father Adrian still be a priest, as well as married to our Rita?"

"That's the general idea, Missus O'Rourke. We can't afford to lose the services of our pastor."

Ma O'Rourke bit her lips with suppressed delight.

Not only was the Master intending to see her daughter married, he was also planning to get her a priest for a son-in-law!

"Sure, that'll be marvellous, me lord."

Liam got up. "Do I need to see Rita about it?"

Ma O'Rourke got up with him. "Leave our Rita to me, me lord. And don't forget we expect to see you at the wedding. I've had a quiet word with the widdy Walsh, and she's of the same mind as meself."

"I'll be there," Liam promised, tongue in cheek. Of course. There was bound to be a reception, even if the actual ceremony took place on paper!

"And ye'll be sending for Rita afterwards, for yer droyt?"

Liam contemplated Peggy O'Rourke's bland smile. How much did these Barley Cross matrons know about the way the village was managed? They were all pretty keen to get their daughters up Barra Hill on their wedding nights.

He sighed. Adrian Walsh didn't have all the crosses to bear. "I'll try not to disappoint you," he promised.

He left, pondering the problem of inducing a clergyman's bride to enter his bed without incurring the wrath of her husband.

Sergeant Fahey and his men returned at the weekend. The recce party had been gone only four days. When the Fist lookout reported four horsemen approaching from the main road, Liam hastened downhill to meet them. The more witnesses the better when Paedar presented his letter to Father Walsh.

The news of the men's return had spread. A crowd waited at the pedestrian crossing outside the Old Market Hall.

Sergeant Fahey reined in his animal. He saluted when he spotted the Lord of Barley Cross.

"What news, Paedar?" shouted Liam, hoping no one would penetrate his deceit.

"We got no further than Ballykilleen, on the Mullingar road, me lord," reported the sergeant. "Sure, most of Ould Ireland is dead as a doornail. We were glad to see some people at Ballykilleen."

"Did you find a bishop?" Liam prompted.

Paedar Fahey looked uncomfortable. "We did, me lord."

That was better . . . so where was the damn letter?

Sergeant Fahey was struggling for words. "This bishop we found has agreed to allow Father Adrian to marry Rita O'Rourke—"

The crowd applauded. Liam found a smile for their benefit.

"Great!" he snarled. "Did he put it in writing?"

Paedar Fahey's hands stayed firmly on his animal's reins. "No, me lord."

God in Heaven! Had the fool not been able to persuade someone to sign the letter!

Paedar added, "The bishop is coming here for the ceremony. She'll be here in a couple of days. And she wants to meet you, me lord."

Liam's hair stood on end. "*She*?"

Paedar Fahey shrank before his Master's fury. "Yes, me lord. The bishop of Ballykilleen is a woman!"

She arrived two days later, on a donkey, followed by ten young women similarly mounted.

Liam stood with his counselors to watch the procession approach along the street. The bishop wore an old velvet mitre and a shabby soutane, the skirts of which were pulled high enough to allow a pair of bare legs to straddle the donkey's back. Suddenly, Liam appreciated how the citizens of Achill must have felt when the Barley Cross contingent arrived in their island.

The Bishop of Ballykilleen halted her animal, adjusted the tilt of her mitre, swung a shapely leg over the donkey's back, and slid to the ground.

Liam figured she was no more than twenty-nine or thirty.

She tugged her soutane straight, and said, "Which of you is Lord Liam?"

The title sounded strange. He stepped forward. "That'll be me, I imagine."

She extended a hand, bearing a large ring on the third finger. "I am Magdalen Malone, Bishop of Ballykilleen. How do you do?"

Liam knew what was expected of him. Hadn't he practiced on poor old Zbigniev? He bowed, and kissed the ring. "I am Liam McGrath, Duke of Connaught, Lord of Barley Cross, and Master of the Fist. I'm pleased to meet you, my lord bishop."

Then he backed off to let Denny and Kevin and the others have a go.

Later, they sat down to a banquet in the Old Market Hall, prepared and served by the ladies of the village.

Liam found himself seated beside Magdalen Malone. Around the cloth-covered boards sat his counselors and their wives, interspersed with the bishop's acolytes. Celia Larkin had brought her brother Joe, who did the village tailoring. Michael, mysteriously spirited down from the Fist, flitted about the table, topping up glasses.

To his astonishment, Liam began to enjoy himself. This was the way life should be, with the good folk of Barley Cross filling their bellies 'round his table. And with eleven new faces to look at—several of them quite pretty. And with a bishopess at his side to bandy ideas with. Perhaps it was the strength of the poteen. Liam found his tongue out of control. Recalling his own verbal deceits, he lowered a forkful of steak and kidney from his lips, and murmured to his companion, "Are you really a bishop?"

Magdalen Malone refrained from comment for a moment, while she dabbled pie-crust in gravy. Then she riposted. "Are you really Duke of Connaught?"

Something went down the wrong hole. Liam choked

and coughed. When he got his breath, he confessed, "Not really, your grace. It's a title my predecessor adopted. I only use it on important occasions, when I want to impress."

"Like now?" she invited.

He flushed. "I suppose so."

"Very fitting," she said coolly. "For I am a genuine bishop. And I have papers signed by the Suffragan Bishop of Mullingar to prove it."

"Jasus!" Liam murmured under his breath.

She sipped at her glass unmoved. "Is this the poteen you drink regularly?"

Liam loosened his collar. "It's the only poteen we have, my lord. Our miller makes it."

"Does he put in anything special?"

"Only the best potato peelings, I hear," Liam said, striving for the light touch.

She didn't appear to notice. "Would he sell me some?"

What kind of bishop was this? Seeking to buy McGuire's poteen! Liam said, "I doubt it, your grace. My man tells me our distiller's production is spoken for up to several months ahead. No doubt you could put in your order."

"With your permission, my lord," she said, suddenly formal, "I would like to speak with your poteen maker before I return to Ballykilleen."

Liam grinned. "Och, ye can try. The job is to catch him sober!"

Over cups of tea at the end of the banquet, she said, "Did Mister Fahey tell you much about Ballykilleen, my lord?"

Liam stirred in two spoons of sugar. "Only that you seem to have a lot of young ladies. That you looked after him and his men well. And that you agreed to come here and marry our Father Adrian."

"I will perform the ceremony," she corrected him. "Father Adrian marries his fiancée."

"That's what I meant," Liam agreed. He coughed to hide his embarrassment. "Since you apparently don't disapprove of a married clergy, have you a husband of your own?"

She gave him a long, cool stare. "Not yet, my lord, I haven't."

He tried again. He needed to find out how they managed the production of children in the bishop's village. He said, "But you accept that the current difficulty in keeping up population figures means tolerating solutions you might not normally agree with?"

The bishop stared at him, a frown wrinkling her forehead.

"I mean," Liam persisted, "you must have solved the problem . . ."

He hesitated. Despite her sex, this was a genuine bishop he was treading on thin ice with. Magdalen Malone ranked Father Adrian. Would have ranked Father Con, had the old priest survived to meet her. Jasus! Why wouldn't she play ball? Did she know how they did it in Ballykilleen? If she didn't, her views on seigneural promiscuity might not tally with those currently acceptable in Barley Cross. But some of her nymphets looked no more than nineteen or twenty, so Ballykilleen had solved the problem somehow.

"I mean," he finished in a burst of recklessness, "you must have solved the fertility problem?"

Her expression remained unchanged, her gaze cool. "That is a subject I wish to discuss with you, my lord. Could we go somewhere and talk privately?"

Liam ushered the Bishop of Ballykilleen into his parlor at the Fist. He turned a key in the doorlock.

"Now then, your grace," he said. "Fire away. We are quite alone."

Magdalen Malone sat down on the cushion normally warmed by Kevin Murphy. She placed her mitre on the floor, on the spot normally occupied by the vet's bottle of poteen. She straightened her soutane, so that her sandaled toes peeped decorously from beneath the hem. She fingered her pectoral cross.

"How to start, my lord? Ballykilleen has a population of two hundred and forty-nine souls, for whose salvation I am responsible. Twenty-seven of those are elderly men, most over sixty, and all crippled or maimed. Fifteen are young people aged between nineteen and thirty—precisely, three lads, and twelve lasses. The rest of my population are middle-aged to elderly women."

She paused. Liam waited, silent. The bishop wasn't quoting statistics for fun.

She continued. "Twenty years ago, all Ballykilleen's ablebodied men were killed or injured in a battle with one of those roving bands of murderers we used to be plagued with. My village outnumbered the bandits, but they had a machine gun. We drove them off in the end, but they crippled the community.

"Soon after that time, Bishop Clancy arrived. He was a fugitive from Mullingar, which had been burned to the ground. He was also a realist. He became our pastor, since our priest had died in the fighting. But Bishop Clancy was not a young man, and he wanted someone to succeed him when he died.

"As you know, only a whole adult may be ordained, and Ballykilleen had nothing but cripples and children left of our male population. So the bishop ordained me. And he made me a bishop, so that I, in turn, could ensure the supply of future pastors."

"There is surely nothing confidential in this—" Liam began.

"I haven't finished." For the first time, Magdalen Malone paused, uncertain of her words.

"Go on," urged Liam. "This is just between you and me."

She chewed on her pectoral cross. "We also lost our last fertile males in that fight with the bandits. No children have been born in Ballykilleen in the last nineteen years. My community is going to die, unless I can find a replacement for those dead fathers."

Liam felt his face grow warm. What had Paedar Fahey told the bishop? Jasus—he had enough to cope with dealing with the brides of Barley Cross!

She continued. "I talked with your Mister Fahey. He told me you have children in Barley Cross. It is obvious that your men are fertile. Paedar tells me it is due to the poteen you drink. So, here is my bargain. I will marry your parish priest to his lady, and I will ordain any candidates you may put up for the priesthood, in return for four dozen bottles of Mister McGuire's poteen, and the option to take more if we need it!"

Four dozen bottles of McGuire's poteen! Liam choked with astonishment. Those Achill lads were an irreverent crew—filling up the bishop with such a load of blarney.

He said, "Paedar Fahey will be getting a rocket from me."

She looked up, startled, "You mean he shouldn't have told me?"

"I mean it ain't true. Whatever McGuire's poteen does to a man—it doesn't make him fertile."

Her face showed bewilderment. "Then why—how . . . ?"

Liam sobered. The net holding his secret got holier every day. But he couldn't let the bishop go back home wondering how Barley Cross managed it.

"Look," he said bluntly, "I don't know how you feel about these things—you being a reverend and all that—but, as Lord of Barley Cross, I am entitled to my *droit du seigneur* with every bride here, on her wedding night."

Magdalen Malone frowned. Her lips tightened. She didn't speak.

He continued desperately, "And whether you approve or disapprove, I exercise that droit. I have to . . . because I am the only fertile male in Barley Cross."

Her eyes widened.

"Some of the villagers are in the know, some ain't. It doesn't matter a damn to me. I'm used to being called a tyrant. But no child in this village learns the truth about his da until he's old enough to understand the why and the wherefore of his conception."

The Bishop of Ballykilleen was nodding slowly now.

"So, your grace," Liam concluded, "I couldn't let you go home believing Paedar Fahey's nonsense. He probably thought he was protecting Barley Cross's big secret. I'm sure we can rely on you not to spill it to anyone."

Her breath was coming unevenly. She said, "You can rely on more than that, my lord. Would you consider exercising your droit in Ballykilleen?"

He hung his head. This was just what he had feared. Why did they treat him as if he were the village pump! He muttered, "I've enough on my plate here in Barley Cross, your grace. Moreover, I can claim some legality for my actions here."

"Ballykilleen would accept you as its lord, if that worries you."

He spread his palms, pleading. "I have a conscience about this droit business. And I have it numbed in regard to Barley Cross. Mainly, I suppose, because I'm following a precedent set up by our previous lord . . . and because, regardless of my feelings, the village needs children."

Her eyes flashed angrily. "Doesn't *my* village need children, too? Do you think it is easy for me to sit here and advocate the wholesale breaking of the sixth commandment?"

He shrugged. "I agree, it can't be easy for you, your grace. But it doesn't make it any easier for me.

I have a wife who is difficult enough about my promiscuity in Barley Cross, without tempting fate by practicing it elsewhere."

Her shoulders sagged. "I cannot persuade you, then, my lord?"

He felt uncomfortable. "I'd like to please you. Perhaps there are other ways around the problem? Couldn't some of your young women come here to get married? Barley Cross has no men to spare, unfortunately, but there's a surplus in Achill. And we've no policy against immigration. Your surplus women could find husbands in Achill, marry them here, and emigrate to Ballykilleen after a decent interval."

The bishop's face grew pensive. "You are willing to exercise your droit on any bride in Barley Cross?"

Liam looked for a trap. That, surely, was what he had said. He nodded. "I reckon I could get away with that."

Her eyes twinkled. "How about a bride-to-be who will be married later in her own village?"

He frowned, doubtful. "Isn't that stretching it a bit?"

She pouted. "I want you to stretch it."

He shrugged. "Okay, I'll go along with that. But don't go blabbing to anyone what you've talked me into."

"Ah, no," she murmured. "I wouldn't do that." She removed her pectoral cross, and placed it carefully on the small table that was never used. She began to unbutton her soutane. "I will be getting married later, in Ballykilleen. I'm a woman, as well as a bishop. And Ballykilleen needs children."

For a moment he could not credit what he was seeing or hearing.

She stood to let the soutane slither down to her feet. Liam stared. "Your grace—you can't . . . !"

She said, "Let's drop the formality, Liam. I'm 'Maggie' off duty."

He watched her step out of her knickers. "Your grace—Maggie—I can't . . . *daren't* commit adultery with a bishop!"

She said calmly, "Adultery for me, Liam. Mere fornication for you. As yet, I'm unmarried."

Heart pounding, he was pleading. "This . . . this is impossible!"

She sat again to remove her sandles. "It may be our only chance, Liam. Prelates and tyrants don't often get five minutes alone in each other's company."

He eyed the tall windows. Drawing the drapes would surely arouse comment. And comment he did not need. He seized the settee, and dragged it around, so that its back faced the light.

"We'll have to be quiet."

She smiled. "I have no intention of singing or dancing."

He struggled out of his jacket. "I—I've never tried to get a bishop pregnant before."

She lay back on the couch. "Neither have I, Liam. Let's make history."

Afterwards, he saw she was crying.

Bishop Malone of Ballykilleen married Father Adrian Walsh to Rita O'Rourke in the village church the next day. The bishop wore her full working fig of amice, alb, girdle, stole, mitre and cope. Her acolytes carried lighted candles, and sang hymns. Adrian Walsh wore his new cassock, a wedding present from the Larkins, confected by Joe Larkin out of the black-out stuff the O'Meara had insisted on in the old days to hide the village lights from bandits. Rita O'Rourke looked gorgeous in the gown her mother and her grandmother had worn before her. The citizens of Barley Cross filled the church, and were happy for their shepherd and his wife. Liam was relieved that everything had gone off so well.

In the presbytery, folding away her vestments, the bishop said, "Now, my lord. Lead me to your distiller."

"But you're invited to the reception," Liam protested.

She tied her garments into a bundle. "I'm sorry, my lord. If I stay for the celebration, I'll not get home before dark. And there's an old man in Ballykilleen who'll be needing the last rites before the night is through."

"But, your grace—you surely have a curate for jobs like that!"

The bishop shoved the bundle to one of her girls. "The old man is my da . . ."

"This way," invited the Lord of Barley Cross.

Mick McGuire was sober, having returned from watching the ceremony, without so much as a sup inside him.

He bent low over the bishop's ring. "How may I serve you, me lord bishop?"

"I want," said Magdalen Malone, loudly and clearly, "four dozen bottles of your best poteen, as soon as may be convenient. And you can send the bill to my lord Liam."

Mick McGuire's expression matched Liam's for astonishment. Then the miller said, "Yes, yer grace. Certainly. As soon as possible. It may take a week or so, but have no fear, Mick McGuire will manage it easily." He paused. "And how will I be delivering it to yer reverence?"

The bishop waved airy fingers. "Just leave it to Lord Liam. He will make all the arrangements."

On their way back to the village, Liam said, "You don't need that poteen. Didn't I tell you . . . ?"

She skipped up the steps from the bridge. "Tell Paedar Fahey that. If I don't take your poteen, he'll be wondering how you persuaded me to perform today's ceremony—and just what price you paid."

"And you've lumbered me with the job of delivering the damn stuff!"

She grinned. "Ah, but I haven't finished with you, my lord Liam. Not by a long chalk. There is merely '*au'voir*,' not 'goodbye.'"

Later, alone in the street, Liam watched the bishop and her acolytes saddle up their donkeys. From the Old Market Hall came the screech of Franky Finnegan's fiddle, and the wail of Danny Cleary's accordion. Barley Cross was celebrating a marriage, temporarily forgetful of its Master and his guest.

Liam waved until the little procession was out of sight. Perhaps he wouldn't mind too much having to meet the bishopess again.

He turned away, to bump into Doctor Denny Mallon hurrying along the pavement The doctor carried his black bag.

"Not going to the reception, Denny?" Liam asked.

"Sure, I'm on my way there now," the doctor told him. "Fintan Dooley is running a temperature. I had to take a look at him before I got down to making a beast of meself."

"Is Finty bad, then?" asked the Lord of Barley Cross.

The doctor shrugged. "Bad enough, Liam. He'll go for sure, one of these days. But I'll hang on to him as long as I can. Finty is one of our founder members, and I don't part easy with *them*."

Liam was silent, thinking. Finty Dooley was one of the select group which shared the secret of Father Adrian's ordination . . . and Finty had proved a clam.

The doctor put down his bag. He fumbled for his pipe. "The bishop is away, I take it?"

Liam nodded.

"Quare sort of fee for a wedding ceremony."

"What's that?" Liam asked, startled.

"Paedar Fahey told me the lady bishop would be after some of Mick McGuire's Superior, in return for marrying young Adrian."

Liam breathed his relief. Maggie had been right.

He nodded. "She stuck us for four dozen bottles. And more if she needs it."

"You'll be putting up taxes to pay for it?" the doctor ventured.

"I'll stick it on McGuire's assessment."

"Ah, no." The doctor searched for his pouch of dried grasses. "The cost should fall on the whole village. Sure we'll all benefit—if it only means a dacent funeral for some of us."

Liam's mind was on other matters. He said, "You work it out, then. I'll sign the instrument."

The doctor abandoned the search for his pouch, and put away the pipe. "Ah—we'll let Celia do the figuring. She's good at the mathematics. I'll be getting along. Will we be seeing you at the 'do'?"

"I'll show up later."

The Lord of Barley Cross stuck his hands into his pockets, and trudged Fistwards. The toilet soap and the perfume had been dispatched to the bride and her mother. Father Adrian's present had been a bit of a poser. The counselors had wanted to give him a little something to show the village's appreciation. Kevin Murphy had solved the problem by discovering a bottle of aftershave in his bathroom cabinet. Now there was just one headache left . . . how to persuade Rita Walsh into the Master's bed on her wedding night.

Liam McGrath sighed. In Barley Cross it was just one damn thing after another!

The Last Battle

The Lord of Barley Cross and his senior henchman paused to peer over the cemetery wall. In the grass near the path, a new slab of Connemara marble glistened in the sunshine.

Doctor Denny Mallon said, "Will you be replacing him?"

Liam McGrath shrugged. "Paedar is expecting promotion. But I don't know that we need a general any more. The Fist guard is mainly ceremonial these days."

The doctor stood, chin on chest, hands in pockets, hunched against the autumn wind. He sniffed. "We've come a long way since the early days, Liam. The Volunteers were a real fighting force in the O'Meara's time. And your stepfather was one of our stoutest warriors."

The Lord of Barley Cross kicked at the nettle stalks by the cemetery wall. Talking about Andy McGrath wouldn't bring him back. He said, "Soldiers are not my only problem, Denny."

Denny Mallon cocked his head to one side. "Oh? And what have I missed?"

Liam made a face. "Only Dermot Carrol."

"And what's young Carrol been up to?"

"He wants to marry Monica Ryan."

The doctor frowned. "What's wrong with that? We like weddings."

Liam scowled. "They're both my kids."

The doctor studied the leaves swirling round his boots. It was easy to ignore the passing of the years. Liam McGrath was now as old as the doctor had been when Liam had inherited the O'Meara's title and duties. And, meantime, Liam's children had grown into nubile men and women. Denny Mallon collected his wits. "I'd say that's something to be proud of."

Liam propped an elbow on the churchyard wall. "Sure it is. And I'll go to the wedding with pleasure. I'll even send them presents. But I won't . . ." He paused.

Denny Mallon peeked up at his lord. "Won't what, Liam?"

The Master of the Fist stared defiantly back at his old friend. "I won't exercise my droit on the wedding night. It's the end of the line, Denny. I decline to commit incest."

The counselors of the Lord of Barley Cross held an emergency session in the Fist parlor to discuss the Master's rebellion.

Liam McGrath was adamant. "No way," he declared. "I'll commit adultery, rape, concubinage and bigamy for you. But I draw the line at incest. You'll have to find yourselves another stud."

Brigit O'Connor, who had been co-opted to the caucus, squirmed on her brocade chair. They had offered her a footstool, but she had spurned it, preferring to swing her dainty feet. "But ye're special, me lord," she protested. "Ye're too important to the

Cross to worry about them things ye're boasting about. Ye're surely not going to mind a bit of incest, if that's what ye want to call it."

"It *would* be incest," Liam insisted. "And I *do* mind."

"Wait now!" Celia Larkin's stick thumped the carpet for attention. "Don't be getting yourselves into a tizzy. Wasn't Monica Ryan's mother in service at the Fist in Dominic Nunan's day?"

They stared at her. It was common knowledge in the village that during his short career as their lord and master, Dominic Nunan had got several of the Fist's kitchen and chamber staff pregnant.

"If she were," the schoolteacher continued, "it's quite possible that Monica is Dominic's child. And if she is, there can be no question of incest."

They turned their gaze to the Lord of Barley Cross. Liam returned it stonily. No question about it: Celia Larkin had changed. At one time, any mention of the Master's amorous proclivities would have had her blushing and demanding a change of subject. He said, "Don't look at me. I can't remember who worked here that long ago. Dammit—maids come and go like wasps in an orchard."

"Ye keep records, surely?" prompted Kevin Murphy.

"I keep nothing," Liam snarled. Even if they were right about Monica Ryan's parentage, it would only push the deadline back by one wedding.

"Michael will know," pronounced the doctor. "Ring for him, Liam. We'll soon find out if Celia has it right."

Liam reached behind his chair to pull on the bell rope which summoned his servant.

Michael appeared with suspicious promptness. Privately, Liam wondered that the man didn't get backache from stooping so much at keyholes.

"Michael," said the doctor. "Can you recall who

was in service here among the maids in Dominic Nunan's time?"

Michael pulled an earlobe in thought. "I can look it up in me records for you, doctor."

"Would that take long?"

"No more than ten minutes."

Denny Mallon looked to Liam for permission, then nodded. "If you would, Michael. It's important that we know."

Michael made a half bow. "Leave it to me, doctor. I'll soon have ye out of yer mystery."

"And bring another bottle if ye can find one," grunted the vet. "This Biddy O'Connor here sups more than Andy McGrath and Larry Desmond could, put together!"

Brigit O'Connor smiled down from her perch. "Since ye're incapable of malice, Kevin Murphy, I'll consider that a compliment. But keep a civil tongue in yer head in future!"

Michael returned with a bottle in one hand and a ledger in the other. He placed the bottle on the floor by the vet, then, licking a finger, began to leaf through the ledger.

At length he looked up. "I'm sorry, doctor. Some pages seem to be missing. I can't find the accounts for when Dominic Nunan was here."

Denny Mallon steepled his fingers. "Too bad, Michael. Thank you for looking. We'll have to check with Polly Ryan herself. She's bound to remember."

That afternoon, a knock on the door interrupted Liam's study of a standard reference on stock breeding. Michael put his head around the jamb. "Excuse me trespassing on yer privacy, me lord. Could I have permission to go down to the village to see Doctor Denny?" The servant put a hand to his jaw. " 'Tis a terrible toothache I have."

Liam smiled. "You're lucky to have teeth to ache at your age, Michael. Get yourself off straightaway."

Michael released his jaw. "I will. Thank 'ee, me lord. If ye want anything while I'm away, young Kelly will come if ye ring."

Liam waved a hand. "Away with ye! I can manage for an hour or so on my own!"

Michael arrived panting at the doctor's home. Tessie Mallon answered his knock. "Surgery's over, Michael," she told him. "Was it urgent? The doctor is taking a nap."

Michael fidgeted with his billycock. "Sure, 'tis dreadful urgent, Missus Mallon. The doctor would wish to be woken if he knew I was here."

Tessie Mallon sighed. Everything was urgent to people wanting to see her husband. "I'll see what he says," she countered.

Michael abandoned subterfuge. "Tell him it's about Monica Ryan."

Tessie Mallon's eyebrows arched perceptibly. She opened the door wider. "You'd better come in, Michael."

Denny Mallon stretched himself awake without rising from the couch. "Right, Michael," he prompted. "Let's have it."

Michael held his hat to his chest. "Have ye been to see Missus Ryan yet about her time at the Fist?"

The doctor smothered a yawn. "Holy heavens, Michael! I've managed to fit in a surgery and my dinner since this morning's meeting. What's the hurry?"

Michael lowered his voice. "Don't go, doctor. Polly Ryan wasn't at the Fist when young Nunan was there. It was months later when she came."

Denny Mallon's yawn ended abruptly. "How did you find that out?"

Michael's billycock twitched. "I told you all a lie up beyond, doctor. Those pages weren't missing from my accounts book. I tore them out before I brought it from the pantry."

The doctor's face was grim. "Why did you do that, Michael?"

The servant glanced over his shoulder as if fearing a witness to his confession. "Why, doctor—if the Master got proof positive that Polly Ryan wasn't at the Fist when Nunan was there, he . . . he might do what he threatened to do."

Denny Mallon nodded. It was tradition that Michael eavesdropped on their meetings. "Would that worry you, Michael?"

Michael fidgeted with his hat. "I'm as loyal a citizen as the next, doctor. If the Master refuses to . . . do his droyts with young Monica, it'll be the beginning of the end for us, won't it?"

The doctor nursed his chin. "So what can we do? Tell him Monica is Nunan's child—without proof. He won't believe it."

Michael's mouth worked with embarrassment. He sought for words. "Doctor Denny—I'd do it meself . . . but t'would be better coming from you—"

Denny Mallon's brow wrinkled. "What would?"

"Why, sir—someone should go and see Polly Ryan and persuade her to tell the Master that Nunan got her pregnant. The Master would believe her."

Denny Mallon ruminated, unshocked by the invitation to entangle another in perjury. How did the Lord of Barley Cross inspire such loyalty? He put his hands behind his head. "Why should Polly Ryan tell the Master a lie? She must be proud of bearing Liam's child—even though we all pretend Martin is Monica's father. And the lass herself won't be keen on claiming Dominic for a da, either."

The servant bit his lip. "She would if she felt like I do."

Denny Mallon smiled. "No doubt, Michael. But we're not all cast in the same heroic mold as you." He mused. "Maybe if I could persuade Polly that it would all be kept confidential—?"

Michael waved his hat. "Aye, sir—and don't forget to remind her what will happen in the Cross if the Master reneges on his droyts!"

Denny Mallon sighed. He swung his legs to the floor. "I'll do that, Michael. It's our strongest argument." He stretched for his bootlaces. "Okay, I'll have a go. And, Michael—?"

"Sir?"

"Burn those bloody sheets you tore from the ledger!"

Up at the Fist, Liam had sent for Sergeant Fahey. In the Master's study, Paedar Fahey came to attention, and saluted.

Liam said, "At ease, sergeant. I want to talk about your future. I suppose you realize you're in line for promotion, now we've lost our general?"

Paedar Fahey attempted a guileless expression. "I maybe gave it a thought or two, me lord. But, sure, I'm not the man to presume on anything."

Liam chewed on a pencil. "One matter bothers me, Paedar. Generals should be level-headed chaps, who don't go off half-cocked."

Paedar Fahey studied the burnished toecaps of his boots. "Agreed, me lord."

"So you see why I hesitate to replace General McGrath?"

The sergeant frowned. "Not exactly, me lord. If ye could make it a bit plainer—"

"Paedar," Liam said suddenly. "Why did you kill Dominic Nunan?"

Fahey's jaw dropped. "Is that what's bothering ye, me lord?"

Liam nodded grimly, glad to have the question in the open at last. He said, "I can't promote a man who kills without warning. Granted, I called for help, and you saved my life. But you didn't have to kill Dominic. That man had a set of genes which Barley Cross needed. Indeed, I wish to God we had him now!"

"Me lord—" Sergeant Fahey's freshly-ironed beret was a crumpled bundle in his fists. "—ye called on Eamon Toomey, not me. But he was too slow. Ye'd have been a corpse by the time he woke up. I had to do something. And I never meant to kill Dominic. He was my friend. I meant to fire in the air, and scare him. There were too many people 'round you to chance for a wound. And, Jasus—I'd never handled a real gun 'til I came from Achill. I might have hit you instead of him. And, sure, I wouldn't hurt a fly!"

"But you fired, and killed him!"

Fahey's shoulders slumped. "The blessed gun went off on its own, me lord. I think 'twas Willie Flanagan's old weapon. He always had the trigger at a hair's pressure. 'Twas bad luck I hit anything at all."

Liam relaxed. A weight he hadn't realized he'd been carrying lifted from his conscience. Dominic Nunan's death had been no one's fault. And dread Sergeant Fahey, the Master's tame butcher, had achieved notoriety by misfortune! If it wasn't so damn tragic, it would be hysterical."

He said, "Don't feel too bad about it. You're just the man I'm looking for—General Fahey!"

Paedar Fahey brightened. His shoulder straightened. "Thank 'ee, me lord."

Liam reached out a hand. "It's my pleasure, Paedar. For years I've been seeking a general who wouldn't hurt a fly."

General Fahey shook his Master's hand. "I'll do my best not to disappoint ye, me lord."

"Disappoint me?" Liam laughed aloud. "You're a bright spark in a gloomy world, General!"

Doctor Denny Mallon delayed his call on Polly Ryan until after dark. The fewer people to notice him enter the Ryan's home, the fewer able to apprise the Lord of Barley Cross that his henchmen conspired to deceive.

Polly Ryan opened the door to the doctor's knock. Her eyes widened. Her mouth opened.

"No trouble, Polly," he whispered. "May I come in?"

She pulled the door wide, and stood back. Denny Mallon slipped into the lamplit warmth. "Where's Martin?"

She closed the door. "He's down at Mooney's. Did ye want him?"

The doctor shook his head. "And Monica?"

"She's over at the Carrol's. And young Billy is off to the play club."

The doctor rubbed his hands together. Polly Ryan was a wife who had been lucky in one of the annual draws held for the Master's favors. Denny Mallon suspected that her husband's pique had prevented her from entering further ballots. Perhaps two vicarious children were as much as Martin Ryan could stomach. "That suits me fine," the doctor told her. "I want to talk to you."

She pushed a chair towards him. "Isn't that what we are doing now?"

He sat down, joints creaking like the chair. "Ahem. Just so, Polly." He cleared his throat. "Barley Cross needs your help, Polly. We're in a pickle."

She folded her arms. "Ye have the advantage of me, doctor."

He met her gaze uneasily. All very well for Michael to think up these schemes. He said, "Yes. Well, it's so, Polly. Without your help, we're sunk."

Face impassive, she said, "What's wrong?"

He hesitated. If Polly Ryan were not party to the great deception which kept Barley Cross ticking over, his next words would have him in trouble. But surely no woman could produce two children without being aware of how they were conceived. He blurted, "The Master has told me he will not be insisting on his *droit du seigneur* when your Monica gets married."

Polly Ryan pulled out a chair for herself. She flopped down heavily. "Why would he do that to us?"

Denny Mallon prayed for guidance. He said bluntly. "The master won't commit incest with your daughter."

Polly Ryan put a hand to her forehead. "Holy Mother! That's a hard one to swally! What made him pick on us?"

Denny Mallon sat very still. "Your Monica is the first of his daughters to be married. The problem hasn't come up before."

"Problem?" she repeated. "But what does it matter, if we're not worried about it?"

Voice urgent, he said, "You were in service at the Fist, years ago. If you'll tell the Master that you were there in Dominic Nunan's time, and that Dominic—" Denny Mallon swallowed, "—raped you—"

She flushed. "But it isn't true! I was never there in Nunan's day."

Denny Mallon sighed. "I know that, Polly, I know. But the Master doesn't know it. He can't remember who was a maid there at the time. And he's the one who counts. If we can convince him that Dominic, and not he . . . ?"

She stared, her mouth framing the unutterable.

He nodded.

Her face crumpled. "I can't go to the Master and tell him a downright lie like that!"

Denny Mallon caught her hand. "If you don't, you'll never see grandchildren of your own!"

Polly Ryan dabbed the corner of her eye with her pinafore. "It's not just the lie, doctor. It's letting the Master believe that Nunan—" She gulped. "—that Nunan did *that* to me! And that Monny is Nunan's child."

Denny Mallon sighed. "Will you let *me* tell the Master that Dominic raped you?"

She peered at him, her face ugly in her distress. "What if he sends for me to see if it's true?"

The doctor shrugged. It was possible. The Lord of Barley Cross was no longer a naive young man. These days he was capable of imputing the worst of motives to his advisers.

He said, "I can't guarantee he wouldn't do just that, Polly."

She sniveled. "Please don't ask me to do it. I couldn't look him in the face after." Her face set. "And Monica is *not* Nunan's child!"

Denny Mallon gave up. He squeezed her hand. "Forget what I asked you to do, Polly. I'll find some other way to get 'round the Master."

She brightened. "Are ye sure, doctor? Ye know I'd do anything to help you . . . except that!"

He found a wan smile for her. "Just forget it, Polly." He got to his feet. "I'll be off now. If anyone asks, I called round to examine Monica. I'll be back to give her a checkup before the wedding day."

The Ryan's door closed behind him. Denny Mallon set off home in the dark, whistling a plaintive air, a little off-key. Next stop would have to be the palace of Bishop Malone of Ballykilleen. The community of Ballykilleen, and its female bishop, had been discovered years ago by Sergeant Fahey. If anyone could influence the Master, she could.

He went alone to see the bishop. The road between Barley Cross and Ballykilleen was well-traveled, with even an eating place and a livery stable at the half-way stage. The risk of attack by road merchants was long gone. The towns and villages he passed through were deserted, or inhabited by shuffling creatures who hid at the sight of him and his gig. He found the bishop sunning herself on the palace steps.

Magdalen Malone and Denny Mallon had early learned to respect each other as rivals for the attentions of the Lord of Barley Cross. She ushered the doctor into her parlor, sat him down, and rang for tea.

He explained his mission.

She said, "If I've got it right, Doctor Mallon, you wish me—a bishop—to urge our Lord Protector to commit incest?"

The doctor eyed her. Sometimes it was difficult to predict which way Bishop Malone would jump.

"That's about the size of it, your grace," he admitted.

"And what persuades you I might accede to such a suggestion?"

Denny Mallon lounged against a cushion, trying to appear relaxed. Just how much her attitude might be a facade, he didn't know. After all, she had condoned bigamy, adultery and concubinage by the Lord of Barley Cross. He laced his fingers, and kept his voice casual. "I see nothing in holy writ which actually forbids incest, your grace. In fact, if we take the scriptures literally—"

The bishop's mouth tightened. "Don't go quoting holy scripture at me, doctor. I know the book backwards."

"Well," he countered, "eugenically speaking, with desirable stock, there is nothing to be said against inbreeding."

Her eyes were like industrial diamonds. "We are not speaking eugenically, either, doctor. We are speaking as a pastor to one of her flock. And we are not certain that we go along with you in this matter."

"But, your grace—" Denny Mallon was suddenly foundering. "This isn't just a Barley Cross problem. In a couple more years you'll have the same situation in Ballykilleen!"

"You submit," continued the bishop implacably, "that what is sinful in one place in one year, might not be sinful in another place in another year?"

Denny Mallon teetered on the edge of the pit. "No—no, your grace. I don't mean that. I mean that circumstances may alter cases. That the good Lord never intended His planet to whirl desolate in space. And that, when He told His apostles 'what you loose on earth will also be loosed in heaven'—he meant exactly that."

Bishop Malone was silent for a moment. Privately she concurred with the doctor. Many of her difficulties were due to people's reluctance to share such views. And she gave the doctor credit for not dragging up her previous rulings on the validity of various marriages in the two villages.

She said, "What do you want me to do?"

Denny Mallon let out his breath slowly. "If you would write me a letter—?"

She snorted. "Do you think I'm mad. To put something like that in black and white? One day I may have to justify *my* actions to a superior. I'll go to Barley Cross myself, and have a word with the Protector."

"I'll tell him you're planning a visit," Denny Mallon said eagerly.

Her smile was grim. "Don't bother, doctor. The mood that man is in, he'd probably try to avoid me. Or at least make sure I didn't get him on his own." She shook his head. "I never met a fellow less keen on sin—even with the church's sanction!"

Denny Mallon warmed to the bishop. Once she got off the fence there was little doubt about which way she voted.

"Perhaps we could trap him into a rendezvous?" the doctor suggested.

The bishop showed interest. "Like where?"

Denny Mallon fingered his chin in thought. "Suppose your grace were on your way over to the Cross, and the Master were on his way to Bally Kay . . . ?"

Her interest became enthusiasm. "There's the Half Way House Eatery the McNultys have opened near Athlone!"

"The ideal place," agreed the doctor. "Isolated—and comforable. I could get Sergeant Fahey to go with him, and hold him there until you arrive."

Face pensive, the bishop nibbled her pectoral cross. "But why would Liam want to visit Ballykilleen just now?"

"Couldn't one of your ladies—?"

She snapped her fingers. "I've got it. Maire Fitz's youngest is sickening for something. He'd go a day's ride for a sick child."

The doctor checked his old wind-up watch. "I've got time to look at the infant. I have my bag with me. And I could give Liam a first-hand report."

The bishop beamed. "That's kind of you, doctor. Our nurse gets a bit out of her depth sometimes. But, don't lay it on too thick when you talk to the Master. We don't want to frighten the man." She paused. "How will I know when he's coming?"

Denny Mallon grabbed the initiative. "Start for Barley Cross tomorrow," he urged. "I'll get the Master going, somehow." He smiled. "If he won't move, we'll surprise him with a meeting at the Fist—and see if he can wriggle out of that!"

The bishop nodded. "Perhaps we should confer more often, doctor. Liam McGrath is often in need of expert guidance." She reached for a gilded tassel, and gave it a tug. "Where's that maid gone with the tay!"

The doctor waylaid Paedar Fahey on his way to the Fist at dawn next morning. When Paedar married Noral Kelly they had moved in with her parents, sharing the Kelly's double cottage on the lane leading to McGuire's mill. The doctor had merely to hide at the head of the lane to be sure of catching his man.

Paedar appeared, puffing vapor. Denny Mallon fell into step with his quarry.

"Fine morning, Paedar."

Paedar Fahey tucked the ends of a woollen scarf inside his jacket. "Ye're up early for a gintleman, doctor."

Denny Mallon shivered, and stamped his feet. The wait had been a cold one. "Not as early as some, Paedar." He thrust his hands deep into his pockets. "Time was when the Fist Guard stood to at first light."

Fahey grinned. "They still do, doctor. I'm excused early parade, now the Master has made me a gineral."

The doctor halted. He offered a hand. "I wasn't aware of your promotion, Paedar. I must have missed the announcement while I was over at Bally Kay visiting a sick child. My congratulations!"

Grinning foolishly, General Fahey shook the doctor's hand.

Denny Mallon swiftly revised his plans. As their general, Paedar automatically became one of the Master's advisers. As a privy counselor, he was entitled to be exempt from misdirection by a fellow counselor.

"We need your assistance," the doctor confided. "I have to arrange a meeting between the Master and Bishop Malone for today."

"Sure, the Master is always glad to see the bishop," commented the general.

Denny Mallon shook his head. "He won't be this time, Paedar. Not when he hears what the bishop wants to discuss."

"And what would that be?"

Fingers crossed, Denny Mallon put his cards on the table.

General Fahey was patently flattered by the doctor's confidence. "Ye get the Master on the Ballykilleen road," he said confidently, "and I'll see he stays in the McNulty's diner until the bishop shows up."

The doctor grasped the general's hand. "I knew you'd be with us."

*   *   *

Two hours later, Doctor Denny Mallon presented himself at the Fist, seeking audience with the Master.

Liam was up and dressed. He met the doctor in the parlor, where the remains of a peat fire smoldered. The Master stooped to drop another turf on the embers.

The doctor opened his bag, and rummaged inside. "Will you lend me Paedar for an important errand, Liam? I have several calls to make in the village, including a checkup on Monica Ryan, and I really haven't the time to go myself."

The Lord of Barley Cross gestured the doctor to a chair. "Paedar's our general, now, Denny. He don't run errands like an ordinary soldier."

Denny Mallon paused in the act of seating himself, his face transparent with honesty. "Ach—I must have missed the announcement. I was over at Bally Kay on a job. Perhaps someone else could go?"

The Master eyed his henchman with impatience. "Go where? What's bothering you, Denny?"

Denny Mallon produced a pill box from his bag. "I have to get these tablets to Maire FitzGerald."

Liam McGrath's face betrayed a flicker of concern. "What's wrong with Maire Fitz?"

Denny Mallon gazed blankly at his Master. "Maire FitzGerald is as right as rain. It's the little fellow— her youngest—who needs the tablets."

Liam leaned forward, his voice urgent. "What's the matter with young Brian?"

The doctor shrugged. "He had a strep throat and a temperature, yesterday. I feared diphtheria, so I gave him a Schick test." Denny Mallon caught Liam's alarmed gaze. "Don't worry. It was *strep pyogenes*— scarlet fever. These sulphanomide tablets will put him right, if I can get them to him. So, if one of your soldiers could—?"

The Master of the Fist got to his feet. "I'd sooner go myself, Denny. You're sure it's not diphtheria?"

The doctor placed the pill box on the table. "Quite sure, Liam. If the little fellow gets these tablets down him, he'll be all right. You've nothing to worry about."

"Like hell, I haven't!" Liam picked up the pill box. "Excuse me cutting you short, Denny. I'd like to get going immediately."

The doctor's eyes grew owl-like. "To Ballykilleen?"

Liam stuffed the pill box into his pocket. "That's where the FitzGeralds live, isn't it?"

"Ahem!" Denny Mallon closed his bag. "I'm grateful for your assistance, my lord."

Liam flung open the door. "Do me a favor, Denny. Find General Fahey, and ask him to get me a horse ready."

"Leave it to me, my lord." Denny Mallon picked up his bag, and went to warn Paedar Fahey.

The Half Way House Hotel had been the residence of a well-to-do jeweller in the old days. The McNultys had knocked down an interior wall or two, put in a polished bar and a few tables and chairs, and erected a sign by the road side. Hannah McNulty did the cooking on a huge, peat-burning stove. Husband Joe waited on table, and served behind the bar. Son Danny looked after the adjoining livery stable. With the proliferation of contacts between the Three Seigneuries, trade was satisfactory. Rumor had it that Joe contemplated a second venture on the Achill road.

As the Lord of Barley Cross and his general drew abreast of the hotel, Paedar Fahey halted his horse. "Time for a break, me lord. Give the animals a blow. An extry half hour won't hurt Missus Fitz's little one."

Liam glanced up at the sun. The light went quickly, these days. "I'd sooner press on, Paedar."

General Fahey grasped his Master's reins. "We've

plenty of time, me lord. And ye ate no proper breakfast."

Liam McGrath sighed. True, his stomach was rumbling. He frowned at the general. "Admit it, Paedar. 'Tis the divil's own thirst ye have!"

Paedar Fahey hid his relief. Sometimes fate dealt the aces just when you needed them. "I wouldn't object to wetting down the dust in me throat," he admitted.

Liam turned his horse in at the hotel gate. "Let's see what the McNulty's can do for us, then."

Magdalen Malone surprised the Master with his teeth into a chicken drumstick. She swept into the McNulty's dining room like a ship under full sail. Liam dropped his bone. Paedar Fahey got to his feet. "Yer grace!"

The bishop bowed to the Lord Protector of Ballykilleen. "Fancy meeting you here, my lord."

He bent over her outstretched hand. "We all have to be somewhere, your grace." He tugged out a chair. "Will you join me?"

The bishop sat down. Liam shouted for McNulty.

General Fahey picked up his plate. He glanced across the dining room to where the bishop's young attendants sat. "I'll leave ye to yer confidences, me lord and yer grace. Maybe yer acolytes would be wanting a little company or something."

The bishop's glance took in Fahey's shoulder stars, and the simpers on the faces of her attendants. She murmured, "You are most kind, general. Don't spoil those girls too much. I have to live with them afterwards."

Liam said, "How is Maire's little boy?"

The bishop faced him. "Much improved, my lord. The nurse saw him this morning. His temperature is down."

Liam patted his pocket. "I have some tablets here from Doctor Mallon for him. Brian should take them, just in case."

She nodded solemnly. "Most certainly he should. It's good of the doctor to prescribe for him."

Liam's eyes narrowed. Bishop Malone was being altogether too polite and accommodating. He said, "And what brings you out on the road to Barley Cross?"

She lowered her voice. "I won't dissemble, Liam. I was coming to see you about this latest foolishness of yours."

Liam blinked. The bishop was sticking her oar in again. He whispered icily, "And just what foolishness would that be?"

She glanced over her shoulder. General Fahey and her acolytes were in animated conversation. She hissed back. "You know quite well that I mean; your refusal to practice your *droit du seigneur* with Polly Ryan's daughter when she marries."

Liam gripped the edge of the table. Keeping his voice low, he murmured, "Maggie—that girl is my own flesh and blood!"

She sighed. "So are my children. But when the time comes—!"

The table shook. "Maggie! You couldn't!"

She eyed him grimly. "Couldn't I, Liam? If it's a case of our survival as a species or nitpicking about degrees of kindred, I choose survival. I don't want to meet my Maker with a charge of conniving at the death of humanity hanging 'round my neck."

He gaped. "But we're not conniving!" He spread his palms. "It isn't us that have doomed mankind. I'm just refusing to—"

She snarled. "Is the man who refuses to jump in the river to save a drowning child not guilty of murder?"

Liam hesitated. "If he can swim—"

Her eyes gleamed. "*You* are the only man we have that *can* swim!"

He groaned. "Quit pushing, Maggie. You don't know what you're asking."

"Don't I?" she began. "Then what do you think—"

She paused. Joe McNulty approached their table, holding a menu card. From his demeanor it was plain that the restaurateur was overawed by the presence of his lord and his bishop.

He bowed to the bishop, and presented the card. "Would your grace care to order? We recommend the colcannon."

She waved a hand. "Just an omelette and a glass of milk, please, Joe. And see what my girls want."

Joe McNulty bowed again. Liam caught his eye. "On my bill, Joe."

The restaurateur shook his head. "All refreshments is compliments of the house, m'lord. We're honored to have you both here."

As soon as he was out of earshot, the bishop leaned across the table. "Liam, you musn't worry about the moral side of this thing. I absolve you from any sin in this matter. The future of the human race is too serious a business for morality."

Liam gritted his teeth. "But Maggie, I don't *want* absolving!"

She toyed with a knife lying on the cloth. "Oh, but you do, my lord. If I may remind you, there are sins of omission as well as commission. And yours, if you commit it, will be a grievous one. I warn you—if you evade your duty to Monica Ryan on her wedding night, I will pronounce anathema on you!"

He stared at her, horrified. "Maggie, that's not fair! You wouldn't do that to me!"

Her eyes were like flint. "If you don't believe me, Liam McGrath, you don't know Maggie Malone!"

He watched her in silence as she ate her omelette. He had been a fool ever to get involved with these Ballykilleen viragos. From the very start, the bishop's one idea had been to dominate him. And now she threatened to ban him from the church. Would she commit incest if she were in his place? Liam groaned. Maggie Malone would do whatever her conscience told her to do.

"Give me time to consider," he pleaded. "I want to talk it over with Eileen."

"You have until the wedding," she pointed out. "I'm merely indicating where your duty lies."

He couldn't face further argument. He brought out Denny Mallon's pill box, and placed it on the table. "Will you give this to Maire Fitz? They are Brian's tablets. There's no point in my rushing to Ballykilleen now the little fellow is recovering."

She picked up the box. "And there's little point in me going to Barley Cross now I've said my piece."

They stared at each other, faces glum.

He got up. "Then I'll say goodbye for now, Maggie."

She didn't offer her hand. "Keep in touch, my lord."

He nodded. "I'll do that."

Across the room, Paedar and the girls were laughing at a joke.

Eileen McGrath said, "Couldn't you pretend to yourself that she's Martin's daughter?" Over the years, the First Lady of Barley Cross had grown accustomed to sharing her husband with the women of three villages. To her, Monica Ryan was just one more in a regiment of unwelcome faces.

Liam hunched over his breakfast. "I'd be fooling myself. I know who's child she is."

Eileen McGrath buttered a slice of toast. "Well, you're the only one that's worried about it. Dear God, Liam! You've swallowed so much in the past— why strain at this gnat now?"

He propped his chin on his hands. "It's no gnat to me," he told her, his voice breaking.

She poured him more tea. The famous O'Connor common sense firmed her mouth. "Then why not get yourself dressed, and go and talk to the girl? See what she thinks about it."

He looked up in surprise. The sanest suggestion yet! If Monica objected to the idea, it would give him a cast-iron excuse. And, if she didn't object . . . well, it was possible to change one's views.

Denny Mallon met his lord at the foot of Barra Hill.

The Master of the Fist halted in mid-stride. "A word with you, Denny Mallon!" he snapped.

The doctor peered up at him, clutching the brim of his hat with mittened fingers. "I was on my way up to see you, my lord," he quavered.

Liam smiled like an assassin about to strike. "That's fine. I'll save you the trouble. We can settle the matter here. What do you mean by trapping me into a confrontation with that bloody bishop?"

Denny Mallon shrank into his overcoat. He gasped for breath. "My lord, I only asked you to take—"

Liam smiled bitterly. "You only got me on the hook with the bishop. She's threatened me with anathema if I don't toe the line on Monica Ryan's wedding night."

Denny Mallon's head emerged from his coat collar. "I was coming to tell you, my lord. You won't have to practice your droit at the wedding."

Liam stood back. "Oh? You've come round to my way of thinking?"

Denny Mallon ventured a smile. "No, my lord. Something else entirely." He paused. Doctor Denny Mallon knew he was about to break the most important news ever to come his way, and he was determined to exploit the opportunity to the utmost.

Liam stared at him, baffled. "Well come on, man—out with it!"

Denny Mallon removed his hat. He held it close to his chest, as though taking an oath. "I examined Monica Ryan yesterday . . . she's pregnant!"

The Lord of Barley Cross stood stock still. "She's *what?*"

Denny Mallon smirked. "She and Dermot Carrol seem to have been anticipating events. He's got her in the family way."

Liam McGrath's face began to split in a huge grin. "You mean Dermot is able to—?"

Wordless, Denny Mallon nodded.

Liam seized the doctor by the arms, and waltzed him around in the roadway. The Connemara drizzle, which had threatened all morning, began to fall in earnest. Tyrant and doctor capered on, heedless of the downpour. They desisted only when Denny Mallon pleaded for breath.

He wiped moisture that wasn't rain from his eyes. He croaked. "We've done it, Liam. We've done it, at last! Pat O'Meara should have lived to see this day. After all these years! Dermot Carrol's got your genes. And he's only the first, you'll see!"

Liam McGrath turned to stare through the rain at his village. His wonderful citizens were going about their business, unaware that the threat had been lifted. The world would not die with the death of their children. He gripped the doctor's arm. "Who else knows, Denny?"

Denny Mallon's eyes twinkled. "Only four of us, so far. You, me, Monica and her mam."

Liam laughed aloud. "Don't tell another soul, Denny! We'll keep it quiet. I'll forget about my droits . . . and Barley Cross can carry on as normal— like it always does!"

As It Was In The Beginning

The last of the Barley Cross giants was toppling. Celia Larkin lay in her cot in the Denny Mallon Memorial Hospital, waiting for a ninety-year-old heart to fail. The others were all gone, now. Denny Mallon, years ago, of the lung cancer he had courted so assiduously. Kevin Murphy, of pneumonia, contracted after a kick from a cow had broken his leg. Poor Andy McGrath, from a succession of strokes. Larry Desmond, God help him, of the drink. And Patrick O'Meara . . . Celia Larkin's eyes clouded with unshed moisture . . . the first and best Lord of Barley Cross, her dear Master of the Fist . . .

Up on Barra Hill, Liam McGrath, the second Master of the Fist—since one couldn't count sad, mad Dominic, still ruled. Still respected—though no longer required—Liam played endless games of checkers with General Fahey, or told stories of the old days to anyone who would listen.

But Liam McGrath couldn't tell the most important story. Celia could recall, as if it were yesterday . . .

. . . the rumbling, clanking, screeching, clattering from beyond the hedgerows which drove the young schoolmistress to hide in a dry gully by the roadside. The noise sounded like a combination of road roller, combine harvester, and a hundred squeaking gates. Celia Larkin crouched low. Any kind of transport could be a threat these days.

She waited some minutes before a long gun barrel lagged with thermal insulation poked its snout 'round the bend. Celia Larkin had never seen a tank before, much less a British Army Main Battle Tank. In her astonishment, she forgot to keep her head down.

The monster halted opposite her hiding place. The roar of its engine died to a low rumble. The driver poked his head through a hatch in the sloping glacis. He called to her. "Is this the road for Castlebar?"

Useless to crouch lower. Celia Larkin stood, brushed dust and grass from her suit, and said, "If you keep straight on you can't miss it."

The man smiled. He wore an oily beret bearing a badge which resembled a ball sprouting feathers, and a jacket covered with green and yellow splotches. "I'm making for Kilcollum in Connemara," he told her.

She stared at his enormous vehicle. Such a monster to carry one man to Connemara! "I've never heard of the place," she confessed.

"Sure, 'tis only a small village," he admitted. "Not many people know it." He paused, as though seeking inspiration for further pleasantries. "Can I give you a lift to anywhere? The roads are not safe for a young lady on her own."

She weighed him up. He had an honest, open face. His smile was disarming. And—most persuasive—his remark about the roads was true. The last car she had hidden from had been packed with shotgun-wielding hooligans.

"How do I get in?" she asked.

He pointed. "If you put a foot on that towing eye, and grab that lamp bracket . . . there are cleats up to the turret. You go through a hatch in the cupola . . . hold on, I'll give you a hand."

She swung her suitcase up onto the glacis beside his head. "That won't be necessary. Take my case!"

She hoisted her skirt, found the foot and handholds indicated, and climbed onto the tank. One of the turret hatches was open. She got in among the machinery.

"I'm in!" she called.

"Where to, miss?" he called back.

"I was hoping to get to Clifden—but that will be a good step past your village, I'm afraid."

"I don't mind running a young lady home."

The engine noise became a roar. She heard him shout. "Don't touch anything in there, miss. You don't want to blow us up!"

Tracks squealing, the tank lurched into motion. Celia Larkin found the noise stunning, the vibration worse than she had expected. The combination of noise and vibration rendered further conversation with the driver impossible. She found a seat, and sat down, wondering what she had let herself in for.

Surely, after her days on the road, anyone would have accepted his offer of a lift. Sligo had been insufferable, the behavior of its citizens growing daily worse. She wanted nothing more to do with it. In lonely Clifden, at the Atlantic's edge, she might find people more civilized, less influenced by the current madness.

When the tank stopped, she nerved herself for further conversation. A hatch opened above her head. The soldier's head showed against the light. He dropped down beside her.

"Time for a break," he told her. "Sit still—I'll put the kettle on."

She watched in amazement as he filled a kettle and plugged it in.

"I didn't know you could brew tea in a tank!"

He grinned. "Sure, there's a deal you don't know about tanks, I would imagine."

He opened a locker, and brought out two plastic plates. "Could you face a ploughman's lunch?"

She hadn't eaten that day, being scared of entering strange eating places. "After that ride," she told him, "I could face anything."

He cut half-inch slabs of cheese, and laid them on slices of bread. He opened a jar, and topped the cheese with pickles. He covered his confections with further slices of bread, and passed one of the sandwiches to her.

"I'm Patrick O'Meara, ex-Second Battalion, Grenadier Guards," he told her. "Who are you?"

Mouth choked with tangy cheese, she gave him her name. "How did you come by this tank?" she asked him.

He grinned. "Stole it from the British government. I've been guarding their docks in Belfast 'til I'm sick of being a cockshy for every idiot who wants his fling while there's someone left to annoy."

"Is that what it's like in Belfast?"

He grimaced. "It's like that all over Ireland, so far as I can gather. Maybe all over the world. No kids born anywhere for the last ten years. People beginning to realize there's no future to look forward to. Nothing left to work for. If we're all going to be dead in sixty years or so, does anything matter any more? Belfast is crazy. The Provos are out in the open shouting a new slogan—'Ours in the end!' We shot a few last week, and they got seven of my lads."

"Sligo is not as bad as that," she told him. "But there have been robberies and muggings. I was a teacher, but my class grew up, and left me without anyone to teach. So I'm going to my sister in Clifden. I hope it'll be better there."

He unplugged the steaming kettle, and infused

the tea. "My parents live in Kilcollum. I haven't seen them since I joined the army. I'm hoping for peace and quiet, too."

She eyed this soft-spoken soldier who stole tanks, killed Provos, and talked of peace. "Why did you steal this machine?"

He grinned impenitently. "Can you think of a safer way to travel?"

They slept that night, all hatches closed, in a pasture hidden from the road by a tall hedge. Next morning he heated water for washing and shaving, then boiled a couple of eggs. They ate breakfast squatting on the glacis.

"I'll have to find some fuel, soon," he told her.

"What kind of fuel?"

He jerked a thumb at the rear of the tank. "That motor will run on anything. Right now we're on diesel."

"How much will you need?"

He grimaced. "I'd settle for a couple of hundred gallons. More, if I can get it. I've plenty of empty cans in the bustle."

Her eyes widened. "Could you pay for that much?"

"No need." He pointed to the long gun above them. "I have a credit card!"

She tried to frown at him. "Mister O'Meara, you are no better than the villains you complain of!"

He indicated once-white tapes on his sleeve. "Sergeant," he told her. "And they can't bust me 'til they catch me. It takes a sergeant for real villainy. Now, come up to the turret, and I'll show you how to work it."

She frowned at him. "Do I need to know?"

He sighed. "I think so."

She wasn't convinced. "For what reason?"

He showed her two calloused hands. "Because I've only these."

A few miles from Castlebar, they found an open

service station. Sergeant O'Meara pulled into the forecourt, and halted his tank by the pumps. A door in the office opened. A man appeared carrying a shotgun.

"Get that thing off my property!"

The sergeant put his head out of the driver's hatch. "I need gas, chief."

The man jerked his shotgun. "I've none to spare for strangers. Get moving!"

Sergeant O'Meara smiled winningly. "I'll settle for a tankful, chief. Diesel or gas—I've got a multi-fuel engine. Don't be hard on a poor traveler."

The man's face contorted. "You heard me, soldier. Get that thing off my forecourt before I blow your head off!"

Sergeant O'Meara raised his voice. "Larkin!"

"Sir?" responded the turret.

"Train on the office!"

"Sir!"

Motors whined. The turret rotated. A long, thermally insulated barrel swung until its business end pointed at the man in the doorway.

"Load HESH, Larkin!"

"Sir!"

Sergeant O'Meara addressed the station owner. "Now, chief, before I give my next order, would you care to reconsider any decisions?"

The man spluttered. His shotgun wavered. He glanced into the office behind him. "My wife is in there."

Patrick O'Meara shrugged. "Then she has two minutes to get clear. I'm not a patient man."

The station operator struggled for his dignity. He brushed a sleeve under one eye. "You British army?"

"On a detached mission," the sergeant confirmed.

"Your commanding officer will hear about this!"

"I'll give you his name and address."

The station operator propped his shotgun against

the door jamb, and crossed to the pumps. He un-
hooked a hose. "Show me where to stick this thing."

Later, as they rumbled towards Castlebar, Celia
Larkin switched on the intercom. Once clear of the
gas station, the sergeant had shown her how to work
it. She addressed the microphone suspended by her
cheek. "What's HESH?"

His voice spoke in the rubber doughnuts over her
ears. "High Explosive, Squash Head. It's used for
blowing holes in concrete bunkers. We haven't any."

"Thank heavens for that," she shouted. "For a
moment, I thought you meant it when you threatened that poor man back there."

"I did mean it," he shouted back. "Could I have
relied on you to shoot if I'd ordered it?"

She ignored the question. "And you paid him with
a chit on the British Army's Paymaster General!"

"He pays all my bills."

Celia Larkin gave up. A Sligo schoolroom was poor
preparation for disputing Sergeant O'Meara's elastic
principles.

They drove sedately down the center of Castlebar's
narrow main street. There was no traffic, few parked
cars. Shop windows were boarded-up. A jeweler's
front was glassless and stockless.

His voice sounded in the doughnuts. "Things don't
look much better here, Larkin."

She said, "Keep going, sergeant. We're being
watched from bedroom windows. Can they harm
us?"

She couldn't see his smile of approval. He said
patiently. "Only if they have anti-tank guns or rocket
launchers, Larkin. I doubt they'll have those kind of
weapons. But you might watch out for Molotov
cocktails—"

"What do I do if I see one?"

In her own way this schoolteacher was a cool character. Education was all she needed. He said, "If

you're nervous, duck down and close the hatch! If you're not—that machine gun beside you is loaded."

Her voice reflected a classroom ring. "Don't be ridiculous, sergeant. Why would I wish to shoot anyone?"

She couldn't see his grin either. "Just a thought, Larkin. Just a thought."

At a steady fifteen miles per hour they rolled along the eastern shores of Mask and Corrib. At Corrib's southern tip, Patrick O'Meara turned west for Galway City.

Insulated from noise by her headphones, and by now accustomed to the tank's vibration, Celia spoke into her mike. "Smoke ahead of us, sergeant."

A black cloud hung above the treetops.

"I see it," he responded. "It'll be Galway Town burning, I suspect. Button up, Larkin!"

They went through the town battened down, crunching over rubble and wreckage. Smoke drifted from buildings which burned unchecked. Celia preferred the magnified picture in her gunsight to that provided by the nine periscopes studding the cupola. She swung the turret from side to side, watching diligently for Molotov cocktails.

Patrick O'Meara, lying in the driver's seat, noted the long barrel swinging menacingly back and forth over his head, and grinned with pleasure. No rioter would tackle his tank while that gun threatened.

On the Oughterard road, clear of Galway, he stopped for tea.

"Well done, Larkin," he told her. "You certainly kept their heads down."

She gaped in astonishment. "I did?"

He opened a secret locker, produced a bottle, and poured a large tot in both cups. The schoolteacher deserved it. "We couldn't have got through so easy without you."

She flushed. He was being gracious. "Nor without you, sergeant."

Patrick O'Meara handed her a cup. "Maybe we've got ourselves a team. Would you like to learn how to handle that gun?"

Celia Larkin was already viewing matters in a fresh light. She recalled the burning hub of Galway, the looted shopfronts of Castlebar, the shotgun-wielding hooligans on the road, and the possibility of Molotov cocktails. She bit her lip. "Do you think it might help?"

His eyes were steady. "I wouldn't suggest it if I didn't think so."

She inhaled a trembly breath. "Very well, sergeant. Show me what to do."

He grinned. "Nothing to be scared of, Larkin. We shoot separate-loading ammo—that's a divided projectile and charge. So you don't have such heavy shells to lift. And there are no empty cases to dump. The bag holding the charge burns up." He pointed. "We keep the charges in water-jacketed compartments under there."

She eyed him hesitantly. "You make it sound so simple, sergeant."

"What's complicated? Aiming is done for you by laser and computer, once you pick the target."

She blinked; "And what do we shoot, if we've no HESH?"

He drained his cup. She was quick on the uptake, this schoolteacher. He said, "Good question, Larkin. We have some smoke shells, and a few rounds of APFSDS."

"APFSDS?" she queried.

"Armor-piercing, fin-stabilized, discarding sabot," he explained. "Very potent stuff."

She drained her cup quickly. The sergeant might be thinking of opening his bottle again. It certainly was potent stuff.

Later, he hauled a suitcase from a compartment in the bustle. He unpacked a uniform blouse and beret.

"Put these on," he told her. "Tuck your hair inside the beret. If we're painting a picture, details are important."

She fingered a row of ribbons stitched above the blouse's pocket. "What were these for?"

He made a business of closing the suitcase, and stowing it away.

"Isn't this the Falklands ribbon?" she persevered.

He faced her. "The British army likes its soldiers to have a bit of color on their gear. Shoulder flashes and the like. To brighten things up."

"And this one?" she persisted.

He swallowed. "That's the M.M." No one made fun of the Military Medal.

"Isn't that given for bravery in action?"

Sergeant O'Meara found it suddenly necessary to get down and check the suspension of the six road wheels on the side of his tank. When he returned, she had donned the top half of his parade uniform.

He appraised the result. "A big improvement, Larkin. No need to stick your chest out. Nature's done that for you. Into the turret, now. Anyone looking quick will think I've got a soldier up there. I'll show you how to work the cupola machine gun, too—in case you really want to impress somebody."

Oughterard, when they passed through, was silent and watchful like all the other small towns and villages had been. Over the intercom, he said, "It must be the tank that scares them."

She said primly, "It certainly can't be me!"

West of Oughterard, the road threaded between misty mountains. Nameless minor lakes puddled the land flanking the road. Turf stacks lined the verge.

She heard him sigh over the phones.

"Nearly there, Larkin."

She surveyed the peaceful panorama. The sergeant's tank was a refuge she would be sorry to

leave. But he would no longer need her assistance
once he got home. One couldn't expect pleasant
interludes to last indefinitely.

She said, "Are we going to Kilcollum first, sergeant?"

He sounded strained. "Why not? You in a hurry to
get to Clifden?"

She examined her conscience. "Not particularly,
sergeant."

"Just as well. I want you to meet my folks."

The road angled around the toe of a mountain
marked Kirkogue on her map. Just off the highway a
cluster of cottages and a castle-capped hill came into
sight.

She said, "I have relatives living there."

For a moment she thought he hadn't heard her.
Then the intercom said, "Take off your phones and
listen!"

She complied.

From the village came the sound of gunfire.

"Someone shooting," she reported.

"Battle stations, Larkin!" ordered the intercom.
"That means down you go, and close the hatch after
you."

She lowered herself into the turret, and closed the
cupola cover. As they turned off the main road,
through the main gun sight she saw, magnified, the
village street ahead. A van blocked the roadway, its
rear doors open. Shotgun-carrying men stood around
the vehicle. Others appeared, carrying boxes which
they dumped inside the van.

"Highway robbery," commented the intercom. "Do
we intervene for your relatives's sake?"

Her pulse jumped at the idea.

"What could we do?"

The intercom grew brisk. "Line up the gun sight
on the van. Don't worry—I'll not ask you to shoot
anyone."

She did as she was bid.

"Switch on the IFCS."

"IFCS, sergeant?"

"Improved fire control system—the computer and the laser sight! Move it, soldier!"

Celia Larkin moved it. Below the optical target ring in her telescope, a green oval sprang into existence. It shifted to encircle the image of the van.

"Target acquired," she reported, getting into the swing of it.

"There's a ranging machine gun mounted beside the big fellow," instructed the intercom. "It's fixed to fire on the same trajectory as the main armament. When there's no one in the way to get hurt, give that van a burst."

Heart thumping, eyes wide with excitement, she squeezed the machine gun trigger. In the gun sight, a flight of bright tracer bullets arched towards the van. The vehicle sank down on one side as a tire burst. "Nice shooting, Larkin," approved the intercom. "That'll do for now."

The bandits had concealed themselves behind their lopsided transport. Celia saw gun flashes.

"Don't worry," advised the intercom. "Those popguns won't penetrate our armor. Load smoke."

"Smoke?" she queried.

"Wake up, Larkin! A smoke shell—like I showed you!"

She hoisted a smoke shell from its rack, and pushed it into the breech of the big gun.

"Don't forget the charge, Larkin!"

She pulled a canvas bag from the special storage, and pushed it after the projectile.

"Close the breech, Larkin!"

She closed, and locked the gun breech, in the way he had shown her.

"Gun ready, sergeant," she panted.

"Fire at will!" ordered the intercom.

The smoke shell went through the van's open rear, and exploded in the driver's seat, collapsing the suspension. A cloud of black smoke enveloped the vehicle.

"Cease firing!" ordered the intercom. "They're retreating."

Patrick O'Meara re-engaged gears, and clanked towards the smoke-shrouded wreck. The roadway around the van suddenly swarmed with people, many masked with scarves or handkerchiefs against the smoke, all transferring plunder back to the shop.

A smallish man, his sleeves rolled up and blood on his hands, approached the tank.

Patrick O'Meara threw back his hatch cover, and stuck out his head.

The man addressed him. "On behalf of the village I thank you for your timely help, sergeant. Those rogues would have stolen all the Glynn's stock. Believe me, you're a welcome sight in Barley Cross."

Sergeant O'Meara lowered his eyes modestly. "We try to please. Are you hurt?"

The man glanced at his hands. "I'm a doctor. This is Willie Neary's blood. They shot him up pretty badly."

The sergeant jerked a thumb at the turret behind him. "I've a medical kit in there if it's any use to you."

The doctor shook his head. "I've medicaments enough, thank you. 'Tis dressings I'm short of. I'll soon be out of shirts if my wife doesn't stop tearing up my wardrobe. . . ."

Patrick O'Meara climbed out of his tank. "I've no shirts to spare, Doctor—?"

"Mallon," supplied the little man. "Denny Mallon—come and meet your debtors. . . ."

Later, over their first hot meal in days, the doctor told them, "We're trying to live a normal life, here in the Cross. But it's damn difficult. Those rogues you chased away have raided us several times already." He looked up from his plate, eyes speculative. "I don't suppose we could persuade you both to stay here? Barley Cross could use a couple of professional soldiers with a tank."

Celia Larkin made deprecating noises. "I'm no solider, Doctor. I wear the sergeant's gear to impress the spectators."

Doctor Mallon gestured with his fork. "You impressed us with your shooting."

She blushed. "It's all done by computer. I'd sooner teach children—if you have any?"

The doctor shook his head. "There's been no work for a midwife in Barley Cross for a dozen years or more." He gazed wistfully at the schoolteacher. "If you could persuade your sergeant to stay on here, we might find you an adult class to teach. There must be many subjects you could lecture on."

"Oh sure! Like sleeping rough, panhandling, shoplifting, or the rival merits of HESH and APFSDS!"

Sergeant O'Meara stirred his tea. "I have to visit my folks in Kilcollum, doctor. Then I'm taking Miss Larkin to her sister's place in Clifden. If my fuel lasts out, I might be back."

The doctor looked suddenly hopeful. "Then you two are not married—or anything?"

Patrick O'Meara stared at his silent gunner. He said, "No, Doctor. Not married—or anything." Inexplicably, the sergeant fell silent.

Later that day, a lone Chieftain tank rolled westward over rain-wet roads. In the misty distance, the Corcogemore Mountains loomed like storm clouds.

Sergeant O'Meara addressed his gunner over the intercom. "Why didn't you tell the doctor you have relatives in his village?"

He couldn't see her confusion.

"I—I wasn't sure I wanted to . . ."

He waited, but she didn't continue.

"Wasn't sure of what?" he persisted.

"That I wanted to . . . get involved . . . *there*," she said slowly.

"What have you got against Barley Cross?" demanded the intercom. "Or is it your relatives you don't like?"

"My uncle is a widower. He has a grown-up daughter."

"But you don't get on with them?"

"Och—I like them well enough."

"But you'd prefer to stay with your sister in Clifden?"

"No . . . not exactly."

"The intercom sighed. "Can't work you out, Larkin. That village could have been a good place for you to settle down in." The intercom hesitated a moment, evidently considering other matters. It continued. "Did you mind the doctor asking if we were married?"

Unseen, she bit her lip. Was he baiting her? Thanking heaven for the electronics between them, she said lightly, "Should I have objected to the question?"

She imagined his shrugging.

"He seemed to think we made a good pair."

Her spine goosepimpled. "Doctors can be quite acute."

The intercom sounded more cheerful. "Ah—so what do you think of the idea?"

"I think it would depend on the attitude of all the parties involved," she said carefully.

The intercom fell silent.

Was the sergeant regretting his rashness?

"Or, at least, one of the parties," she amended. "Since one can only speak for one's self."

The intercom thought about that for a moment, then it said. "Perhaps we should leave it there, Larkin? 'Til we've paid a call on Kilcollum. When you've met my folks, you might feel more able to form an opinion."

"If you want to," she mumbled. Was he thinking she might not like his people? Surely a Grenadier Guards sergeant wouldn't worry about what a school-teacher thought of his parents. "I'm sure your parents are very nice people," she said meekly.

The intercom sighed. "Message received and understood, Larkin."

Later it began to whistle an old Irish air about a low-backed car.

"—and filed for reference I hope," she added to herself, piqued by his lack of concern.

The signpost, like so many in Ireland, pointed the wrong way, and was barely legible. Unhesitatingly, Sergeant O'Meara rotated his tank off the main road, onto a stretch of tarmac less than a dozen feet wide.

"Four miles to go, Larkin," the intercom announced cheerfully.

There had been no more than a score of homes in Kilcollum. Each was a gutted shell, roofs caved, supporting beams charcoaled.

Sergeant O'Meara halted the tank. Over the intercom, he said, "Cover me, Larkin."

He climbed out of the hatch, a large revolver in his hand. Celia rotated the turret to bring the co-axial machine gun to bear on the road ahead of him.

She watched him peer through the broken windows of the first dwelling. Grass was already growing over the debris within. The sergeant moved quickly from house to house. At the wreckage of the third home, he crumpled.

She forget the gun, and was out of the turret and running. She found him kneeling by the wall of an overgrown garden. Sprouting from the weeds were two wooden crosses. They bore the names Padraic and Ellen O'Meara. She waited in silence until he looked up.

He gestured at the crosses. "Meet my folks, Larkin."

She touched his shoulder. "Come back to the tank, sergeant. It's not safe here."

He gazed about the ravaged village. "There's no danger now, Larkin. The murderers are long gone."

She tugged at his sleeve. "Come away, sergeant."

He got to his feet, dazed. "I can come back later, and tidy this place up."

She said, "We'll both come back. I promise."

He allowed her to lead him back to the Chieftain. "Why would they do that to a tiny village, Larkin? Why burn every house?"

She shook her head. "We live in a sick world, sergeant."

The drive to Clifden was silent. He should have been modifying his plans after what he had seen in Kilcollum. Why didn't he speak? Then she could tell him she no longer wanted to live with her sister in Clifden. She ached to hear him whistle the Low-backed Car tune again. The intercom stayed dead.

When the spires of the town came into view, she heard his voice. "Whereabouts in town does your sister live, Larkin?"

She gave him the address, wishing she didn't need to.

The house stood in a side street. He halted the tank outside the front door. She got down from the turret. He stayed in his driving cubby, head out of the hatch, watching her. Eyes peeped at them from behind curtains. Several men congregated on the nearest corner, but no one approached the tank.

She called to him, "Aren't you coming in with me?"

He shook his head.

She mounted the steps to her sister's home. The front door was ajar. From within came the sound of a woman screeching in anger, and the basso rumble of protest from a man. Hand on the knocker, Celia hesitated. She heard the noises of altercation, and the crash of breaking pottery. She dropped her hand from the knocker.

He was still watching her from the tank, his face expressionless.

She stumbled back down the steps. "I think I've made a mistake, sergeant."

He jerked a thumb. "Get aboard!"

She climbed back to the turret, conscious of the eyes on her. Safe in her refuge, she switched on the intercom. Voice tremulous, she said, "What do we do now?"

"That doctor made you a fair offer."

Her thoughts were in a turmoil. No home in Kilcollum, now, for the sergeant. No haven for her in Clifden. What did he plan to do? Seek revenge for the murder of his parents? If she didn't want to lose him, she had to make up her mind quickly. She said, "Let's go back to Barley Cross, sergeant."

He said, "I have a job to do."

The doctor's question was forgotten, she knew. It didn't matter to the sergeant, now, whether they got married—or anything.

Her eyes were moist. "You—you've still only one pair of hands, sergeant."

The intercom remained silent.

She repressed a scream. "Did you hear me, Sergeant O'Meara?"

"I heard you," said the intercom.

"You can't fire the gun, and drive this tank at the same time." Her voice quavered. "You—you told me we were a team!"

"We are a team," affirmed the intercom.

"Then let's stick together like a team!" she sobbed.

"Right," said the intercom, suddenly brisk. "We'll stick together. And we'll kill all the murderers in Connemara."

The gears whined. The tank reversed up to the main road, backed out, and turned east.

In a rear periscope she saw strange vehicles.

She called over the intercom, "There's a tractor with a big gun on it behind us. It's got something on tow."

The Chieftain came round in its own length.

Patrick O'Meara stared at the potential menace.

Celia trained the main armament on the target.

The intercom said, "It's parked. Keep your head down."

Patrick O'Meara drove slowly towards the armed tractor. A platform had been constructed between the big drive wheels. On the platform, a light anti-aircraft gun pointed skywards. In the driver's seat, a man watched their approach. An automatic rifle rested on his knees.

Sergeant O'Meara halted the tank. He called, "Hi, chief! Would you be interested in a spot of government surplus?"

"Like?" said the man.

"Like a tank," said the sergeant.

Only the man's eyes moved. "Ye'll be wanting the boss. He's in Finnegan's bar with the boys."

Patrick O'Meara appeared to meditate. "Do you think he'll be interested?"

The man's eyes rolled to take in the length of the Chieftain's rifled 120mm gun. "Have ye any ammo for the cannon?"

"A few rounds."

"Ye'd better wait 'til Healey gets back. Where are ye from?"

Patrick O'Meara eased himself out of the hatch. He propped his back against the turret. He stretched his legs along the glacis. "I'm a stranger round here," he confessed. "I pinched this bugger off the British Army. Someone must have a use for it."

The man relaxed. "I reckon the boss will take it, if you'll wait."

The sergeant linked hands behind his head. "Och— I'm in no hurry. What's that you have on the trailer?"

The man kept his eyes on the sergeant. "Armor plate. A warship went aground in the bay. We salvaged those plates. Healey was going to make a tank out of this tractor. Looks like you might have saved him the trouble."

"Is he at war with someone?"

The man glanced at the road, beyond the tank. "He's at war with anyone that don't agree that he's boss of Connemara."

Celia shot a quick glance at the rear periscopes. The road behind was empty. Clifden's citizens had evidently decided that neither tank nor tractor were of consuming interest. Celia put her eye back to the gunsight.

Voice casual, Patrick O'Meara said, "Did you ever meet up with a gang from out Kilcollum way?"

The man sneered. "That lot? They were no problem. We burned 'em out months ago."

Sergeant O'Meara stiffened. "Were you there?"

The man grinned. "Was I there—Jasus!"

Patrick O'Meara's hand moved inside his jacket. Suspicious, the man swung up his rifle. Celia squeezed the trigger of the co-axial machine gun, sending a stream of tracer over the man's head. Instinctively, he ducked. Patrick O'Meara's bullet took him square in the chest.

The man gurgled, dropping his rifle. The sergeant slid back into the driver's cubby of the Chieftain. Gears whined as he reversed alongside the tractor. Ignoring the figure slumped over the steering wheel, he got out, and uncoupled the trailer.

Celia threw up the cupola hatch, and poked out her head. "What are you doing!"

He looked up, his expression calm. "Watch the road, Larkin. Those shots will bring out the rest of them. I'm taking their armor plate. We can use it in Barley Cross."

He dragged the towing hawser from the side gantry of the tank, and hitched the trailer to the rear of the Chieftain. Someone began firing from a shop down the street. Celia ducked back inside to swing the gun 'round. The sergeant climbed back into the driver's cubby, ignoring bullets spanging off the armor.

The intercom came alive. "You okay, Larkin?"

She tried to stop trembling. "I—I think so."

"Button up—we're getting out of here."

The motor roared. The Chieftain nudged the tractor out of the way. Towing the stolen trailer, it rumbled towards the villains spewing from Finnegan's bar. She watched them scatter for cover at the sight of the tank.

The intercom said, "Give 'em a squirt, Larkin!"

Lips quivering, she chided, "Isn't one death enough, sergeant?"

The intercom muttered a blasphemy. "They killed my parents, Larkin. You said we were a team!"

The schoolteacher inside her submitted. They were a team. Teeth chattering, Celia Larkin squeezed the trigger of her co-axial gun, swinging the turret from side to side, spraying the road with bullets.

"Jasus!" exclaimed the intercom.

Before the belt ran out, the turret was facing to the rear, and the road was dropping behind them. She wasn't sure she could see any bodies. She hoped she couldn't. There was no pursuit.

"Nice shooting, Larkin," commended the intercom. "That cooled their courage anyway! I'll load a fresh belt when we get clear."

Celia Larkin swallowed a lump in her throat. "Maybe you'd better show me how to do that, too," she choked.

Later, trundling along the lonely road below the twelve bens, he began to hum The Low-backed Car.

Five miles off Recess, a loose tread began to clang. He killed the motor, and got out to inspect the damage. She filled the kettle, and plugged in. Tea was ready when he poked his head over the open cupola.

"Did you notice whether they had a blacksmith in Barley Cross?" he asked.

She passed him a steaming cup. "He was shoeing a horse as we left."

The sergeant blew on the hot liquid before sipping it. "We'll be needing his services."

"Something you can't fix?"

He nodded. "It's a—" He broke off to stare back along the road. "Those villains have followed us."

She poked her head out to see.

Far down the road tiny figures clustered 'round a vehicle. She reached down for the binoculars. The tractor had halted. There were men on the gun platform, others standing in the road.

"How far are they, do you reckon?" asked the sergeant.

She hoped he wasn't planning what she feared he planned. "A couple of miles?" she suggested.

"About that," he agreed. "Make room in there, Larkin. They probably think they are out of range."

Feeling helpless, she watched him load a round of armor-piercing, fin-stabilized, discarding-sabot shot.

He said, "Put on the 'phones, Larkin. This'll make a noise."

The shell ploughed into the verge beside the tractor, throwing up a spout of soil. The tractor tipped, then toppled, to lie on its side. Through the glasses she saw the figures scatter to safety.

"Pity AP don't explode," commented the sergeant. He heaved himself out of the turret, and climbed down to wriggle back into the driver's seat. "Stand by with the cupola gun, Larkin."

He swiveled the tank in the width of the road, and rumbled back towards the abandoned tractor.

She said over the intercom, "Where are we going now?"

He was humming softly. "I want their flack gun, too."

Did he think of nothing but guns and vengeance? She said, "Why did we shoot at them this time? They couldn't hurt us."

He continued to hum, unperturbed. "Don't be too sure. The Russkis have a 37mm gun that can shoot two and a half miles, straight up! I wasn't giving those rogues time to get their gun into action. Anyway—they were following us. Barley Cross has enough troubles, without us bringing them more."

She gulped with relief. Maybe she had misjudged him. "You only fired to frighten them off?"

The humming ceased. "Not at all, Larkin. I fired to kill them. I just don't shoot as straight as you do."

Celia Larkin held her tongue. This was what she had pleaded for. She and the sergeant were a team.

The doctor was waiting for them in the main street. He waved. "Welcome back. Will you be stopping this time?"

Patrick O'Meara cut the motor. He eyed the little man. "Are those jobs still open, doctor?"

Denny Mallon crowed with delight. "Come and meet Barley Cross's government."

In his surgery-cum-living room, he introduced his friends. "Larry, Kevin and I have been trying to run the village since the county council lost interest in us. Larry is our minister of defense. He'll put you in the picture."

Larry Desmond stretched long legs towards the turf fire glowing in the grate. "Jasus, Dinny—all I know about defense is that shotguns aren't much use against automatic rifles, and the best thing to do when the shooting starts is keep yer head down. The villagers can do that without an old soldier's advice."

Sergeant O'Meara lounged on the doctor's cushions. One week of roughing it in a tank was sufficient to teach appreciation of such luxury. He said, "I have half a dozen FN rifles aboard my wagon. I lifted them from the guard room before I took off."

Kevin Murphy rubbed reddened hands before the fire. "A sensible precaution for a rebel, sergeant. I believe they shoot deserters in the British Army."

Patrick O'Meara ignored the jibe. He was no rebel. He was a reasoning being who had recognized the futility of trying to control the uncontrollable. He said, "In my mob they'd probably crucify them."

Kevin Murphy flexed his fingers in the heat. "A typical autocratic reaction—"

Larry Desmond cackled. "What would your lot do, Kev—guilloteen 'em? Comes the revolution, ye'll all eat peaches and cream whether ye like it or not!"

Patrick O'Meara hid his contempt. With these two garrulous fools running things, no wonder Barley Cross was anybody's football! He said, "I've also a few Kalashnikovs and a couple of Armalites I captured along with the AA gun. Those villains must have clobbered an IRA gang to get weapons like that. The AK47's take the standard Nato round, which is useful. I could arm a platoon for you."

Denny Mallon got out a bottle and glasses. Celia refused with a shake of her head. He poured for the others, saying, "Just tell us what to do, sergeant. We'll follow your instructions."

Patrick O'Meara smothered an impulse to get up and walk out. These three were only playing soldiers! Organizing the village's defense in the face of such complacency could be harder than fighting villains. It was time they learned that survival demanded discipline. He shot a glance at his gunner. Celia still wore his best blouse. She gave him a rueful smile. Gunner Larkin's convictions had taken some hard knocks recently. And Sergeant O'Meara admired the way she had faced up to them. He sighed. But Barley Cross was their only chance of staying together. He would have to deal with these clowns.

He said, "I'll want twenty full-time volunteers to train into a standing army."

"Done!" approved Larry Desmond. "I'll guarantee 'em."

"And we'll need a refuge for non-combatants. Who owns the castle up beyond?"

Denny Mallon sipped his poteen with a grimace. "It's an old O'Flahertie stronghold. A chap called Higgins converted it into a home, some years back. When the troubles started he and his wife went off to Dublin looking for their kin. We've seen neither hair nor hide of them since."

Patrick O'Meara made his voice brisk. It was the fuel business over again. You couldn't afford to hesitate. He said, "We'll take it over. If we put that armor plate over the doors and windows, build a few gun emplacements, we'll have a fortress which will shake a fist at the whole of Connemara!"

Larry Desmond waved his glass. "Hold on, now! What if Higgins and his wife come back?"

Kevin Murphy raised a restraining palm. "It'll be done in the name of the people. Higgins will have to accept *force majeur*."

He lay back, and let them argue. It had to work—in spite of them. At the first lull in the polemics, he said, "And if I'm your Military Adviser, we start training first thing tomorrow."

In three months, the sergeant had a fighting force which proved itself in a raid on a mobile gang camped near Lough Corrib. Larry Desmond had been promoted to general, getting him out of the way. Kevin Murphy had been given charge of the four-legged transport. Andy McGrath, a foot-loose bachelor who had seen service in the Irish Army had been made up to sergeant. Two captured machine guns taken at Corrib had been set up on the battlements of the O'Flahertie stronghold—already christened O'Meara's Fist—and Celia Larkin, now living with her widowed brother, had given up gunnery in favor of instructing a group of villagers in the nuances of Modern Art.

Barley Cross's Military Adviser sat at his desk in a downstairs room of O'Meara's Fist, plotting a raid on Tuam for medical supplies.

A knock on the door interrupted his musings.

"Are you busy, Pat?" inquired Denny Mallon. "I'd like a word with you."

Patrick O'Meara pushed his plans up the table. "Come in, Denny." The doctor had proved to be a sensible man, once his fellow governors were off his back. Patrick O'Meara had plenty of time for him.

The doctor's face was unreadable. "I have mixed news for you. Celia Larkin came to see me today."

Patrick O'Meara hadn't seen the schoolmistress for weeks. Since being appointed Military Adviser he had been busy creating an army. He growled, "What's she been up to?"

Denny Mallon pulled out a chair, and sat down facing the sergeant. "She came to consult me in my professional capacity." He paused a moment, as though reviewing a decision. Then he said, "She's had a miscarriage."

Patrick O'Meara froze.

"She's all right," the doctor assured him. "I've sent her to bed for a few days. And no one knows what's happened but we three."

Voice scarcely audible, Patrick O'Meara whispered, "Was it me, Denny?"

The doctor's voice was equally subdued. "Who else, Pat? Celia is not a loose woman. And, in any case, we're all sterile here. Have you done this before?"

Patrick O'Meara hesitated. "With Celia?"

The doctor shook his head angrily. "No—I mean with any other women."

Barley Cross's Military Adviser chewed his lip.

"There was a girl in Belfast—she claimed I'd got her pregnant. She got shot in a riot." He glanced guiltily at the doctor. "What's it mean, Denny?"

The doctor leaned towards him. "It means you are fertile! You may be the only fertile man in Ireland."

Patrick O'Meara studied his palms, then looked up. "What do you expect me to do about it?"

Denny Mallon spread his hands on the table. "I don't know yet, Pat. But we can't ignore such an opportunity. You'd better not go on any more raids. . . ."

Two days later, the doctor summoned them all to his home. Wrapped in a thick cardigan, pale-faced, Celia Larkin sat close to the fire.

The doctor rubbed his hands together briskly. "I've called us together because we have a problem. Our Military Adviser has discovered he is fertile. And, since I know he has his eye on a certain young lady, I feel he should be dissuaded from his honorable intentions."

Patrick O'Meara marveled at the neatness of it. No mention of how or where. As long as the others weren't too curious. . . .

General Desmond looked up from the glass he was filling with the doctor's poteen. He seemed not to have heard the doctor's first piece of news. "Why should we object to his marrying, Dinny? Is it any business of ours what the man does in private?"

Patrick O'Meara blessed the old fool.

Kevin Murphy ahemmed. Vets weren't as easily bamboozled as generals. He murmured, "Might I ask how you come to know so much about our Military Adviser's personal matters?"

Denny Mallon pursed his lips. Was Kevin demanding classified information? Or was he just airing a well-known penchant for sticking a nose into other people's business? The doctor decided to take him seriously. "How I learned is covered by my Hippocratic oath, Kevin. But rest assured, I can confirm Pat's claim."

"Who's he fancying?" queried the general. "Maybe we should discuss it with the lady."

The doctor frowned in mock reproof. "Hold on now, Larry. Who Pat fancies is his own business. I just feel he ought not to marry at all."

"All right, I'll buy it," agreed the general. "Tell us why he shouldn't wed."

The doctor steepled his fingers. "If our Military Adviser is fertile, shouldn't he be encouraged to spread his gift as widely as possible? Wouldn't we all be happy to see a few children around the village again?"

"Ah!" The general's face cleared. "Now I see what you're driving at." He frowned. "But surely that would mean polygamy—or something like it?"

"I hope not," interpolated Patrick O'Meara. "I was raised decent. No heathen antics for me!"

"There's our problem," said the doctor. "We need to fix it so that the O'Meara genes are distributed all over the village."

"It would help if he was a ram," grunted the vet.

The general rolled the words on his tongue. "O'Meara the Ram. Now there's a title with a fine ring to it!"

"I prefer Military Adviser," commented Patrick O'Meara.

"Even if Pat is willing—" began Celia Larkin

"Who said he was willing?" interrupted the Military Adviser.

"—there are the women's feelings to consider. He couldn't marry them all. And, if they were not willing, it would be rape. And, if they were, he would be committing adultery—or fornication."

General Desmond turned 'round in surprise. "I'm astonished to hear such talk from you, Celia!"

She snuggled deep into her cardigan. Larry Desmond could stuff his astonishment. She had talked this over with Denny Mallon. The main task was to talk Pat O'Meara into playing stud. She said, "You'll have to put up with my sexy talk, Larry. What Denny has just told us means that Barley Cross could have children in its streets again. The village might even survive the general demise we all fear. In a few years, I could reopen the school. But we have to work out a way to bring it about."

The general grunted. "That's easy. Line 'em up. Send 'em in by numbers. Shoot them that won't toe the line!"

The Military Adviser opened his mouth to speak, then closed it again. Patrick O'Meara was beginning to plan.

Celia Larkin was laughing. "We don't live in Soviet Russia—or wherever it is they go in for that type of behavior."

"Nothing wrong with Soviet Russia," grunted Kevin Murphy. "If they found a ram there, the women would have more sense than to turn their backs on him."

The general grinned. "But that is exactly what—!"

"Please gentlemen!" Denny Mallon intervened. "Let's avoid lewd talk. We have a lady present."

Celia Larkin spread her hands before the fire. There was a way it might be done—if a certain person was prepared to forego the future she had striven for. Did the survival of a community rate higher than one's personal happiness? Silently, gazing in the glowing coals, Celia Larkin decided on a sacrifice.

She said, "There used to be a custom called *jus prima noctis.* . . ."

Kevin Murphy choked on his poteen. "That's bloody medievalism—pandering to a depraved aristocracy—!"

She smiled sweetly. "Can you think of a better way to spread a survival gene?"

Inside Kevin Murphy the vet conquered the politician. He muttered, "Bajasus, I never looked at it in that light!"

Larry Desmond poured himself another drink. "Do ye think our Barley Cross women would go for such a foreign-sounding thing?"

Celia Larkin shrugged. "It would only concern brides. *Jus prima noctis* means the 'right of the first night.'"

"Ah!" exclaimed the general, looking wise.

"But he would need high rank to exercise it," she continued. "Only rulers had the *droit du seigneur*—"

"The what?" demanded the general.

"Same thing," the vet told him. "It means the boss gets into bed with the underling's wife."

Celia Larkin ignored the interruption. "If we made him Lord of Barley Cross—?"

"Duke of Connaught would be more impressive," murmured the doctor.

"I could fancy King of Connemara, meself," snorted the general, getting into the swing of it.

"You can't make kings," pointed out the vet. "Thrones have to be inherited. But you can create lords or dukes."

"Let's make him both," suggested the general. "What the hell—they're only labels!"

The Military Adviser woke up. "Hey, no way! You make me boss—I'm a real boss!"

"For goodness sake, Patrick—!" began the doctor irritably.

"He's right," Kevin Murphy intervened. "We daren't fool the village with a dummy lord. If we make Pat top man—that's what he'll have to be. And he can live up at his Fist and boss us like a real medieval monarch."

"Or like a tyrant?" suggested Celia Larkin.

"Or like a tyrant," agreed Kevin Murphy.

"That's agreed, then," said the doctor hastily. "When and how do we bring it off?"

"Soon as possible," grunted the general.

"We need a peg to hang his promotion on," mused the vet. "A victory of some kind—like Napoleon after Austerlitz."

"Napoleon was emperor *before* Austerlitz," corrected the schoolmistress.

"Would I have to crown myself?" queried Patrick O'Meara, betraying more than a nodding acquaintance with Gallic history.

Denny Mallon tugged at his chin. "Perhaps you ought to go on that Tuam raid, Pat, if we must have a victory to celebrate. But don't get yourself killed! Come back with the loot, and we'll treat ye to a Roman Triumph."

Larry Desmond slapped his thigh. "Bedam—I niver knew I was acquainted with so many scholars!" He turned to the object of their conversation. "How would your Coldstream Guards react to that, Pat? From deserter to Lord of Barley Cross is a couple of leaps!"

Patrick O'Meara scowled. "*Grenadiers*," he corrected. "And they'd still crucify me for it—probably between a couple of rogues!" He stared pointedly at the general and the vet.

Celia Larkin stirred restlessly in her hospital cot. Memories were crowding in. She watched the tank she knew so well return from the Tuam raid, exuberant villagers clinging to it, clanking down the main street to halt before the Old Market Hall. She saw Andy McGrath, trusted to drive, wave from his hatch on the glacis. She heard the volunteers cheering in answer to the crowd's applause. And saw Patrick O'Meara perched in the cupola, face grave, waiting for the planned ceremony to begin.

Denny Mallon stepped forward.

Flinty Hagan, rifle waving, beat him to the punch. "Hi, doc! We've grabbed enough pills to cure all the plagues of Egypt, and not a man among us so much as scratched!"

Denny Mallon swallowed his prepared text, and started over. He flourished a clenched fist. "Well done, lads! We're proud of you!"

Larry Desmond pushed between bodies to stand beside the doctor. The crowd fell silent, expectant. The general shouted, "We ought to promote Pat for this, Dinny!"

Denny Mallon shrugged. "We don't need two generals, Larry."

"Och—I mean higher than a general," protested the old soldier. "He should be our top man after today."

Well coached, Tessie Mallon called, "Why not make him Lord of Barley Cross?"

Celia Larkin meant to echo the demand, but her voice wouldn't work.

An unexpected ally in the crowd shouted, "Pat O'Meara, Lord of Barley Cross!"

The volunteers on the tank took up the call, chanting it.

Patrick O'Meara climbed out of the turret. His men made way for him, jumping to the ground, surrendering the platform.

He spread his arms. "Fellow citizens—you have proved you can stand on your own feet! I'll lead you, if you want me to. But it might not always be to victories. I might ask you for sacrifices."

"Ask away!" shouted his men, from the crowd, drunk with success.

He grinned. "I know what *you* can do. Didn't I train you?" He waved his arms. "But I mean every man and woman in Barley Cross."

His words were drowned in a roar of approval. There hadn't been an occasion like this since Barley

Cross reached the quarter finals in the All Ireland Hurley Championship.

Mick McGuire, miller and distiller, lost his head. "Into Mooneys with ye all!" he called. "The drinks are on McGuire!"

Celia Larkin watched, dry-eyed. She had lost him. Sergeant O'Meara no longer belonged to her.

He caught her eye, and grinned. He pulled a pair of leather gloves from inside his flak jacket. "A lady left these in my turret. I carried them into battle like a knight's favors. I hope she'll leave them with me to bring me luck in the future."

She recognized her navy-blue gloves. She flushed. The new Lord of Barley Cross was tucking them inside his jacket. Celia Larkin abandoned modesty. She set her foot on a towing eye, gripped a lamp bracket, and heaved herself onto the armored deck. She held out a hand, "I'll take one of those, my lord."

He gave her the glove. Putting his mouth to her ear, he whispered, "No regrets, Larkin?"

She took the glove. Lips trembling, she kissed him on the cheek. "No regrets, Pat. Good luck in your new job."

She heard the crowd applauding. He murmured, "I'll need it—especially with the brides."

She said, "You've won their hearts already. There'll be a queue."

He waved to the crowd, his eyes on her face. "It isn't them I fear—it's their husbands. Aren't I training them to be killers!"

One last memory to torment a failing mind. A church bell tolling in the night. Celia Larkin throwing a mac over her nightdress, hurrying through the dark street to O'Meara's Fist. The shuttered front door wide open, an oil lamp flickering on the hall floor. And the Lord of Barley Cross lying on the bottom stair, head cushioned by a servant's jacket.

When she entered, Michael stepped back. "Don't try to move him, ma'am."

She bent over her lord. Patrick O'Meara was still conscious.

"Pat—it's me, Celia."

He recognized her, and smiled. "I went dizzy on the top step. I think my back's broke."

Footsteps were pounding up the hill. She said, "Denny's coming. He'll help."

His eyes rolled. "I'm not sure I can wait for him, alanna. Hold my hand."

She took his cold fingers between her palms. Tears blurred her sight.

He whispered, "I never really loved anyone but you, Larkin."

She held his hand until they took him away from her.

In her hospital cot, Celia Larkin wondered if it had all been worth while. She had given him up so that they could make a tyrant out of him. And they had repeated their presumption with poor Liam McGrath. Through the open window came the shouts of children at play—children no one had ever expected to see. And she knew, if she had her chance, she would do it all over again.

In her mind, she heard familiar voices grunting in agreement.

"Amen . . . amen . . . AMEN!"